THE
PLAYGROUP

BOOKS BY LEAH MERCER

A Mother's Lie
Why She Left
A Secret in the Family
The Mother Next Door

Who We Were Before
The Man I Thought You Were
The Puzzle of You
Ten Little Words

THE PLAYGROUP

LEAH MERCER

bookouture

Published by Bookouture in 2024

An imprint of Storyfire Ltd.
Carmelite House
50 Victoria Embankment
London EC4Y 0DZ

www.bookouture.com

ISBN: 978-1-83790-984-1
eBook ISBN: 978-1-83790-983-4

To Sami, the best story-generator and plot-fixer a mother could wish for.

PROLOGUE

The fire started slowly, shy tendrils of light lapping at the dark. It grew stronger and brighter, its smoky fingers stretching out. The flames gleefully followed, dancing up walls and consuming the happy faces of children pinned there for posterity, transforming smiles into ash that spun away into the night. Cries rang out as the black carried them off, and she cocked her head at the sound. Those weren't real. Children weren't here now, were they? No, there couldn't be.

She stood in the middle of the room, transfixed – but not with horror, and not with fear. She should move. She should run, but where could she go? Everything – everyone – else was gone.

The flames got closer, smoke wrapping everything in a gauzy haze. The heat reached out towards her, and she breathed it in, welcoming the warmth into her body. She'd loved this place. She'd believed it would give her all she needed. She'd trusted it with her future; with her *family's* future. But now... now even this safe space was no more.

It should burn. It *would* burn. She wouldn't stop it.

She tilted her head, encouraging the fire forward.

ONE

LENORE

'Almost there, baby girl.' Lenore Morgan glanced at her daughter in the rear-view mirror, happiness stirring inside – happiness she hadn't felt in forever. Ever since Florence had been born eighteen months earlier, life had been more a nightmare than the dream of motherhood bliss she'd expected. Finally, though, she was ready. Ready to be the mother she wanted to be; ready to enjoy her daughter. She might be alone, but she could do it.

Shame James didn't agree, she sighed, pushing back the short chestnut bob she'd had cut right before she'd told him she was leaving. The new style made her feel more confident and capable than her old limp brown hair, even though, at first, she'd felt like an imposter underneath the crown of glossy strands. She'd told herself she *was* that woman, though, as she'd held firm through the endless nights when James had softly pleaded with her not to take their daughter. To realise she still needed him, like she always had. To not threaten all the gains she'd made – they'd made – since the illness had gripped her.

'It took you so long to get back on your feet,' he'd said in a gentle tone, as if she was a piece of china that might break. 'I know you think you're fine, but it's only been a few months since we've got your meds right. Do you remember what you were like without them? What you were like to Florence without them?'

Lenore had dropped her head, shame blossoming inside. He didn't need to remind her. It was something she would never forget. She breathed in, recalling the panic she'd felt that day when she'd believed all eyes had been peering through the window, silently judging her. *You can't do this. You're not a good mother. You can't do this.* She'd grabbed every sheet she could find and covered the windows, but she couldn't drown out the voices. James had been so upset when he'd come home from work to find her cowering on the floor with Florence, mumbling those words and gripping the baby so tightly she was—

Lenore pushed the memory from her mind. That wasn't her. That was the illness, and she'd been fine for way more than a few months. She knew James still worried, but his watchful eye every hour of the day was a constant reminder of when she hadn't been well. And while she'd appreciated his vigilance – she'd *wanted* his vigilance, both for her and for Florence – it dogged every interaction until she knew the only way she could finally trust herself as a mother was to be away from him, even if for a short while. She needed to do this both for her and her daughter.

'You're not actually leaving, are you? You're not really going?' he'd asked hours earlier, when she'd corralled Florence into the car with her much-loved stuffed toy, Freddie. She'd carefully buckled her daughter in, making sure the straps were tight enough. James had nudged her aside and checked again, adjusting one though she knew it was fine. Any lingering doubts fled. She couldn't live like this. She had to learn to trust herself. It was *time* to trust herself. If she didn't begin to believe in herself as a mother now, she never would.

'I promise I'll keep her safe. I promise she'll be fine – *I'll* be fine. It's not for long, and you can visit soon.' Lenore swallowed as she spotted his incredulous expression. Despite all her preparations, he'd clearly never believed she would follow through. Guilt swept through her that, after everything, she was still hurting him. 'I'll... I'll miss you so much. I'm sorry. I just have to do this.' Part of her couldn't believe she was leaving either. She hadn't been away from him for longer than an hour or two since she'd been diagnosed with post-partum depression a few weeks after Florence's birth. He'd been there for her, supporting her through the darkest times – not just recently, but when her parents had died years ago too. She'd been happy to let him hold her up, but somewhere along the way, she'd let her own muscles weaken, despite knowing she could stand on her own.

Fear flashed through her as she gazed down at her daughter. It was one thing to test your strength alone, but when someone you loved with all your heart depended on you... could you risk *them?*

She shoved the question aside. She would never risk her daughter again. She was well. She could do this. A fresh start; a place where no one knew her was just what she and Florence needed. And when she had righted herself in her new role as mother, she'd come back to James. She'd prove to him she was capable, and they could have that perfect family life they'd dreamed of. This would strengthen them as a couple too. She'd leaned on her husband so much. Maybe soon she could support him when he needed it.

She rolled down the window to let in the spring-fresh air, smiling at Florence's squeal as the wind tossed her golden curls. Soon, they'd turn off the winding road and into the heart of Mapplestow, a village about an hour from London: close enough for James to visit, but not so close that he'd camp out there each day. After scouring the internet for something that might suit her meagre budget, Lenore had come across a Facebook post from an old classmate looking to let her two-bedroom place while she was on sabbatical overseas, offering a paltry price in exchange for a trusted house sitter.

Lenore had fallen for the house the instant she'd seen photos: roses flanked the weathered red-brick exterior, perfectly manicured grass spread out like a blanket around it, and the door was painted in her favourite turquoise colour. It was close enough to other houses not to be isolated, but not too close to feel constantly overlooked like she had in their tiny flat in the middle of London.

The arrangement was flexible, so she paid for a month with the agreement she could extend her stay if she wanted. At the moment, it was hard to imagine being away for a day, let alone a month, but she needed this space. As if he could hear her thoughts, James had shaken his head, saying it was a waste when she'd probably be home again in a week. She'd met his eyes, thinking that, however long this took, it would *never* be a waste if it helped her finally be the mum she wanted.

Driving away from the flat, watching James get smaller and smaller in the rear-view mirror, had been one of the hardest things she'd ever done. She'd felt untethered, as if she might float away without him by her side. But then she'd caught sight of her daughter in the back seat, and excitement replaced uncertainty. The days ahead stretched out in front of her, not full of darkness and dread but with light and potential – time with Florence to fill however she wanted.

She'd always envisaged having a whole new circle of mum friends, but she'd been in no state to socialise after Florence was born. Maybe she could find a part-time temp job in a café or volunteer somewhere, nothing too intense but enough to show James she was ready to go back to teaching when she came home again. And perhaps she'd get to know some of her neighbours, unlike London where you had to live beside someone for at least five years before so much as nodding to them. She'd always dreamed of living outside the city one day.

'Wow, look at that,' she said, more to herself than to her daughter, who was busy twisting Freddie's ears together. A building with ivy climbing up the stones and a pointed roof complete with chimney was perched by the side of the road. Surrounded by fields of rolling green and framed by forested hills, it looked straight from a fairy tale.

Lenore's eyes widened with delight when she saw the sign spelling out 'The Nest' in big golden letters, with 'Co-op Nursery' below, positioned in curlicued script beside a stylised photo of a nest and the cutest little birds nestled inside. A nursery! James had told her from the moment she'd got pregnant that he didn't want their child being raised by faceless strangers who couldn't care less about their charges. They'd always agreed that when – if – Lenore went back to work, James's mother would take over Florence's care. He'd resisted the hospital's recommendation that Lenore and Florence stay in the mother and baby unit after her diagnosis, instead taking a leave of absence from his job so he could be there to care for them.

But nothing was how they'd planned, and this place looked miles from the dingy inner-city nurseries of London. She didn't want to be away from Florence for more than a morning or two, but this would be ideal if she did want to get a little job – although if it was anything like London, the fees would be more than what she'd earn. She flicked on the signal and pulled off the road into the car park. It was a bit out of the blue to turn up like this, but she might as well check it out while she was passing. Besides, the place was so inviting that she couldn't resist its pull.

Florence chortled and pointed at the birds on the sign, her chubby cheeks stretching in a wide grin. Lenore swept her out of the car seat and inhaled the country air.

'Come on,' she said, getting a good grip on her daughter's hand. Lately, Florence had a habit of tearing off, as if she was trying to escape from prison. Lenore rang the buzzer, shifting from side to side as she waited for someone to answer. Peering in, she could tell this nursery was perfection. Daffodils perched on the windowsill; children's framed artwork, photos and thank-you cards were arranged on each surface; and the walls were painted in a springy green colour that reminded Lenore of fields beneath scudding clouds. It was like being transported into a dream.

Her phone vibrated, and she slid it from her pocket.

Are you okay? Have you started unpacking? I'll come tomorrow to help. Remember, Florence needs her nap at 2.

Lenore sighed, staring at the screen. She knew this was hard for James. It was hard for her as well. But she'd asked him to give her a day or two to settle in – she needed that time to right herself. Didn't he trust her to go for one hour on her own? Then guilt bubbled up again. Of course he was anxious. She'd put him through so much. He hadn't just worried about Florence. He'd worried about her too.

A memory slunk into her head of how she'd lain in the over-flowing bath, sinking further and further as everything faded, and she shook it away. She wasn't there. She was here. As she gazed back into the Nest, peace slid over her. She'd text James back later and reassure him; tell him all was fine and he didn't have to come. She knew it was difficult, but he *had* allowed her this time apart to find her feet. That was an encouraging sign. She'd show him he'd been right to give her this chance.

TWO

ALICE

Alice Culver leaned back in her chair at the Nest's office, tapping her short nails on the desk. She couldn't believe that almost ten years had passed since she'd set up this place. It felt only weeks since she'd decided driving her two young kids miles away to the nearest childcare place was ridiculous. Mapplestow should have its own nursery, and she would be the one to make it happen.

She hadn't the capital to start the business on her own, so the community co-op model had been perfect. Everyone, whether they had children or not, could become a member in exchange for a share in the company and having a say in how the business was run. Parents with kids at the nursery would also be expected to volunteer each week, helping to keep costs low. Amazingly, the project had come together much faster than she'd ever thought possible. Demand for the nursery had surprised her, and after finding the premises and hiring a manager to run it, the Nest opened its doors. Getting it off the ground had been only half the battle, though. As the person who'd spearheaded the whole project, it had to thrive.

And thrive it had. In those ten years, the Nest had grown

from taking in children solely from the village to catering for those from miles away. The nursery had the best reputation anywhere outside of London, and Alice couldn't set foot in the local area without someone thanking her for starting it. In truth, she'd only wanted somewhere trusted for her kids so she could focus on her law career, not that it had helped in the end. But now the Nest was more entrenched in Mapplestow than the local pub, and that was saying something.

As the founder and board chair, she had to make sure it stayed that way. It couldn't fail. That was why she'd been at the nursery almost every day for the past few weeks when she should have been slogging away in her London office. It wasn't that she was needed here; far from it. When it came to the daily logistics of running the place, she trusted the manager, Georgie, and her assistant, Beth, without a doubt. But what good was having the best team in town if the nursery itself ceased to exist?

Ceased to exist because of *her*?

She had to find a way to bring in more money – and fast.

A buzz from reception interrupted her thoughts, and Alice got to her feet and smoothed her shirt. She strode down the corridor before Georgie or Beth had the chance to respond. Alice loved talking to parents and seeing their awe-stricken expressions when they first entered the Nest. With fluffy cream carpet, sage green walls covered with framed children's artwork and a mixture of photos of the kids they'd had over the years, it was a perfect paradise. She'd move in here if she could.

Her family certainly wouldn't miss her, she thought, a familiar pain shooting through her. Simon and the kids never knew whether she was home or not. The three of them had formed a tight unit after Simon had been made redundant from his accountancy job and decided to stay home, even if the kids were already in school by that point. She'd tried for a while to make it back each day for supper, only to discover they'd eaten without her, all three barely glancing up from their tablets when she entered. Any attempts at conversation were met with monosyllabic grunts, and she'd end up eating alone in front of the telly.

The final straw had been during half-term last May when Simon booked a caravan at the seaside for the three of them without asking if she could come. Simon had looked surprised by her hurt, saying he'd never imagined she could take a week off when the courts were sitting. He'd asked her over and over to join them, but she'd been too upset to agree. The realisation that she'd been phased out – a mirror image of what had happened at work – had hit hard.

She didn't like to admit it, but sometimes she felt a little lonely. People in the community admired and respected her like she'd always wanted, but there was no one she could sit down with and have a good cup of tea and a natter. Georgie and Beth were the people she spoke with most, but they had their own lives, and as chair of the co-op board, she was effectively their boss.

Thank God for this place. Funny how she'd started it for her children, and now it had become a refuge for her. Please may it stay that way.

'Hello!' she said, as she opened the door, arranging her face in a welcoming smile. She didn't recognise the slender woman with the short bob, but she did recognise the look of wonder. Before she could say more, the toddler the woman had been clutching tightly streaked to the little table in the corner where they kept crayons and paper.

'Sorry about that,' the woman said, scurrying over to put a hand on her daughter's shoulder, as if she couldn't bear to be without her. 'Usually, she's shy in new places. She must really like it here!'

'Oh please, don't worry,' Alice said. 'How can I help you? If you're after a place, I'm afraid we're full up at the minute. But we can put your name down on our waiting list.' She loved pointing out the Nest's success.

The woman ran a hand over her hair. 'Oh, of course. A place as great as this, I can imagine you do have a waiting list. I'm Lenore, by the way. Lenore Morgan.'

'And I'm Alice, the nursery's founder,' she said, drinking in Lenore's admiring stare. 'Lovely to meet you. Would you like to give me your details and I can get you on that list?'

'That would be great,' Lenore said. 'I'm staying in the village for a bit. I'm a teacher, but I'm looking for a part-time job or maybe a volunteer position somewhere. And I know Florence would love it here.' The barrage of words came out slightly stilted, as if she wasn't used to speaking.

A teacher? Alice's mind spun. She'd toyed with expanding the number of kids they took on, but that would mean hiring someone else full-time. She'd put out a few feelers, but no one half decent had responded. But maybe a solution was in front of her. This woman wanted a job and a nursery, and she wanted staff. If she worked here in return for a place for her daughter, then Alice could bring in at least ten more kids. Maybe she could convince the board to raise the fees to reflect Lenore's added level of experience. It wouldn't be a lot more money, but it would be something.

It would be a start.

'You know, we might be able to do something,' she mused aloud, pretending she was still thinking about it.

Lenore's face lit up. 'Really?'

Alice smiled. 'We're looking for extra staff to accommodate all the kids who want a place. I can't think of anything more fun than working here! If you can do mornings, afternoons, or better yet, the whole day, then I'd love to offer you a job. Pending reference and qualification check, of course,' she added. 'We can't offer you more than minimum wage, but in return, we could take your daughter for no cost.' She paused, letting the woman take in every word. She probably had her at 'no cost'. Lenore's hair was professionally cut and the colour was fresh, but that was about the only thing that looked new. Her jeans were faded, and her jumper was nubbly and worn.

'That sounds perfect,' she said finally, and Alice nodded. That was exactly what she wanted to hear. Lenore would be a great backup for Georgie and Beth, and Alice could tell parents that they had an actual qualified teacher in place. Already her mind was calculating how much more money they could bring in. She held out her hand, her fingers closing around Lenore's. At last, something was going right. 'Welcome to the Nest.'

THREE
GEORGIE

Georgie wiped the counter a final time and glanced around the room, breathing in the late-afternoon silence. The whole place vibrated with life when the kids were here, but she loved the peace once the nursery emptied and everything was returned to its rightful place, ready for tomorrow. At the Nest, every morning was a brand-new universe, filled with potential... a fresh start with no hangovers from the day before. After ten years of managing the place, she still appreciated the beauty in that, now more than ever.

If only real life could be that way, she thought, sinking into a chair and trying to focus through the haze surrounding her. If only she could awaken the next morning with a clear head and happy heart. If only her daughter could get up and be cured. Then everything would be fine. Molly would live a wonderful life, and everything would be normal once more. Maybe she and Kasper could actually talk again without her feeling like she had to be positive and optimistic about the hammer that had hit her family – without her feeling like she had to match his strength or let him and everyone else down.

Georgie closed her eyes, remembering the day their teenage

daughter had been diagnosed with multiple sclerosis. Molly had been having balance issues for weeks, but they'd put it down to growing pains. When she'd fallen at home one evening, they'd taken her to the A&E, and a weeks-long process of tests had begun. The illness had taken over their homelife, though Molly refused to discuss it with either of them. It was as if by ignoring it – and them – she was hoping it would simply go away.

But it didn't, and it touched every part of their family. Mornings were the worst, with Molly in tears when her fingers fumbled with buttons the way they never used to, or when she couldn't put on make-up with her shaking hands. Then Georgie would have to help, and more often than not, they'd end up in an argument. Georgie would stand there in tears as her daughter took out her frustrations, their once-close relationship in tatters.

In fact, all of Molly's relationships were in tatters. Georgie had watched her popular, outgoing fifteen-year-old pull away from her friends until she spent every second in the bedroom, gaming with strangers. Even her older brother, who she'd always been close to, couldn't get through to her. She might be trying to pretend her condition didn't exist, but in doing so, it seemed to be eating her alive.

But today, Georgie could finally see a glimmer of light in the darkness she'd been plunged into. A new woman, Lenore, was going to start working here. Alice said she was a qualified teacher, so maybe... maybe Georgie finally would be able to broach the subject of taking time off. She loved the Nest – loved the direction it had given her after staying home with the kids – but she was needed at home again... to be there for her daughter; to support her as much as she could. To help her seventeen-year-old son Theo, too, who was barely getting a look-in these days. Every once in a while, she'd try to talk to Alice about it, but Alice was always busy and never had time. Lately, she seemed more preoccupied than usual, spending long hours in the office at the Nest. She just smiled, told Georgie she was the best, then went back to staring at the screen in front of her.

Georgie knew she wasn't the best. Not then, and definitely not now. She needed this break, not just for her family, but to give herself a chance to absorb what had happened and to rebuild her strength. Ever since the diagnosis, she'd been running at full tilt on all fronts but feeling like she was failing at everything. If she could slow down for a second, then maybe... Maybe she could eat a proper meal, get her mousy-brown roots done, look like a normal human instead of the white-faced zombie she saw in the mirror most mornings. Maybe she could get a handle on herself.

She *had* to get a handle on herself. She couldn't let what she'd become – a foggy, shaky version of herself – affect anything here, somewhere that had been such a blessing to her. It was the only place that remained unchanged in her life when everything else had shifted. And though she might be leaving, she had to make sure it stayed that way.

Everything will be okay, she reassured herself, shaking off the thoughts. Beth was always around to keep an eye out, and anyway, it wasn't like the children could come to any harm in the Nest. It was as secure as Fort Knox, with a fenced-in garden and electronic gates. They'd even had cameras installed in the playroom and nap room with the notion of streaming everything so parents could see what their kids were up to at any given moment of the day. They'd had so many technical issues that they'd given up streaming, though, and parents didn't seem interested anyway. Alice had told her not to bother.

Still, Georgie liked that the cameras were there as a backup. Beth often forgot to switch them on when she opened in the morning, but Georgie always remembered. Everything at the Nest was geared towards making both children and parents as secure as possible, and the co-op lapped it up.

'Right, I'm going,' she said to Beth, getting to her feet. 'Are you okay to lock up?'

Beth nodded, and Georgie thought how she seemed tired lately too. The glossy olive skin Georgie had always admired was looking pale and lacklustre. Normally, Georgie would have fretted whether all was okay; maybe attempted to talk to her about it, though she knew Beth wasn't one for heart-to-hearts. They got on amazingly well, and Beth worked tirelessly beside her, but after five years, Georgie didn't know much about her homelife. Conversation rarely strayed from surface level – last night's supper or village gossip – something for which Georgie had been only too grateful for recently. She didn't want to talk about anything serious here – not Molly's MS, not anything else.

'I'll see you tomorrow, then,' she said, aware she was lingering. She should get home to her family. They needed her. But the instant she left, the reality of her world would come crashing in.

You'll be fine, she told herself, forcing her legs out the door. *Just hold it together, and you'll be fine.*

Well, maybe not fine, but okay enough.

For now.

FOUR
BETH

Beth waited until she heard Georgie's car pull away from the nursery before sitting down and taking out her phone. For the millionth time, she looked at the calendar app, counting the days since she'd had her last period. It was thirteen days late now, and she was usually right on schedule at twenty-eight. Could she actually be pregnant? She'd been dying to check every day she'd been late, but she'd been afraid to be disappointed.

She certainly felt like she was pregnant. Fatigue pulled at every muscle, her breasts were heavy and tender, and she had the odd twinge or two in her abdomen. But she'd had that before, and it had come to nothing... just like all the other times. Just like the times she *had* been pregnant but had lost the baby within weeks of finding out.

She and Rich started trying before she'd moved to Mapplestow, unable to wait until their official wedding day. Beth had laughingly protested that she didn't want to walk down the aisle with a bump. Rich had grinned and told her she would look beautiful, adding that his kids from a previous marriage, Tiff and Jonah, would love a little brother or sister.

She'd rolled her eyes at his cheesiness, but secretly she'd adored it. She'd never been loved so much, so intensely, with the kind of unshakeable faith that Rich had in her. A baby together seemed so right. But it hadn't happened for months, and then she'd had an early miscarriage. And another. And then nothing.

'Don't worry,' Rich would tell her, when yet another month had passed and it still hadn't happened. Sometimes, as she lay beside her husband late at night, she would wonder if this was payback for what she'd done in the past – payback for finally having the life she'd always dreamed of and who she'd betrayed to get it. Rich already had two children, so there had to be something wrong with her. Then she'd tell herself not to be an idiot. The past was dead. She'd taken great care to bury it. No one – not even Rich – knew who she used to be, and no one ever would.

She took a few deep breaths to calm herself, then rummaged in her handbag and drew out a pregnancy test. Unable to wait any longer, she'd stopped by the chemist on her way to work this morning, cursing herself for not having a whole stack at home so she could dodge the inquisitive gaze of the woman who worked there. But she hated how the tests stared at her every month, silently asking why they weren't being used... silently accusing her of not being pregnant.

Well, finally she was about to find out.

She went into the tiny staff toilet and closed the door, then removed the stick from the packet. She'd done this so many times that she didn't have to read the instructions. One minute later, the test was resting on the countertop waiting to be read. Beth jiggled her leg, willing herself not to look at it until a few minutes had passed. She wasn't pregnant, of course, she told herself. She was just checking. She was just checking, and—

Before she could stop herself, her eyes slid to the results window, and one word met her eyes. *Pregnant*. She slumped over, tears streaking down her cheeks as the word echoed in her mind. She was pregnant. Maybe the past hadn't cursed her after all. Maybe she and Rich could finally have that child they'd wanted. Please may it last this time, she prayed silently, her hand sliding down to her stomach. She'd do anything to have this baby. She'd do anything to keep it safe.

The buzzer from the front door sounded, and Beth jumped. Who could that be? The kids had left ages ago, and everyone knew the nursery locked up at six. It rang again, and Beth hauled herself to her feet. Now of all times! She just wanted to sit, protected by the four walls keeping her and her baby cocooned from the rest of the world.

'Hello,' she said, her brow furrowing as she spotted a slender woman with short dark hair at the door. A toddler, about eighteen months with blonde curls, was tugging at her hand. 'I'm afraid we're closed at the moment. I was about to lock up.'

'I'm so sorry to disturb you,' the woman said. 'I'm Lenore Morgan. I'm going to be working here. This is my daughter, Florence.'

So *this* was the woman Georgie had been talking about; the one Alice had been thrilled to get on board. Beth smiled down at the little girl. She was so cute – in that sweet spot where she had enough baby fat to still look cherubic but gaining in independence and on her way to becoming a character. Her own grin got bigger as she thought that maybe in another year and a bit, she would have a daughter like this too. *Please*, God.

'I think she must have left her soft toy here earlier,' Lenore was continuing. 'We've looked everywhere for it, and this is the last place it could be. I really hope it's here.' She sighed. 'We've just moved to Mapplestow today, and she's off her normal routine. I think she's overtired, but she's so excited about everything she couldn't sleep.'

Beth met Lenore's eyes, huge in her pale face. Despite the glossy sharp hair, she, too, looked overtired. But like her daugh-

ter, there was an energy fizzing about her, as if she'd shifted a
weight and *had* to move. Beth remembered when she'd first
moved to Mapplestow. She'd felt exactly the same. A zing of
connection ricocheted between them.

'Thank goodness you hadn't left yet,' Lenore said, shaking
her head. She stroked Florence's curls, then hugged her
daughter closer, and Beth could see the depth of her love for the
little girl from that one gesture. 'Go have a look where you were
doing your drawing. Maybe you left it there.' She gestured
towards the table in the corner, and Florence let go of her hand.
But instead of heading to the table, the toddler streaked down
the corridor and into the toilet where Beth had just been, probably attracted by the light that was streaming out from it.

'Florence!' Lenore hurried after her. 'I'm so sorry. She loves
to run off. She...'

Her voice faded as Florence came out waving something in
the air, and Beth's heart dropped. Oh, God. It couldn't be.
Was it?

'Florence, what is that? Put that down, please. Florence!'
Lenore's soft voice grew firm, and Beth could only watch in
horror as Lenore grabbed it from her daughter's hand. Beth
froze as realisation swept over Lenore's face, then she turned
towards her.

'Is this yours?' Lenore asked. 'You're pregnant? Congratulations!' The excitement rang in her voice, and Beth met her eyes.
She wanted to tell the world, but before she could stop herself,
she was shaking her head. She couldn't say anything – not yet.
She had to keep this secret, if only for a few weeks. She had to
know if this time, it would work.

'Oh, I'm sorry.' Lenore stepped back. 'It's just that I can
remember how excited I was; how happy.' Her face darkened
for a second, then her smile returned so quickly that Beth
wondered if she'd imagined it.

'It must belong to one of the volunteers,' Beth said weakly, aware it was a lame explanation. But what else could she say? In the rush of emotion, her brain was barely functioning. Luckily, Lenore seemed to buy it, putting the test on a nearby table and turning to her daughter.

'Florence...' Lenore pointed under the table. 'I think I see Freddie!' Florence rushed over and scooped up a fluffy dog that had somehow been wedged between the table and the wall, beaming in delight. 'Thank goodness.' Beth could see the relief on Lenore's face. 'Come on, let's let this lady get home.'

'It's Beth,' Beth said, realising that she hadn't yet said her name.

'Beth.' Lenore smiled, and once more that connection sparked between them – the feeling that this place was a fresh start for them both; that they both had things in their past they'd wanted to shrug off.

And now... now, this *was* a fresh start. Beth put a hand on her stomach, a smile growing on her face despite the fear inside. Now was the time to focus on her child; her future, with nothing more to interfere.

She prayed again it would last.

FIVE
LENORE

'Looks like your first two weeks have gone well!' Alice smiled as Lenore waved goodbye to a little girl who'd wanted to stay with Lenore rather than go home with her mum. Far from being upset, though, the mum had patted Lenore on the arm and laughed.

'If that's not the best endorsement for a nursery, then I don't know what is!' The mum had swept her toddler into her arms, then looked up at Lenore. 'She's loving it here since you started. Not that she didn't love it already,' she added, glancing over at Alice. 'But she's really taken to you. Oh, and I meant to tell you! We're having a mums and toddlers meeting this Saturday morning, if you're free? We'd love for you and Florence to join.'

Lenore had nodded, happiness flaring inside. This was exactly what she'd hoped for when she'd moved here. 'I would love to. Thank you.'

'And I'll bring you that extra playpen we have kicking around at home,' the mum added. 'This one doesn't use it any more.'

'That would be perfect.' She couldn't turn her back for a

minute at home without Florence dashing off somewhere to cause more destruction.

'See you tomorrow, then!' The little girl had reached out to Lenore for a final cuddle before her mum managed to prise her away and get her into the car.

'Hiring you was a stroke of genius, if I do say so myself,' Alice said, as they watched the car drive away. 'You're fitting in here perfectly.'

'She really is,' Georgie said, coming up behind them. 'It's hard to believe you've only been here for two weeks. I don't know what we did without you!'

Lenore smiled, loving the kind words, but thinking they'd got on just fine. Georgie had all systems down to a T, with one day flowing easily to the next. Parent volunteers came and went according to the rota on the wall, each one bursting with enthusiasm to take part in the nursery that they, too, owned a share in. And each one had welcomed Lenore and Florence to Mapplestow with open arms, from the mum who owned the local café and snuck them all in treats to the one who ran the post office, letting the kids dress up in the uniforms and deliver the village post. The Nest was a community in the truest sense of the word. Finally, Lenore felt a part of something... a sense of belonging that made her safe and secure, even if she was miles from her husband.

And the best thing about her new world was the three women she worked with. Although it had only been a short time, it felt like they'd been in her life forever. It had been ages since Lenore had such supportive people around her – she'd always been busy with school in the day, then collapsed on the sofa with James each night. But although Alice was busier than she'd ever been, she had still found time to drive Lenore home from work one day when her car had broken down unexpectedly, needing a few days in the repair shop. Alice had pulled strings there, too, making sure the mechanic put her at the top of the list and gave her a 'friends and family' discount to boot.

Anyone who worked at the Nest was a member of the family, she'd told Lenore, waving off her thanks. Lenore had touched her arm, grateful to have someone who wielded so much influence in the community as her boss.

With Georgie by her side, Lenore really did feel like a member of the family. Georgie radiated kindness and caring, and the kids idolised her, following her and clinging on to her. She cared for Beth and Lenore, too, always making sure they'd eaten enough on their lunch break and that they left at a reasonable hour after tidying up. When Georgie had heard that Lenore still needed some furniture for Florence's bedroom, she'd got her daughter's old things out of storage and brought them round. The look of delight on Florence's face when she'd seen the pink furniture covered with Peter Rabbit made Lenore smile, even now.

Florence had been so enamoured with her bedroom that she'd refused to leave, so Lenore and Georgie had hunkered down on the floor for a quick cup of tea before Georgie had to head back to her family. Laughing together as they watched Florence's antics made the small house come alive, and Lenore felt more at home than ever.

She'd paused a split second before accepting Alice's job offer, unsure how long she would be here and not wanting to let anyone down. She'd thought she'd need more time to settle, but nothing could have helped her settle faster than working at the Nest. Seeing how the other parents looked at her admiringly made her confidence grow with Florence, and her daughter was responding to her new certainty like a leaf unfurling, turning her little face towards the sun of her mother's love.

It had been a huge change to do everything at home on her own, and it had taken a while to bite back the impulse to ask James what he thought. He'd been far from thrilled to hear about the nursery, only softening when Lenore told him she'd be there at all times too. He'd been by a few times to visit their daughter, helping Lenore unpack and assemble Florence's cot in her bedroom. His arrival left her on guard for any ambush of the old doubt that had hovered over their interactions. She could almost hear his thoughts as he glanced around the lounge: that rug could trip up their daughter, the coffee table had too-sharp corners, the TV remote needed to be put up higher. To his credit, though, he hadn't said a thing, and hope had burst through her. Already he was learning to give her space to be a mother and trusting her to cope without him. This break was doing just what she'd hoped – for both her and him.

With every day, the uncertainty and fear that had followed her since her illness was receding further into the past. She could do this. She was capable. She was finally on her way to believing that she was a good mother, and she was only getting started. She knew James wanted her home again – the one week he'd predicted she'd need had passed. She wasn't ready yet, though. With more time, she'd be stronger still.

'Mummy!' She turned to see Beth holding Florence tightly by the hand. Florence had settled in so well to the place she'd named 'Nestie', calling both Beth and Georgie 'Auntie'. She'd taken a particular shine to Beth, running to find her the second they entered the nursery. Lenore could understand that. Ever since the first day they'd met, she'd felt a connection between them – an understanding and calm that she hadn't had with many others, even if they hadn't spoken much about their lives outside the nursery.

'Hey, honey. You ready to go?' She reached out to take Florence, jerking back when she noticed Beth's face was pale and sweaty. 'What's wrong? Are you okay?'

Beth reached out to steady herself against the wall. 'Come on. Come sit down.' Lenore handed Florence to Georgie, then led Beth to the playroom at the back. With the kids gone for the day, silence swirled around them.

'Sorry. Just felt a bit dizzy there for a second.' Beth smiled, but it looked more like a grimace.

Lenore put a hand on her back, feeling the muscles tense beneath her. Whatever was happening, this was more than just dizziness. She tilted her head, remembering how Beth had barely eaten anything for lunch today. 'Maybe you've caught a bug from the kids?' There was always something going around. 'If you're up to it, it might do you good to eat. I can fix some toast for you with that raspberry jam Jo brought in.' Jo was the mum who owned the café. Lenore's stomach grumbled just thinking about a lovely slice of fluffy bread slathered with jam.

But it obviously didn't have the same effect on Beth, because she covered her mouth, then lurched for the loo. Lenore watched her go, brow creasing. Come to think of it, Beth hadn't eaten much yesterday either, and she'd looked distinctly peaky. As a responsible caregiver, there was no way Beth would come to work if she knew she was ill. An image of that pregnancy test from the first day they'd met burst into her mind. *Could* that have been Beth's? It made sense that she might not have wanted to tell Lenore – they'd practically been strangers then. But now... now they were colleagues and well on their way to being friends.

She waited until Beth trudged out of the loo, then handed her a glass of water.

'Thank you.' Beth took it gratefully, gulping down a mouthful. 'I'm so sorry.'

'You don't need to apologise.' Lenore touched her arm. 'You can't control morning sickness.' She winced, thinking that wasn't exactly the way she'd wanted to ask if Beth was pregnant. 'If that's what it is?'

Beth stared at her a minute, then nodded. 'It is.' Despite her pale face, a smile was spreading, like she couldn't hold it back any longer. 'I'm pregnant.'

'Oh, wow! That's wonderful!' Lenore hugged her, keen to share the excitement. She'd been thrilled to find out about her own pregnancy, eager to delve into motherhood. She'd rung James from the staffroom, unable to wait until breaktime to tell him the good news. He'd cooked all her favourites that night and treated her like a queen the whole nine months, both of them dreaming out loud about their future. If only they'd known.

They would have that life they'd envisaged, she reminded herself. She'd go back to London, and they'd be fine. Sadness pricked at the thought of leaving, and she forced a laugh as she pushed it away. She'd only been here two weeks, for goodness' sake! It couldn't compare to home. Because London *was* home. Still, despite telling herself that, she couldn't stop the thought that she felt more comfortable here after two weeks than she had after years in London.

Maybe James would move to Mapplestow? Maybe she'd never have to leave? She tilted her head, indulging the fantasy. He could commute to London like Alice did. She could keep working at the nursery and stay in the community, strengthening budding friendships and giving Florence plenty of space to grow. It would be the best of both worlds. Perfect family; perfect place. Would he ever agree?

'It is wonderful.' Beth's words cut into her thoughts. 'But, well, my last two pregnancies ended in miscarriage. And then I didn't seem to be able to get pregnant again. So...' She ran a hand through her hair. 'I'm worried. I... I want this baby so much. I don't want anything to happen to it. And I feel like it's all down to me to keep the baby safe. I don't know if I can do that.' The words came out in a whisper, and Lenore squeezed her hand. If anyone understood, it was her.

'I know. Trust me, I know. But I think...' She drew in a

breath, wondering what she could say to make Beth feel better. 'I think you have to believe in yourself. In your baby, and the connection between you.' She spoke the words as much to Beth as to herself. 'I went through a very tough time after Florence was born – doctors, medication, all that.' Her shoulders sagged, and for an instant, she could feel the darkness on top of her. But then she remembered she wasn't back there any more, and she shrugged it off. 'It was hard, but I'm stable now. I'm doing all I can to get ready to build our life together. Your baby is worth whatever fear and uncertainty you might feel. I can promise you that.'

Beth nodded, colour returning to her cheeks. 'Would you mind keeping this between you and me?' she asked quietly. 'It's just, with all that happened in the past, I'd really prefer to wait until I know everything is okay.'

Lenore's eyebrows shot up. 'Of course! I won't say a word.' She gave Beth a quick hug again. 'Congratulations once more.'

'Everything okay?'

Lenore and Beth looked over to see Alice and Georgie in the doorway. Georgie was holding Florence's hand, and Florence streaked over to Lenore. She scooped up her daughter and held her tightly, breathing in her scent. She *did* believe in the connection between them, and with the help of these women and the Nest, she was well on her way to having the life she'd dreamed of.

Of being the mother she'd dreamed of.

She smiled at the women around her. 'Better than okay,' she said, hugging her daughter closer. 'Everything is great.'

SIX

LENORE

The sun streamed down, and the first hints of green-glazed branches appeared as Lenore made her way to the nursery to pick up Florence. She'd spent every second with her daughter this past month, but she hadn't been able to put off registering with the village's doctor any longer. They might only be here for a short while, but London was too far if – when – Florence caught one of the many viruses circulating in the nursery.

Lenore drew in a breath, wondering how long she *would* be here. London felt shrouded in the dark claustrophobia of her illness, while this place... she could feel light flooding in. Here, she was more than the struggling mum she'd been in London. She was a member of the community, part of the Nest's co-op network, and standing on her own two feet for the first time in almost two years. She wasn't just becoming a more confident mother; she was becoming a more confident person.

After a month, the thrill of having a job again and doing something productive still hadn't worn off. As soon as she pulled on the cheerful polka-dot top with the embroidered Nest logo, she felt a calm slide over her – a calm that helped her cope when James texted, asking when she thought she might come home and if he could put Florence to bed that evening. Guilt would clutch her once again, even as she told him she needed more time. She'd paid her friend for another month at the house, that same guilt mixed with relief flooding through her... relief that she could stay a bit longer.

She did miss James, though, especially at night when Florence was sleeping. She'd loved watching Netflix together of an evening, laughing at his constant commentary rubbishing whatever show they'd chosen, and curling up under the duvet at night as they planned for the next day. They had been happy. They'd had a good life – a life where she'd felt safe and loved, through the darkest times. And with each day that passed, she was more hopeful than ever that they could have that again... and maybe more, as equal partners who could bolster each other.

Bolster each other in Mapplestow? The thought had started as a fantasy, but the longer she stayed, the more wanted it to be real. The Nest was the ideal job that allowed her to be with Florence and work too. She couldn't have dreamed of a better set-up. James might be resistant at first – he loved London – but once he saw how well she and Florence were doing here, she was sure he'd at least consider it. He'd always been the one to steer their course. Perhaps it was her turn? She'd wait a little longer and then try to broach the subject with him.

Lenore smiled as the red bricks of the nursery, glowing in the sun, came into view. She glanced at the time: half past three. At this hour, Georgie would be reading the kids a story while Beth and a volunteer would be cutting up the afternoon snack of mixed fruit and berries. If she hurried, she'd be able to help.

She bit her lip, thinking of Beth. She'd hoped the confessions they'd shared would bring them closer. But when she tried to talk to Beth about her pregnancy – or even the usual questions about where she'd grown up and how she'd met her husband – Beth clammed up. Maybe she regretted telling

Lenore she was pregnant in the first place, and she was embarrassed to share more. In a way, Lenore could understand. She hadn't meant to tell Beth about her struggles with Florence either. She'd wanted this to be a fresh start, and the fact that Beth knew a bit about her history marred that.

Time would help them both, she thought. Beth's pregnancy wouldn't be a secret forever, and she'd have bigger things to think about than Lenore's past. Maybe she could ask Beth over for a cuppa one night. It wasn't like there was much time at the Nest to chat anyway. With all the kids around, it was chaos. *Controlled* chaos, Georgie always liked to say, and Lenore agreed. Georgie was the perfect manager, running everything on a tight schedule and keeping all the volunteers in line too. The place was a dream, and Lenore couldn't believe her luck in getting a job there.

She squinted as a movement up ahead caught her eye. Was that... was that a child? Racing from the nursery car park towards the—

Oh my God. Her heart stopped as the pink jumper slid into focus. The pink jumper Florence had been wearing that morning when Lenore had dressed her: the one which had almost made them late when Lenore couldn't find it and Florence had refused to be dressed in anything other than 'pink, pink'.

Horror flashed through her. It was Florence. It was Florence, and she was about to go into the road. Where were Georgie and Beth? Where was *anyone*?

'Florence!' Lenore shrieked. '*Florence!* Get away from the road!'

But Florence kept moving, her little legs churning in furious motion, as if an invisible force was propelling her forward. Lenore went faster, everything fading away but her daughter, praying with all her might that no car would round the bend. It must have only been a second, but it felt like time was

suspended as a car came flashing down the road and a shrill
squeal of brakes rent the air, scattering birds from treetops.
Lenore heard a scream, but she couldn't be sure if it was from
her or the universe itself as the car bore down on Florence and
her daughter disappeared underneath it.

The world went dark, closing in around her until the only
thing she could feel was the pounding of her heart, each beat
filled with horror and dread. The only thing she could see was
her daughter. Somehow, she was moving towards the crumpled
form on the asphalt, her arms and legs obeying not her clouded
brain, but the instinct to save her child.

Florence had to be okay, she told herself, clutching at the air
to try to breathe. She had to. There was no other option. She
couldn't lose her. Not when she was finally on the path to
becoming the mother Florence needed her to be.

'I'm so sorry,' a man was babbling. He hovered over Georgie,
who was now kneeling beside Florence. 'I couldn't stop in
time. I...'

But Lenore barely heard him; barely saw him. Every fibre
was trained on one thing only. She dropped down beside her
daughter, fear churning inside as she scanned Florence's
familiar form, every inch of the body as familiar to her as her
own. *Please be alive. Please.* Her arm was at a funny angle, and
her leg was bent awkwardly under her body. Blood trickled
from her nose, but the pink jumper was surprisingly still pris-
tine. She'll be happy about that, Lenore thought in a daze, relief
flooding through her when she noticed Florence's chest still
moving up and down.

Thank God. Thank God, thank God, thank *God.*

Lenore gripped her daughter's hand and sagged onto the
pavement. Sounds around her suddenly rushed in, as if she'd
been in a bubble until finding out if her child was living or
dead. It felt like she was being assaulted on all sides, from the
driver's endless apologies to the 999 operator blaring from the

handset, telling them the ambulance was on the way. Lenore wanted to curl up on the hard pavement beside her daughter, to crawl under the blanket Georgie had thrown over her, the cheery colours and happy cartoon characters looking so out of place beside Florence's pale, still face. She screwed her eyes closed tightly and squeezed the small hand inside her own, willing all her strength – all her life – to be conducted into her daughter.

Finally, she heard the sirens approaching, and she opened her eyes to see the kind face of the paramedic.

'Are you Mum? How old is she?'

Lenore blinked. Her mind was blank. In that moment, she couldn't grasp onto any words. Florence was everything. She'd always been here. There had never been a moment she hadn't existed.

'She's eighteen months,' Georgie said from behind her, and she closed her eyes again. Eighteen months. It sounded so short, like nothing at all, and yet it was a lifetime. It had changed her. It had changed everything.

'Mum. *Mum.*' A voice broke into her thoughts, and she looked up to see the paramedic staring down at her. That was her, she thought. She was Mum. She was Florence's mother, even if it had taken a while until she felt she could be. 'You need to let go,' the paramedic said, nodding down at her hand still clasping Florence's.

Lenore stared at her fingers wrapped around her daughter's tiny ones. She hadn't been there like she should have been for so long after her daughter's birth, but she was now. How could she let Florence go? How could she ever do that again?

Georgie touched her shoulder, and Lenore slid her hand away. Carefully, the paramedics strapped Florence onto a board, then manoeuvred her into the waiting ambulance, as gently as if she could break apart any second. Lenore hated the thought that her sturdy little girl was so fragile.

'Is she going to be okay?' She could barely speak, and her throat tightened more when she noticed them trading glances.

'Let's get her to hospital,' one paramedic said. 'Come on, get in.' He took her arm and pulled her into the ambulance, sitting her down on a metal seat in the corner. She looked out at the road, where a patch of blood marked where Florence had fallen. The discarded blanket lay there as limply as her daughter had.

Then she glanced over at Georgie. Their eyes locked, and Lenore thought how Georgie looked like a ghost, her face white and pale, her eyes wide and pupils dilated with fear and shock.

'Why was she in the road?' Lenore asked, her voice emerging raspy and low. 'What the *hell* was she doing in the road?'

Then the doors slammed shut and the ambulance pulled away, the siren obliterating everything.

SEVEN

GEORGIE

Georgie watched as the ambulance pulled away, the siren wailing like a child in pain. Her body trembled and her legs gave out. As she sank to the ground, she saw that her top was smeared with blood – Florence's blood. Nausea rose, and she barely managed to stop herself from being sick right there on the side of the road. What had just happened?

She blinked, trying to piece it all together: the squeal of the tyres, the piercing scream, charging out to the road... For a split second, she'd wondered if this was a hallucination, if this was really happening at all. But the anguished cry of the man who'd hit Florence had wrapped around Georgie, forcing her back. She'd knelt down beside the little girl, sagging with relief that she was still breathing. Out of nowhere, Lenore had come running, then Georgie had snapped into action and told the driver to call 999.

Why was she in the road? What the hell was she doing in the road?

Lenore's anguished questions seared into her brain. How *had* Florence got into the road? Georgie tilted her head, trying to roll back to the time before the accident. She and Beth had decided to take the children to the garden for some fresh air and games. If she was being honest, she'd needed fresh air too. Something to help her cope. *Anything* to help her cope.

The children had streamed outside to the garden, and she'd paused in the silence, then gone outside. She'd stood for a minute on the steps, staring up at the sky, watching it whirl around her and losing herself in the clouds. Finally, she'd crossed the small path between the building and the car park, then touched her fob onto the garden gate and pushed into the vast expanse of green. Beth had been playing in the mud with the three- and four-year-olds, while Georgie had watched her younger charges toddle around, content with pulling up grass and shredding dead leaves. The next thing she'd heard was the squeal of tyres and that awful scream from the road.

But how had Florence got there?

Georgie slowly got to her feet and went inside, her head throbbing. She had to try to be clear. She had to be present, now more than ever. She had to try to understand and make sense of this.

Beth appeared at her elbow, her face white. 'Is she going to be okay?' she asked, shaking a maraca to entertain the child in her arms. All around them, kids were toddling happily in the playroom, grabbing toys and chewing on books. The joyful noise was a sharp contrast to the scene that had occurred outside, as if there were two universes that existed. Georgie would give anything to stay inside this one, to wrap herself up in the comforting layers of the Nest and stay here forever.

It was how she had always felt, right back from the very first day she'd started working here when it had opened. She'd been a stay-at-home mum then, and although she loved it, running the Nest meant she was at the heart of so many families' lives. It gave her a sense of importance she'd never had before.

'I don't know,' Georgie said, in response to Beth's question. Florence might still have been breathing, and she was lucky to have survived the crash; but she'd looked so *broken* lying there on the pavement that it was hard to believe she would be okay.

'But how did she get out there?' Beth was asking, her eyes wide. 'I'm certain she was in the garden with me.'

'She was.' Georgie shook her head, confusion clogging her every thought. No one had been left inside, and Florence couldn't have escaped from the garden on her own. Once the gate was closed, there was no way a child could open it. Because she *had* closed the gate. *Hadn't she?*

She pressed her hands to her temples, as if she could drill clarity into her skull. Everything was hazy, the horrific events of the past hour floating around her like a nightmare. But it was real. It was real, and she had no idea how it had happened.

'Did you call Alice?' Beth asked in a low tone, her face tight with urgency. 'The police are outside, taking photos and talking to the driver. They're going to want to speak to us.'

Oh, God, the police. Georgie's brow furrowed as she took in Beth's shaking hands. Why was *she* so worried? Georgie was the one who... guilt and shame mingled with shock flowed into her, almost knocking her over with their force. She hadn't been fit to work with children, no matter how much she'd told herself she could hold it together. What had she been thinking?

Could she have left that gate open? She'd closed it. She must have done. Please God, let her have closed it!

Her heart pounded and she could feel sweat breaking out, a cold clammy film on her body. What should she say? That she had no clue? Would the officer know just by looking at her that she hadn't really been paying attention? Fear flashed through her.

They both froze as a buzzer rang in reception.

'Hello?' Georgie's gut clenched as Malena's voice rang through the corridor. She must have used her key to get in – she was a frequent volunteer at the Nest, often coming in on weekends to restock the pantry for the week ahead. A dedicated board member, she'd been one of the first people to support Alice's idea of the Nest. Her twin boys had gone through the nursery, and Malena credited the Nest for allowing her to rise to the rank of sergeant within the police. Although her kids were almost teens, she was still deeply involved. That was the power of the Nest. It drew people in. Everyone was invested in its success.

But today, Malena wasn't here to volunteer. Georgie blinked, thinking it was always so odd to see the normally flamboyantly dressed woman in her police uniform, her mad curls tucked back into a neat bun. 'Hi Georgie, Beth.' Her tone was sombre. 'How are you both holding up?' She stared hard at them, and Georgie felt the urge to wipe the sweat from her face. Or would that only make her look more guilty? She waited for Beth to answer, but Beth was cowering behind her. Beth had always been shy with parents, but this was a bit much, even for her.

'It's awful,' Georgie said finally, praying her words sounded clear and not as far away as they did to her. 'I really can't believe it.' That much was true anyway.

'I've just been talking to the driver. He's in pieces,' Malena said. 'He says he rounded the corner, and the child was in the road. He tried to stop, which is evident by the tracks on the road, but he couldn't do anything in time.' She shook her head. 'Poor Florence. Poor *Lenore*. Was she working here at the time? I recognised her car in the car park. I live just a few doors down from her, and I've seen it on her drive.'

Georgie tried to focus on Malena's words. 'She wasn't working here this afternoon,' she said finally. 'She'd taken time off to register with the surgery.' Her lips felt numb, the words difficult to form. 'She must have just come back to pick up Florence.' Her gut churned again as she imagined Lenore returning, eager to see her daughter, then watching the horror unfold in front of her. *Had* she seen her daughter get hit? Or had she parked up after the accident had happened? She'd been there within seconds... hadn't she? Everything was clouded.

'I haven't had a chance to talk to Lenore yet,' Malena was saying. 'Florence has been taken into surgery, and Lenore's not in a fit state at the moment. Do either of you have any idea how Florence got on the road? I know this place is ultra-secure – sometimes, I can barely remember all the codes and keys.' She shifted her weight. 'Had Lenore taken her out to the car park? You only need one second of distraction with kids that age before something bad can happen, don't you?'

Georgie felt herself nodding, although she knew Florence had been with them in the garden. She waited for Beth to contradict Malena – to say that Florence had been here; that Lenore hadn't been in the building – but she stayed quiet too. For a minute, she felt a mad urge to say that Lenore *had* picked up Florence, and Malena's explanation was exactly right. She tilted her head. Lenore's car was here after all. Maybe that was what had happened? But no, she would remember Lenore coming in to get her daughter. She wasn't that out of it. God, she had to get a grip.

A sharp cry rang out from the corner where two kids were biting one another, and Malena grimaced. 'I don't miss those days. Look, the last thing we want is another kid to get hurt because I'm taking you away from your duties.' She looked at her watch. 'I've got to get back to the station, but I want to talk to you both later.'

'Okay.' Georgie's breath left her in a whoosh. Thank God she didn't have to say anything at the moment. Beth was right: she had to ring Alice. If she left London now, she could be here in an hour. And by then... by then maybe Georgie's mind would be clearer and she'd be able to figure out what had actually happened – before Malena called by again.

'It really makes you want to go home and hug your own kids, doesn't it? At least I would if mine would let me.' Malena hefted up her trousers. 'Like I said, I'll be in touch. I'll leave you – I think you'll have a difficult afternoon once word gets out about the accident, and it won't take long. You're going to be overrun with worried parents.'

Georgie bit her lip. She hadn't thought of what would happen when the parents arrived to pick up their children. Alice would know what to do, though. She always did.

She needed to get here fast.

EIGHT

ALICE

'Culver! Where's that brief?'

Alice smoothed her long dark hair, trying to quell the impatience snapping inside. She hated when people called her by her surname, and she hated it more when that someone was half her age. Okay, maybe not half, but it felt like that. More and more, eager young graduates seemed to be taking over the firm, pushing her further down the ranks. She should be on top of them – on top of *everyone* – if she actually cared enough to put the hours in.

The truth was, she hated this job. Actually, she hated being a lawyer. She hated sitting at a desk reviewing long, complicated documents so thick with legalese her brain would hurt within seconds. She hated sitting in an office for hours, discussing whether one word made a difference. She was a big-picture person, and details were too trivial to waste time on.

She'd only gone into the profession because of people's admiring expressions when she mentioned her future career goals, and now everyone thought she was some hotshot lawyer. Her father had been so proud, telling everyone – right down to the woman at the supermarket till – what his daughter did for a living. Even though he'd died a few years ago, his voice still rang in her ears. *This is it. You've made it.* It was too late to roll back and say she'd made a mistake.

Thank God for the Nest. Watching it grow made up for all those years of boredom at the office. Sometimes, she dreamed of quitting here and working at the nursery. Then she'd tell herself not to be silly. Her family relied on her income. Her high salary was what had allowed Simon to stay at home with the kids in the first place, and though she'd felt pushed out, she had to admit they'd thrived. He could get another job, but he showed little inclination, and this wasn't the time to upset the family dynamic. Maybe in another ten years or so when the children went off to university. Her heart sank at the thought of working here for that much longer.

'I put the paperwork on your desk ages ago,' Alice said, pushing back her chair. She hadn't, but Pritesh wouldn't realise for at least another hour. She'd been too busy trying to think about how the Nest could survive the next year, let alone the next ten. She might have found a way to raise a bit of extra money with Lenore on board, but it still wouldn't be enough.

'Well, I can't find it. I—'

She held up a finger, cutting him off as her phone started to ring. Before she could answer, it clicked through to voicemail. She tapped to listen to the message, horror filling her as she listened to Georgie's rushed words. An accident? At the Nest? What the *hell*?

It couldn't have been too bad, she reassured herself as she waved away Pritesh and punched in a request for an Uber. Nothing awful could happen at the Nest – she'd made sure of it, first for her own daughter and then for her son. And she trusted Georgie, she thought, grabbing her coat to head to the nursery. Every inspection they'd had was outstanding, and Georgie always followed each rule to the letter.

Alice jabbed at the phone, desperately trying to ring

Georgie as the Uber started its journey. Why wasn't she picking up? She sat back, watching as the city faded away and fields replaced buildings. She hated London. No one knew who you were, and no one cared. Other people might like the anonymity, but she didn't. When she'd found out she was pregnant, she'd jumped at the chance to move back to Mapplestow, telling Simon they could afford a much bigger place with a garden. She might be a big fish in a small pond, but at least here she was something.

She raised her eyebrows as the Uber slowed. They were still a good distance from the Nest, around the next bend. 'Why are we stopping here?' she asked, her voice vibrating with impatience. 'Can we carry on, please? I have an emergency to get to.'

'The road is reduced to one lane up ahead,' the driver said. 'There's too much traffic. I'm happy to wait, but it might be faster to walk.'

Alice craned her neck, noticing for the first time the row of cars stretching in front of them. They must be doing roadworks, although she hadn't heard about them. A woman at the council had a daughter at the Nest, and she always warned Alice about anything that might affect the nursery.

'All right, I'll walk. Thanks.' She got out and slammed the door behind her, grimacing as her high heels sank into the soft grass at the side of the road. Hurrying, she rounded the bend, squinting at the sight in front of her. A tow-truck was removing a car blocking a lane. Alice stared at the long skid marks snaking across the road, stopping almost directly in front of the Nest. *The accident.*

Could this be what Georgie had meant – there'd been a car crash in front of the Nest? She must be worried about how parents would come to collect their kids. What a nightmare, Alice thought, glancing at her watch. They still had a bit of time to sort it out before pick-up, but they'd need to come up with an action plan. She spotted Lenore's car in the car park, and she exhaled. Thank goodness Lenore was here too. Parents really liked her, and they listened.

She opened the door to the nursery, the powder-scented air surrounding her. Of course they never used talc, but for parents, the scent of it was comforting, evoking happy memories of cosy childhoods. When she'd first opened the doors of this place, she'd made sure that scent greeted all who entered. It was even more important than the colour of the walls: without knowing why, parents immediately felt at ease. The Nest was a refuge from the world outside, a world of responsibility, of burden. Listening to the cheerful sounds of laughter and the banging of the xylophone, it was hard to believe anything bad could touch this place. Alice would make sure it never would.

'Oh, thank God you're here.' Georgie rushed into the reception, and Alice recoiled. She looked awful. Her face was pale and gaunt, her eyes wide and unfocused, and her straggly sandy hair was escaping from the ponytail better suited to jaunty preteens than a mother of two. But that wasn't the worst of it: the shirt and trousers she was wearing were covered with splatters... Alice narrowed her eyes. Splatters of blood?

She told herself not to be silly. It had to be paint. The children must be having one of those watercolour lessons Georgie loved doing. Georgie would never allow herself to wear a blood-stained shirt with all the kids around... would she? She eyed the woman in front of her, thinking this was not the Georgie she knew. Was she in shock?

'What happened?' she asked, trying to keep her voice calm as dread stirred inside.

Georgie swallowed, and Alice noticed she was so thin that she could see her Adam's apple working. 'Florence got out and into the road.'

Alice's mouth dropped open. *What?*

'And then a car hit her.' A whimper escaped Georgie, and she put a hand to her mouth, tears streaking down her cheeks.

'We called 999 and an ambulance came and took her to hospital.'

'She's alive?' Alice could barely get the question out. This couldn't be happening. This couldn't have happened. She wouldn't let it.

Georgie nodded, and relief whooshed through her. At least Florence wasn't dead. That was something. She drew a breath in. 'You said Florence got out,' she said slowly. 'What happened?'

'We were taking the kids to the garden,' Georgie began, lifting her tear-stained face to look at Alice.

Oh, God. Alice felt the dread inside balloon. The garden. Between the building and the garden gate was a small path that led out to the car park. And from there, you were smack onto the road.

'Who was here? You, Beth and Lenore?' The words rattled from Alice like a machine gun.

'Not Lenore,' Georgie answered. 'It was just me and Beth.' She lowered her head, her face contorting. 'She's back with the kids.'

'All the children were with you in the garden? You're sure no one was left inside?' Alice stared hard, and Georgie nodded once more. 'And who was the last one in?' Her eyes bored into Georgie, as if she could see inside her head.

Georgie blinked. 'It... it was me.'

'Well, there's only one explanation,' Alice said. 'You must not have closed the gate.' She couldn't believe this. She didn't want to believe this. How could this have happened? But it had, and she had to deal with it.

Georgie dropped her eyes. 'You're right,' she said in a small voice. She swayed, and Alice thought she might fall over. 'I must not have. I was distracted for a second; I was thinking of what to make the kids for their afternoon snack.' She let out a shaky sigh. 'I must not have closed it. Alice, I'm sorry. I'm so—'

'Did Beth see you leave the gate open?' Alice interrupted. She needed to know exactly what she was dealing with here.

Georgie shook her head. 'No. She had no idea how Florence got into the road. She didn't say anything to Malena anyway.'

Alice felt panic crash through her. 'Malena?' Malena had been nothing but supportive of the Nest from day one, but she *was* a police officer.

'She was here investigating. We didn't have time to talk since it was just me and Beth with the kids. She said she'd want to speak with us, though.'

'Don't say a word, okay? I'll talk to her.' She and Mal went way back, from playing together on the secondary school netball team to attending the same prenatal classes. When Alice had mentioned that she'd started a nursery in the village, Malena had thrown herself into recruiting co-op members far and wide. She'd been on the board for years, and everyone liked and trusted her. She knew the Nest's protocol and security systems inside out. She knew they couldn't be at fault. Still, she had to do her job. Alice would have to come up with some explanation for the accident. But *what*?

Silence fell as Alice's mind whirred. It would be so easy to tell everyone that Florence had been hurt because one lone employee had slipped up; that one moment of inattention had unfortunately led to tragedy. But any admittance of negligence or fault on the part of the nursery, and inspectors would pounce to make sure all procedures and safeguards were in place. And... and then they would find the secret. The secret she'd been trying so hard to keep hidden.

The secret that needed to *stay* hidden before it ruined everything. Because parents had no idea that the building they deemed perfection – the building they all owned through the co-op to house their little darlings – was tainted. The asbestos wasn't harmful, Alice had been assured when she'd first looked into buying the place. It was only dangerous if someone disturbed it, and since it was in the space between the ceiling and the roof, there was no need to worry.

She knew without a doubt, though, that if she had told the co-op members the building that would shelter the most precious things in their lives contained a material that could cause disease and cancer, they never would have gone for it. So she'd kept the information to herself, eager to get the project underway and knowing no other building within miles came close to their requirements. After her latest demotion in the office, this had to work out.

Everything had been fine, and it probably could have stayed that way for years if a crack in the nursery's outer wall hadn't appeared. She'd had a survey done a few weeks ago and been told the upper part of the wall needed rebuilding in the next couple of months – which meant disturbing the asbestos. There was no way around it. She'd have to get it removed, and that wasn't something that could be done overnight – or in secret. She'd no idea what story she could come up with to justify closing the nursery and keeping any nosy parkers away from the site while the work was completed.

The cost was astronomical too. There was some money in the sinking fund, but keeping costs low meant any contingency fund grew very slowly. Maybe she could get the board to agree to raising the fees, but it would take months before they had enough, and they didn't have months. That wall needed to be fixed or it could become a hazard itself.

Her actions weren't criminal. Plenty of buildings up and down the country had asbestos in them, from schools to hospitals. But this wasn't just a building. It was the Nest. And if the members found out, they'd pull their kids faster than she could blink. They'd never trust her – or the nursery – again.

What would inspectors think when they saw the crack in the wall? Would they ask why repairs were being delayed?

What would happen if they found out about the asbestos... the asbestos Alice had kept quiet about for years?

Even if inspectors didn't probe too deeply, the media loved stories about children injured at nurseries. She still remembered reading how a child had escaped to wander the streets for hours, and that child had been returned safely. Imagine the media's glee when they discovered a child had been seriously hurt – and might die. Alice shuddered. Once a nursery was tarred with safeguarding issues, whether it actually was the nursery's fault or not, parents would pull their children. She wouldn't have the money to fix the asbestos, and the building would be unsafe. She'd have no choice but to close.

That couldn't happen. That *wouldn't* happen.

No way could she say the nursery or its staff had been at fault without risking everything. She'd have to come up with something – quickly. In the meantime, she needed to make sure Georgie kept her mouth shut.

'I know how much this place means to you,' Alice began. 'You're such an important person here.' That much was true anyway. While Alice knew the other mums looked up to her, they sometimes seemed a little intimidated. Georgie was everyone's friend. As long as she was here providing stability, people would trust them, no matter what the truth was. She could barely believe what had happened herself. 'Anyone can have a slip-up. You've done such great work, and I'd hate to see it all ruined by this.'

Georgie's eyes grew wider. 'Really? Alice, I...' Tears came to her eyes. 'But what can we say, then?' She looked at the clock on the wall. 'Parents will start to arrive in a few minutes.'

Alice nodded. They had to act fast. 'First things first, you need to change.'

Georgie looked down at the shirt she was wearing, and if possible, she went whiter. 'Oh, God.'

'Don't mention the gate. I won't, and you shouldn't either.

Not to Beth, and not to anyone. What happened, happened, and no one is going to benefit from you taking the blame. We need you here, more than ever. I'll think of another explanation for the accident.'

Georgie took in a shaky breath. 'Thank you so much, Alice. You don't know how much this means to me. I've been going through a lot, and this... to have your confidence and appreciation is everything.' Georgie looked like she was about to collapse into her arms with gratitude, and Alice took a step backwards. She didn't need gratitude. She needed Georgie to stay quiet. 'And...' Georgie blinked rapidly, like she was trying hard to grasp onto something. 'I might have an idea about what we can say.'

Alice cocked her head. 'Really?' Usually, she was the big-ideas person, but she'd listen to anything now.

'It was something Malena asked. She spotted Lenore's car – Lenore must have parked up when the accident happened. Malena wondered if she'd already come to pick up Florence... if she'd been trying to get her into the car and Florence got away from her.' Georgie paused. 'The car is still there. Everyone will see it when they come get their kids. You know how Florence loves to tear off whenever she can. Everyone knows that. So it *is* believable. And of course, Lenore will disagree, but—'

'But we can say that it's natural not to want to accept responsibility, and that we all understand,' Alice finished, holding Georgie's gaze. She might just have something there. As much as everyone liked Lenore, she was still an outsider. People didn't know her well, not like they did with Alice, Georgie and Beth. Besides, everyone loved the Nest. They would *want* to believe that nothing bad could ever happen here.

Malena would want to believe it too. As one of only a few officers assigned to their borough, she was always talking about how under-resourced and overstretched her small team was – how they rarely had the time they needed to fully investigate incidents. She'd do what was necessary for her job, of course. But if she was presented with an explanation corroborated by everyone except the person who'd caused the accident – and with no other conflicting evidence – then further investigation wouldn't be needed. Besides, as far as Malena knew, this wasn't a crime. It was a terrible accident, and that was all.

If the three of them stuck together, they would be fine. Lenore might protest a bit, but with her child in hospital, she would be focused more on her than the cause of her accident. And Alice would make sure she knew her job here was waiting for her, with the whole community behind them once Florence pulled through. Because she would pull through, and why would Lenore implode the brilliant life she'd been building just to disprove their story?

'I'll speak with Beth,' she said. 'We need to make sure she knows what to say. We need to make sure she sticks to it. What happened today impacts her too. Maybe you didn't close the gate properly, but she should have noticed Florence getting out. Saying it happened when Florence left our care is best for all of us.' She squared her shoulders, as if bracing for war. 'I'll tell the parents as much. Let me handle them. You and Beth stay in the back.'

As Georgie returned to the children, Alice felt a sense of calm slide over her. This was a terrible situation, but everything would be okay.

The Nest would be fine.

For now, anyway.

NINE
LENORE

'Is she okay? Where is she?'

James's face twisted with panic and fear as he tore down the corridor towards her. Lenore didn't have a chance to answer as she hurried alongside the paramedics wheeling Florence into the A&E. The journey here had felt like forever, but, in reality, it had only been fifteen minutes to the nearest hospital in Guildford. The siren had blared, and the ambulance had jerked back and forth, but all Lenore could focus on was her daughter, willing her to keep breathing. Her eyelids fluttered, but they remained closed. Apart from that, she was deathly still.

'It looks like she has a leg fracture. We're going to do a CT scan to see if there's any internal damage,' the doctor was saying, and Lenore tried her best to listen. 'And then we can go from there.'

'But she'll be all right, won't she?' James's voice matched the terror she felt inside. 'She's not going to die?'

Lenore swallowed at the expression on the doctor's face. 'We need to see what's going on inside of her,' he said gently. 'And then we will be better able to update you on her condition.'

Amidst the beeping and the commotion around them, Lenore only took in one thing: he hadn't said no. Florence could still die. She could lose her daughter, just as their life together was beginning.

Her legs went limp, and she started to sink to the floor as their daughter was wheeled away. James grabbed her arm and propelled her into the waiting area. She let herself feel his strength and support, grateful to have him here despite the distance she'd put between them. This was their child. This was their entire world.

Then his grip loosened. He ran a hand over his face, guilt and pain mixing in a mask of misery. 'I shouldn't have let you take her,' he said, his voice rasping out from deep inside. 'I knew it was wrong. I knew you weren't ready.' He shook his head, his eyes locking onto hers. 'You promised you'd keep her safe. You *promised* she'd be fine.'

Lenore's mouth dropped open. *What?* Did he think that she'd hurt their daughter? The worry and shock on his face was the same as when he'd rushed home to find Florence limp in her grip. He'd turned to her then, too, with this expression, mouthing words she couldn't hear. Florence had slipped from her arms, looking just as lifeless as she did now.

But she hadn't been trying to hurt her baby, the therapist had made her see. She'd been trying to shield her and keep her safe. She'd never harm her daughter intentionally, and her actions weren't her fault. It was the fault of the illness.

And this wasn't her fault either. 'James, Florence was at nursery when the accident happened. I wasn't even there.'

'She was at the nursery without you?' James's face hardened. 'You told me you were going away because you wanted bonding time with Florence. I never would have agreed to the nursery in the first place if I'd realised you were going to leave her there alone. They simply aren't safe.'

Lenore dropped her gaze. She knew how James felt about

nurseries, but this was the Nest. Never had she seen a more secure, safety-conscious workplace – she was certain James would agree if he saw it. And Georgie had eyes in the back of her head, something Lenore had discovered when she'd surreptitiously taken her mobile out one day to check something. Georgie had barked at her to put it away and get the lunch ready, and Lenore had been amazed. Beth was the perfect assistant, always working, always on hand, always there.

Lenore shook her head. 'I only left her this once, just to register at the surgery,' she said. 'I don't know how she got hurt. But it is a good nursery. It really is.'

'A good nursery?' James's voice rose. 'When a child ends up in hospital? If that's your idea of a good nursery, then there really is something wrong with you.'

Lenore drew back as his words hit, but she wouldn't allow them to penetrate. She had been ill, but she wasn't any longer. She *had* been ready, and the last month had been everything she'd hoped for. No one could have predicted what had happened at the Nest, and she couldn't let any doubt or guilt from the past engulf her again. Nothing would drag her back there.

'Excuse me.' The doctor poked his head into the waiting area and cleared his throat, clearly uncomfortable at having interrupted them. 'Would you like to have a seat?' He motioned towards the chairs, and Lenore's heart sank. It couldn't be good news if he was asking them to sit. Legs shaking, she eased herself onto the chair. 'We've done the scan on your daughter, and it shows an area of internal bleeding in her abdomen.'

Lenore drew in a breath. Oh, God.

'She also has some cracked ribs, as well as a collapsed lung.' Lenore willed him to stop talking. She couldn't take any more. Her poor girl.

'We are going to operate shortly to clear the blood, and then we will keep Florence sedated to give her body time to recover,' the doctor said, but it felt like he was getting further and further away, as if his words were coming from somewhere else. 'We're about to take her into surgery, if you'd like to see her before she goes in.'

Lenore nodded. She and James followed the doctor down the corridor to where Florence was lying on a gurney. She was pale and still, her dark eyelashes looking even darker against the white skin. Surrounded by the bevy of machines bleeping and whooshing, it was hard to find a way to reach to her hand, but Lenore touched her fingers. They were warm and clammy, a reminder that her daughter was alive – that somewhere in there was the little girl who loved any animal with ginger fur and who chortled without fail at Lenore's funny faces.

The daughter she loved with all her heart, and who loved her in return.

And when she came out of surgery, Lenore would be waiting for her. Waiting, present and able, to be the mother her daughter deserved.

TEN

BETH

'I'll see you tomorrow, okay?' Beth poked her head into the office, praying Alice would say she could go. Every bit of her felt shaky and uncertain after the accident, as if the very ground she was standing on was trembling, as if it could give way at any moment. She knew only too well what that felt like from the past.

She still didn't understand what had happened, but did that matter? All she could think about was Florence.

Florence. A little girl Beth loved more than all the other kids here, despite only knowing her for a few short weeks. And Florence loved her too: her face lit up when she spotted Beth, and she'd streak across the room for one of Beth's legendary cuddle-and-swings. It was Beth's lap she'd settle in for story time if Lenore was busy, and Beth who would pat her tummy until she drifted off at nap time. When Beth dreamed of her own little girl, it was Florence's face she saw when she closed her eyes.

And although they'd never again exchanged secrets like the day she'd said she was pregnant, of all the mums she'd met since moving here, she'd connected with Lenore the most. Beth might have lived in Mapplestow for years, but she still felt very much an outsider – especially since most of the women she knew had been friends first with Rich's wife who, even though she'd passed away nine years ago, still loomed large.

It was the reason Beth had been hesitant to move here after Rich had proposed, but his kids were already settled, and Beth had such a great relationship with them that she hadn't wanted to jeopardise it. Occupying the same space as Cherie hadn't been easy, but she loved the village. After growing up in care, the neat streets and vibrant shopfronts were like something from a storybook.

And the very best thing had been the Nest. Working here had been like going back to her childhood and getting the kind of life she'd never had; a do-over. It let her meet other parents and their children, to be enveloped in the community in a way she never could have otherwise. She may never have a group of girlfriends to go out with, but women trusted her with their *children*, the most precious things in their lives.

But trading confidences with Lenore had made her realise that she did miss having a close friend, something she needed even more since finding out she was pregnant. She'd yet to tell Rich, worried about disappointing him if things went wrong. Lenore was the only one she'd confided in. Talking about it had made her nervous, but having someone who knew about the baby made it real – gave it added strength to keep growing. Watching Lenore and Florence was like a mirror of herself in the future.

And now... now, her very worst thoughts about the future felt like they could come true.

Alice barely looked up from her desk, where she was busy rifling through some papers. 'Do you have a second? I need to speak to you.'

Beth's heart sank as she stepped inside the office. The last thing she wanted to do was talk to Alice. Was she going to blame Beth for what happened? Because it hadn't been her fault. She'd been in the garden, engrossed in playing with her group of kids when she'd heard the squeal of brakes and then a scream. Georgie had raced out leaving Beth behind, and when she'd heard the siren, she knew something bad had happened. Beth had been too muddled to clock that it had been Florence who'd been missing, and when Georgie finally came back in with blood streaking her shirt and saying she'd been hit, Beth could barely catch her breath.

Georgie didn't know what had happened either. What the hell had gone wrong? She started to shake, and Alice motioned her towards a chair.

'Have you heard how Florence is?' Beth asked, praying everything was okay. It had to be. She placed her hands on her stomach, cradling her own baby inside.

'No, nothing yet.' Alice stared hard at Beth, and Beth shrank back, as if distancing herself from a coming blow. Was Alice going to fire her? After all, she had been on duty. 'Do you know how Florence got into the road?'

Beth shook her head. 'I can't figure it out.' Fear and panic shot through her. *Was* she going to be in trouble? Would the police need to talk to her? She didn't want to answer questions. She didn't want to take part in an investigation. Not with her past... a past not even Rich knew about. A past she'd tried so hard to forget; to slough off. A past she wasn't going to let catch up and destroy this idyllic new life.

Especially not when she was pregnant, with a baby she and Rich wanted so much.

'There must be some explanation,' she started, desperation lacing her voice. If she could come up with something, then perhaps they could avoid more investigations. 'Maybe—'

'I've been speaking to Georgie,' Alice interrupted. 'She told me that Lenore had come to pick up Florence. Her car is still here, actually. So the accident must have happened when

Lenore was getting Florence into the car. Georgie says Florence likes to run off, and it's just a short distance from the car park to the road.'

'But...' Beth stopped herself from saying she was sure Florence had been in the garden with her, and she hadn't seen Lenore take her out again. And if Lenore had come to get Florence, why hadn't Georgie told her that when she'd asked what had happened?

She held Alice's stare, her mind spinning. Georgie had been in a state after the accident. She hadn't been thinking clearly. Maybe in all the confusion, she'd forgotten to say that Lenore had picked up Florence. Lenore's car was here after all. And Beth had been busy with her own group of kids. Maybe she'd missed seeing Lenore come by.

A mix of emotions tumbled through her, almost taking her breath away: relief, sympathy and pain. If the Nest wasn't involved in what had happened, there'd be no reason for the police to investigate it... or her. She was safe.

But Lenore... Her heart squeezed as she thought of what her friend must be feeling. Beth didn't know the whole story of what she'd gone through in the past, but the mention of medication after Florence had been born and the fact she was here on her own pointed to a traumatic first year. Beth knew she'd wanted a fresh start and to build a life with her daughter. The love between them had been so palpable, it was hard to envision Lenore struggling after Florence's birth.

And now her daughter might die. She might die, and if Alice was right, it was because Lenore had turned her back for a moment. One small lapse, one small mistake, and she would lose the one person that meant everything. Beth kept her hand firmly on her belly. She had to focus. She had to stay strong. She couldn't let the same thing happen to her.

'I should call and see how Florence is doing,' she said, backing away from Alice. She needed to hear that the little girl was alive. That she and Lenore still had their life together in front of them, the same way she and her own baby did.

'Yes, you should. Why don't you do that?' Alice said. 'I'd like to know too.'

'Okay.' Beth drew her phone from her pocket and brought up Lenore's number.

'And remember, it's going to be very hard for Lenore to deal with the truth,' Alice said, and Beth winced at the harsh words. 'She's going to be angry. She's going to be looking to blame others. She might try to blame you.' Beth's heart picked up pace. Would Lenore blame her? Would she have to talk to the police after all?

No. She couldn't let that happen.

'Or she might have blocked it out completely. She'll need you to be strong to get through this,' Alice was continuing. 'She needs a real friend to help her come to terms with what happened. She's lucky to have you.'

Beth nodded. Heart beating fast, she tapped Lenore's contact and listened as it rang, praying Florence was okay.

'Lenore!' she said when she picked up. 'Oh my God. How are you? How's Florence?' Alice mouthed at her to put it on speaker, and she flicked the button despite her discomfort at having Alice listen in. The way she was focusing on every word was unnerving.

'She's alive,' Lenore said, her voice cracking. 'She's still alive.'

Beth sagged at the words.

'She's in surgery,' Lenore continued. 'She had some internal bleeding.'

Oh, God. 'That's terrible, Lenore. I'm so sorry this happened. We all are.' Beth paused. 'And how are you doing?' She bit her lip, wondering how Lenore could stand the guilt. She knew what that felt like. 'Please don't blame yourself,' she said. 'Please. It could happen to anyone. I know it's hard, but—'

'What do you mean? Why would I blame myself?' Lenore's voice shook with emotion, and panic leaped inside Beth. Was Alice right? Did she not remember what had happened? Though after what she'd been through, Beth could hardly blame her. She understood only too well how trauma and shock could cause black holes... black holes that could threaten to swallow you if you didn't fill them in fast. But could she really push the terrible reality at her friend when her child was in surgery fighting for her life?

'Look, why don't we talk later?' she said finally. 'Call me when Florence is out of surgery. We're all thinking of you both and sending lots of love.'

'No.' Lenore's voice was hard. 'I want to know what you mean. I didn't do this. I don't know how Florence got onto the road, but it had nothing to do with me. You were there. Georgie was there. Who else was working this afternoon?'

Beth felt Alice stiffen beside her. *One small lapse, one small mistake, and she would lose the one person that meant everything.* She had to speak carefully here. If Lenore believed the Nest was at fault, Beth had no doubt it would lead to a hunt to find the culprit – a hunt that could mean further police investigation. And that investigation could jeopardise everything: the Nest, her baby, her *life*.

As much as she didn't want to hurt her friend, she had to tell her the truth. She had to make sure she understood her role in the accident.

'What happened this afternoon was awful,' Beth started in a slow voice. 'And I'm sure you must be in bits. I know I would be. But you'd already picked up Florence, hadn't you?' She continued without giving Lenore time to respond. She had to get through this, and then she could hang up the phone, go back to her home, and be done with it all for the day.

'She must have got away from you somehow and run into the road. It can happen so quickly, I know.' Beth gripped the phone tightly. 'I'm so sorry. You know that we're wishing her well – we are all behind you. Please don't hesitate to let me know if I can do anything.' She was babbling, her words more formal than they should be for a woman she'd connected with, but she couldn't bear to think of Lenore's reaction.

'What?' Lenore's voice shot through the line like a bullet. 'Beth, that's not true. I didn't cause the accident. You know I didn't! I hadn't picked up Florence.'

Alice leaned forward, her eyes boring into Beth, and Beth swallowed. She didn't want to destroy her friend, especially now. She should be with her at the hospital, not trying to rub her face into the tragic situation.

'I know it's hard. I can't imagine. But the sooner you come to terms with the truth, the better it will be. You must know that yourself, from everything you've been through in the past.' God, she hated using what Lenore had told her in confidence against her, but she couldn't risk the police nosing around. She had to make sure Lenore accepted this. 'I need to go, I'm sorry, but please keep me posted on Florence. I'm thinking of you, we are all thinking of you.' And with that, Beth ended the call before she could hear Lenore's response.

'I know that can't have been easy, but you did the right thing.' Alice leaned back in the chair, tilting her head. 'You mentioned something Lenore had been through in the past? What's all that about? Is she okay?'

Beth dropped her gaze, wishing she'd never brought it up – especially in front of Alice. 'She mentioned some difficulties after Florence was born,' she said quickly, lest Alice should think it was something worse. 'But she got treatment quickly and everything is fine.' *Was* fine anyway. Because how could she be all right after this?

'Ah.' Alice swivelled back towards her desk and rifled through some papers. 'Right, you look exhausted. Why don't you head off? I'll see you tomorrow.'

Beth got to her feet. What had she just done? Instead of comforting her friend and providing support, she'd dropped a bomb right into the middle of the trauma. Maybe it was important Lenore accept the truth, but if she really had blocked out what happened due to the shock, then she'd be in pieces at a time when she'd need her strength more than ever. What kind of friend did that?

But Beth had no choice. She had to tell her; she had to stop anyone from finding out her past. A memory flooded into her mind of years ago – the face of another she'd sacrificed to save herself – but she pushed it away. She wasn't that woman any longer. She was a wife, a nursery worker, and about to become a mother.

So, why did she feel the past hanging over her, like a threatening mist that could envelop her at any time?

ELEVEN
LENORE

Lenore hung up the phone and stared at it, as if the handset could help her understand what had just happened. What *had* just happened? Had Beth really said Lenore had caused the accident? The words swirled around her head, slowly intertwining with James's voice and the way he'd looked at her – how he, too, had thought Florence must be hurt because of her.

He was wrong, though, and so was Beth. She hadn't gone inside to get Florence. She hadn't taken Florence out of the nursery to the car. For God's sake, she hadn't even taken her car. It had been such a nice day that after registering with the doctor, she'd decided to walk back to the nursery. She'd only just rounded the bend when she'd seen her daughter in the road.

But why would Beth say all that when she knew it wasn't true? Lenore chewed on her bottom lip as her mind spun. Could Beth have mistaken Lenore's car for another parent's? It was an easy enough error, given Lenore's small black Vauxhall was hardly unique. Or maybe... maybe Beth was worried she'd messed up – so worried she was trying to pin it on Lenore.

Maybe she was the one who'd let Florence tear off outside; who'd turned her back for an instant.

If so, Lenore could understand that she was afraid, and that she might not want to say she'd been responsible. Perhaps she was fearful she'd lose her job, but wasn't she going off on maternity leave in a few months' time anyway? Lenore knew she loved the Nest, but surely not enough to try to gaslight Lenore. They might not have known each other long, but she'd thought they'd connected; understood each other. To hit Lenore with such lies when her daughter was lying in hospital, well...

The sooner you come to terms with the truth, the better it will be. You must know that yourself, from everything you've been through in the past. Beth's words rang in her ears, and hurt and disbelief poured through her that Beth would use her struggles after Florence was born against her. Those words about coming to terms with the truth cut more deeply than she could ever know. They were exactly what James had said when she'd refused to believe that she'd almost harmed Florence.

James had found them huddled together on the floor. After he'd eased Florence from her arms, she'd sat dazed and numb beside him in the car as they raced to the hospital. When the nurse had asked her what happened, she hadn't been able to speak. She didn't know what had happened. All she could hear was the voices in her head. *You're not a good mother. You can't do this.* Over and over, as Florence had wailed and the eyes stared accusingly from the windows around her.

Then James had told the nurse what he'd seen, and she'd held her hands over her ears and started screaming.

That had been when they'd taken her away.

It had taken months of work with her therapist and endless talks with James until she finally accepted what she'd done. He'd been desperate for her to get well again. For him, her lack of accountability and confusion about that day was a sign of the illness still gripping her. It was only when she told him she remembered that he'd let her stay alone with Florence again, just for an hour or two.

She had almost hurt her daughter before. She did accept that. But this wasn't her fault, no matter what Beth had said.

It *wasn't*.

She thought of Florence in surgery, fighting for her life, and anger gripped her so strongly she started shaking all over again. How could Beth tell her she'd caused this? Did she think Lenore was so confused, so distrusting in her own capability as a mother after what she'd been through that she'd simply believe it?

Had she told those lies to Georgie and Alice too?

'Who was that?' She jerked as James gestured at the mobile in her hand. She hadn't noticed him come back into the waiting room – he'd been pacing the corridor outside. Her heart jumped as she met his eyes. How much had he heard? In the time they'd been waiting, his anger at whoever had caused the accident had been growing, as if it was a lightning rod for all his fear and pain. He'd started talking about heading to the nursery tomorrow to find out who was to blame.

What if he discovered the nursery thought *she* was?

'Just the Nest calling to see how Florence is,' she mumbled, praying he hadn't heard more. She held her breath until he simply nodded, his face twisting in fury at the mention of the nursery.

They both looked up as the doctor came down the corridor. His face sagged with exhaustion, and Lenore's heart pounded. Had Florence made it through the surgery all right? Every inch of her ached to hold her daughter in her arms, to draw her close and never let her go.

'And?' James's face was white.

'She's stable,' the doctor said, and Lenore felt her muscles sag in relief. Florence was still here. She still had her daughter. 'We managed to deal with the bleed and reinflate the lung. The leg fracture is severe, and that may need more attention later on down the line. We've given her plenty of medication to keep the pain under control and to help her sleep, and we'll keep her as comfortable as we can. But in time, she should make a full recovery.'

Lenore gripped onto James, emotion flooding through her. A full recovery. Thank God. Thank *God*. 'Can we see her?' She couldn't bear to think of her daughter all alone, even if she was unconscious.

'Yes, but then it's probably best if you both go home and rest,' the doctor said gently. 'You'll need all your energy for the road ahead.'

Lenore followed the doctor, thinking that energy wasn't a problem. There was no way she could rest.

'She's in here,' the doctor said, motioning to a cubicle in the corner of a ward. He pulled back the curtain, and Lenore rushed towards her daughter on the bed, desperate to touch her; to feel her breath. It was all she could do not to drag her away from this terrible nightmare, back to where everything would be okay – back to the life of light and happiness they'd had just hours earlier.

Beside her, James was shaking. 'I'm going to the Nest as soon as it opens,' he said, anger twisting his face. 'I'm going to talk to everyone there and find out what happened. And then I'm going to the police. Whoever did this – whoever hurt my daughter – is not going to get away with it.'

Lenore swallowed, fear shooting through her. If he went there, he was sure to hear Beth's ridiculous story. Would he believe it?

She stared at him as thoughts ran through her mind. He knew she was much better. He'd seen how well she'd coped these past few weeks without him, and she'd thought she was starting to gain his trust. But then... then earlier today, he'd said he never should have let them go, and that she wasn't ready.

He'd really believed she'd hurt Florence. Yes, he'd been in shock when he'd said those things, but clearly his doubt still hung heavy over the fragile foundation of belief she'd managed to build. She understood that. Doubt hung heavy over her, too, despite the load getting lighter day by day.

Would Beth's version of events break that foundation? Would it allow his doubt to seep in? *Would* he think she had hurt Florence; that she wasn't ready after all? She couldn't bear it, if so. She wanted him to believe in her. She needed him to.

'Let me talk to the nursery,' she whispered, her voice sounding loud in the hush of her daughter's room. 'I work—worked there.' After Florence had been hurt so badly on the premises, Lenore knew they could never go back. Sadness and anger struck her like a physical blow. The Nest had given her a sense of purpose and belonging. She had been part of the family, like Alice had said. And thanks to Beth, a woman she'd tried to help by sharing her past, that had been taken away.

The bright future she'd been building in her mind was also crumbling. The Nest had been an integral part of her vision of settling with James in Mapplestow, the lynchpin in the whole plan. Without the nursery and the community that came with it, what was the point? She wouldn't have the perfect job. She wouldn't have that sense of belonging. She'd be an outsider once more: the woman whose child had a terrible accident, whether people believed it was her fault or not. This place would be tainted with darkness too. Tears swam in her eyes, and she swiped them away. At least her daughter was alive, she told herself. She could cope with whatever came next.

'I know the people who work there. They're way more likely to open up with me than with you.' She shifted, praying Alice and Georgie would listen to her and not Beth. They'd have to, given she'd never got Florence in the first place. 'Then we can talk to the police if we need to.' Hopefully, though, Beth would come clean about the accident and nothing more need be done.

Her heartbeat raced as James paused, his eyes raking over her. 'Okay,' he said finally. 'I guess that makes sense. Do you think you're up for it, though? You've had such a shock. We both have. I just want to make sure you're all right.' He rubbed his face.

'I want to,' she said. 'I'll be fine.' He was right: she was exhausted and in shock. But now, all that mattered was moving forward – towards the family she'd hoped they could be.

Towards the family she hoped they *would* be, when all of this was over.

TWELVE
GEORGIE

'Hey, honey. You okay? You look completely wiped out.'

Georgie put down the mobile and turned to face Kasper, trying to stay steady on her feet. He was right: she was completely wiped out, both mentally and physically. The weight of what she'd done pressed heavily on her, and she wondered how she would ever move freely again.

She'd been so grateful to Alice for agreeing to keep quiet about who really was at fault. There would be no investigations, no stress. She could remain focused on her family. Instead, though, she'd potentially damaged another family by coming up with the story that Lenore had been to blame. A story Alice had readily bought into, giving Georgie a reprieve.

But how long would that hold out if Alice discovered the real reason Georgie hadn't closed the gate? Yes, she'd been distracted. She'd been unfocused. But it was more than dealing with her daughter's illness.

And if anyone knew what had really happened – the truth of why she'd left the gate open – then the consequences would be unbearable.

She never should have taken those pills. Not the very first

time, and not today. She'd never meant for them to become a habit, but... Georgie dropped her head, remembering when she'd first had one. She and Molly had just finished their usual slanging match, and Georgie had felt herself about to break down. She'd rushed into the toilet and closed the door, rummaging through the medicine cabinet to find some ibuprofen for her pounding head. Her fingers closed around a bottle at the back, and she squinted at the label. OxyContin, from an operation her mother had had last year. She'd stayed with them but only taken her pain meds when it was absolutely necessary, then left them behind.

Without thinking, Georgie had gulped one down. It had been a godsend, making everything fuzzy and unreal. So when she'd felt that same anxiety and the overwhelming urge to scream creep over her once more, she hadn't been able to resist downing another. And then another, and another, until living from pill to pill was all she could think about... apart from Molly's illness. But the pills dimmed the horror of that, as if she was staring at a car accident through a dirty, smeared window, unable to see all the gory detail, yet knowing it was brutal.

But nothing could dim the horror of what she'd done. She'd told herself no one would ever know; pledged never to tell Alice the truth. But then she'd remembered that even if she kept quiet, Alice could still find out. All she needed was to check the video Georgie religiously turned on each morning.

God, she was so stupid. With everything that had happened, she hadn't thought of the cameras covering the nap room and playrooms until she'd got home. If anyone saw what had really gone on, she'd face more than losing her job. She might face criminal charges, and what would that do to her family? They'd be more devastated than they already were.

Had she turned her back when taking the pill like she usually did, or had she been so desperate that she'd forgotten? Had the camera shown how dazed she was?

'Honey?' Kasper's voice cut into her thoughts.

'Sorry, I've a million things on my mind,' she said, manoeuvring into a chair before she collapsed. She'd tell him about the accident later. She needed to sit for a second. Then she had to get back to the Nest and delete that video. Alice might have forgotten they still used the system, but Georgie wasn't taking any chances.

'You relax,' Kasper said. 'I'll sort out supper. Spag bol okay?'

Georgie nodded, thinking how lucky she was to have him, though eating was the last thing on her mind. She hadn't felt like eating for months, and the weight was falling off her. But her son Theo would gulp everything down in seconds, while she and Molly just picked at it. It was amazing how much he could put away. She drew in a breath as Kasper clanked around the kitchen, whistling a jaunty tune. It was incredible how the world around her seemed so normal, yet everything felt changed.

'Kas?' She hauled herself to her feet. 'I forgot something at the Nest. I'll be right back.' Hopefully, Alice would have gone home.

'Okay.' Kasper continued whistling as she grabbed her keys and made her way to the car. She opened the door and leaned her head against the steering wheel, trying to gather up her energy.

It was only a short drive to the Nest, and she probably could have driven there with her eyes closed, she knew the route so well. This village was engrained into her mind – she'd always lived here, and even if she had once longed to leave, she loved it now. It had been the perfect place to grow up, the perfect place to raise a family... and the perfect place to manage the best nursery for miles. For the first time in her life, she had a place where people listened to her; followed her instructions.

Tears came to her eyes, and she swiped them away, trying to concentrate on the road. How could she not have closed that gate? How could she not have seen Florence running out? But most of all... how had she thought she could take the drugs at work and all would be fine? She would live with that guilt for the rest of her life, and she prayed that Florence would recover.

A police car drew up behind her, and she gripped the wheel tightly. She'd been driving okay, hadn't she? She slowed and the car went by, and relief shot through her. The last thing she needed was to be stopped. She could feel the bottle of pills pressing into her pocket.

After what felt like forever, she pulled into the Nest's car park. Thankfully, Alice's car was gone, and the lights were off inside. In the falling darkness of the spring evening, with birds singing in the soft hazy dusk and the fields and trees looming greenly behind the little brick building, it looked downright idyllic. But it would never be idyllic again. It would always be the place where she'd failed a child.

Failed herself.

Georgie got the key from her pocket and went inside, going straight to the office. She switched on the light, then turned on the computer, clicking on the file where the video was saved. She scrolled through the day, smiling at the kids and admiring how natural Beth was with them all. She hadn't been too sure when Alice proposed taking on a salaried assistant; she'd liked being the only one with full-time responsibilities to direct the parent volunteers. But Alice had been right when she'd said the nursery was growing fast and she could do with help.

Georgie had given in, silently agreeing she was finding it harder to keep up. Beth, with her gentle nature and positive attitude, had been a great addition, even if she'd never be the kind of woman Georgie could pal around with, laughing and giggling. There was a guardedness about her that Georgie only saw drop when she talked to Lenore.

Remembering why she was here, Georgie fast-forwarded the video until the moment right before they started taking the

kids to the garden. She sat back, watching Beth begin to herd
the children outside, then saw her grainy image in a corner,
shaking as she took a bottle out and swallowed a pill. She stag-
gered a few steps, then went out onto the steps, her head tipped
upwards, looking like a zombie.

Georgie let out a cry and before she could think about what
she was doing, she hit 'delete'. She couldn't watch herself like
that. She couldn't. It was one thing to know what it was like to
take the pills – to feel what it was like – and another thing to
watch. It was like being hit in the face with evidence of your
worst possible fears; of seeing yourself do the worst possible
things. And at the moment, she was filled with enough guilt and
loathing. She couldn't bear more. Breathing in, she went to the
recycling bin on the laptop and deleted the file again, just like
her son had showed her when she was trying to free up space on
her ancient laptop at home.

Gone. She sat back, tears running down her cheeks. The
video was gone. No one apart from Alice would know a fraction
of what had happened. And no one would know the real truth.

It was a small comfort – no comfort, really, in light of what
she'd done. But at least she wouldn't have to risk hurting her
family, at a time when they needed her more than ever. And as
soon as she was home, she was going to flush the rest of the pills
down the toilet.

Half an hour later, she crept past Kasper and Theo eating in
front of the TV in the lounge and went up the stairs to the
toilet, desperate to get rid of the pills before the urge to take
another took hold. She scrambled in her pocket to get the bottle,
but the pocket was empty. Brow furrowed, she tried the other,
but that was empty too.

Georgie froze, panic needling inside. Where was it? Had
she put it in her jacket, maybe? She padded down the stairs to

where she'd hung her jacket by the door, the panic growing as she rifled through it. Where the hell was that bottle?

She grabbed her jacket and shook it. Nothing came flying out; nothing rattled across the hardwood floor she so carefully protected. Desperate, she patted down her trousers, her pulse racing. There was no bottle of pills here, that much was obvious. But she knew she'd had it when she'd gone to the Nest to check the video. So, where was it?

Fear shot through her as a thought entered her mind. Could it have fallen out there? She took a deep breath, forcing aside that terrible possibility. Maybe it was in the car? Yes, that must be it. She crept out of the house, the cold air hitting her arms, and scoured the car, but there was no sign. Georgie collapsed in the driver's seat, shaking not just with the urge for another pill but with alarm. The bottle must have dropped out at the Nest. If someone found it, what would happen?

She jangled the keys in her hands. She had to go back there – right now. She had to get the bottle before anyone else did. It didn't have her name or the kind of pills on it; she'd been careful to decant them into an empty bottle. Whoever found it wouldn't know who it belonged to, or what the pills were. There were so many women in and out of that place, volunteering and picking up their children, that it could belong to anyone.

But Alice knew she hadn't closed the gate properly. She knew how unlike Georgie that was. What if she put two and two together? *Would* she continue to protect Georgie if she knew what had really happened?

'What are you doing?' Kasper's worried voice cut into her thoughts, and she looked up to see him standing in the doorway, framed by the golden light of the house. 'We've got a plate all ready for you inside.'

'Oh, I thought I'd left my mobile in the car,' she said, forcing a laugh. It was amazing she'd managed to pluck that excuse from the haze of her thoughts.

Kasper tilted his head. 'It's inside on the table, where you put it when you came in,' he said slowly.

'Oh yes, of course it is.' She let out another feeble laugh. 'I don't know what I was thinking.'

Kasper's eyes raked over her. She ran a hand through her hair, conscious she must look a mess. 'Are you okay?'

Georgie blinked, tears coming to her eyes. In the falling light, she prayed he couldn't see them. She was far from okay, but how could she begin to tell him what had happened? He was so strong; so solid and dependable. While she... she was falling apart. Anyway, she didn't have time to talk. She needed to get to the Nest.

'I was trying to find you,' Kasper said. 'Molly's calling. She went to sleep as soon as she got back from school – she was exhausted. She had some bad dreams, and she wants you to sit with her. I told her I would, but she wants you.'

Georgie drew in a breath. Molly's meds often gave her terrible dreams, and she always called for Georgie, just like she had when she was young. Georgie would sit beside her daughter until she drifted off, often keeping up a running commentary on the day's happenings at the Nest until she was certain Molly was asleep. It was one of her favourite times of the day. But now...

'Mum!' The cry cut into her, and she got out of the car. She had to be with her daughter. She'd go to the Nest early in the morning before anyone came. No one would be there tonight anyway.

Her secret was safe for the time being.

THIRTEEN
BETH

'Kids are asleep. Well, pretending to be anyway.' Rich plopped into a chair across from her and reached out to squeeze her foot. 'Want to do some baby-making?' He waggled his eyebrows comically, and despite all that had happened that day, Beth couldn't help smiling. She loved his sense of humour – the way he lifted her up and made everything around him seem light and happy.

He was the world's best father too. At thirteen and sixteen, Tiff and Jonah were well past the ages of needing their dad to put them to bed, but he still insisted on tucking them in and making sure their tablets and phones were stowed safely away, although they usually snuck them out again. She loved how protective he was of them – and of her. He would die before he let anything happen to his family.

'Look, I know it's been a brutal day.' Rich's face went soft. 'If that was one of ours, I can't imagine... How is the little girl anyway?'

'It's pretty serious. Lenore said she was in surgery when I rang.' Guilt swept over her once more when she recalled her friend's anguished tone, and how Beth had been the one to say her daughter had almost died because of her. How could she have done that? Yes, Lenore needed to know the truth, like Alice had said. But... Beth touched her stomach. She hadn't done it for Lenore. She'd done it for her.

To protect her present from her past.

Before she could stop it, the face that had haunted her for years flashed into her mind. His eyes from across the courtroom had cut through her, staring at her with such hatred it was like a physical blow. And when she'd left the stand after testifying against him, he'd hissed that he'd never forget this. He would ruin her life, the way she had ruined his.

So far, though, he hadn't managed. She'd moved to Guildford where no one knew her, going to college to get her childcare qualifications. She'd always loved working with kids: they were so enthusiastic, so willing to see the best in people, and they didn't care that she lived in the worst bit of town or that she had to hit the local foodbank to have something to eat. She'd met Rich when he'd come to the nursery where she'd been working in order to wire an extension that had recently been added. They'd chatted each day, and he'd started bringing her coffee, then lunch, and then he'd asked her out for supper. Despite keeping to herself for fear of someone finding out who she really was, she hadn't been able to help saying yes.

'I've been watching you with the kids,' he'd said with his kind, open smile that first night over spaghetti carbonara at the local Italian. 'I mean, not in a creepy way,' he added, holding up his hands. 'I love how kind and patient you are with them, how gentle. And they obviously adore you.'

She smiled, basking in his description of her. After so long of being seen as the bad one, his words were a balm to her soul.

'You know, you can tell a lot about people from how children respond to them. They follow you everywhere. You're a

good person, that's for certain.' He reached out for her hand,
and she shifted on the chair. Because he wasn't right. She wasn't
a good person. She *had* harmed someone. A memory of the day
she'd realised she had to leave popped into her head – a body,
sprawled on concrete – and guilt and fear pounded into her.

'It's been a while since I've had someone in my life,' Rich
continued. 'Cherie, well... she passed a few years ago.'

Beth had sat up, nearly dropping her food in her lap. His
wife had died? Rich was a widower, with two young kids? God,
how sad.

'And I haven't wanted to bring anyone round.' He made a
face. 'Those dating websites and the people on them are brutal.
I once went to meet a woman who said she was thirty, but when
I got there, she was in her sixties! I mean, for the love of God! If
you're going to lie about that, what else are you capable of?'

Beth nodded, trying to keep her face neutral.

'I haven't known you very long,' Rich said. 'But I have this
feeling about you, like I trust you already. I'd love it if you
would come meet Tiff and Jonah. I can cook you something that
will be a million times better than this.' He made a face at the
half-eaten pasta on their plates, and Beth laughed. She hadn't
wanted to be the first to say that this stuff was awful.

She stared at him, her mind whirring. This would be the
moment to tell the truth about the evil she'd been caught up in,
but she couldn't bear to burst the bubble of how he saw her –
the way he saw her. She wanted to be that person. Hell, she was
that person. The past was dead and buried, and there was no
point dredging it up again.

So she smiled and said yes, and that had been the start of
her new life as a wife, a step-mum and eventually, an assistant at
the Nest.

She loved the life she had now. She loved the person she
was now. And... she rubbed her belly. With this baby, finally,

her world was going to get better still. She couldn't bear to imagine Rich's face if the truth about her past came out: the sheer look of betrayal and disbelief that she wasn't the woman he'd thought she was.

And she couldn't bear to think of how the people around her would look at her: the same way they had when she'd been growing up, as if she was worthless. She drew in a breath as another thought hit. What would happen to her job at the nursery if anyone found out about her past? No way would she be able to keep working there, even if her criminal record had been expunged years earlier. The other parents would never want her around their children.

Her life – the life she'd built for years; the life she wanted to bring her baby into – would be gone. And she couldn't imagine raising her child in the terrible circumstances she'd grown up in herself.

She'd done the right thing, she told herself, taking in big breaths. Well, maybe not the right thing, but the only thing. Lenore might not accept the truth at the moment, but once the shock had worn off, she would.

'Are you okay?' Rich was staring at her with a concerned expression.

'I'm fine.' She wiped away the sweat which had beaded on her upper lip, the same way it always did when she was fearful or nervous. The day she'd got married, she'd practically sweated out a whole bottle of champagne, she'd been so worried something might go wrong. It hadn't, though, and it had been the best day of her life. She hated that she was lying to her husband for almost the first time in their marriage.

Soon, this would be behind her. Soon, she'd tell him about the baby they were about to have. She'd have everything she ever wanted. All she had to do was hold firm and ensure everyone knew that the blame lay with Lenore and not the nursery. There was nothing to investigate; no employee had been at fault. It had been a tragic accident caused by a parent, and nothing else.

Her future – her *baby's* future – depended on it.

FOURTEEN

ALICE

Alice forced a bright smile and waved goodbye as she climbed into her car later that night. It was already ten o'clock and she shouldn't have had that glass of white wine, but she'd needed to encourage Malena to relax. Grabbing a bottle and swinging by Mal's house under the pretence of thanking her for keeping everyone so calm at the Nest had been a stroke of genius, if she did say so herself.

She'd rung Simon to tell him and the kids she'd be home later than usual, but he hadn't answered. These days, she was lucky to exchange a few words with him before sleeping. She used to love that Simon was so low maintenance, unlike some of the other men she'd dated in law school who expected her to return their texts within seconds. When they'd finally spoken after running into each other every morning in the coffee shop around the corner from her office, Alice had been expecting him to ask for her number – or maybe even a date.

Instead, he'd just grinned and handed over her coffee. She'd been the one to ask him out; the one to text. She'd loved that she'd been in charge and that he wasn't running after her. No demands; no pressure. She had enough to worry about with law school, and Simon's easy-going, laid-back manner made her feel comforted and secure. In a world where she strived every day to impress and achieve, he was the one person she could count on to be there, regardless of when they'd last texted.

She'd asked him to marry her the day she'd graduated, practically organising the whole thing before he'd said yes. Any other man might have baulked at the thought, but Simon just laughed and said it was his dream scenario: all he had to do was turn up.

A memory flashed into her mind of their wedding day, and she shifted as a bit of discomfort needled. Her dad hadn't been able to travel due to his arthritis, and Simon's friends weren't exactly her biggest fans, brushing off her attempts to win them over. She'd been too busy at school to really make any firm mates, so they'd decided to elope.

It had been a spring day like this one, chilly with a fresh wind, and when they'd gone up the stairs of the registry office, she'd tripped and fallen, bruising her ankle. For anyone else it might have been an omen, but Alice had made the decision to marry Simon, and nothing was going to stop her or ruin this day... despite the fact that she had to hobble down the aisle. Or Simon's tiny hesitation and flick of the eye before saying 'I do' that no one else would notice unless they knew him as well as she did.

But he had said 'I do', and they'd gone for a night in the Dorchester Hotel, a luxury neither of them could afford at that time but had decided to splurge on. She'd guzzled champagne, then climbed in the bath, taking advantage of the tub that her bedsit didn't have. She'd lain there, trying to regain the comfort and security she always felt around Simon – around the man who was now her husband. That little twitch on his face had meant nothing. She shouldn't be even thinking about it. It was normal to have cold feet. What man didn't? They'd be fine.

And they *had* been fine, Alice thought. They had a home, a

family and a marriage where they loved and respected each other. Although of late they were more like ships in the night, Alice didn't doubt Simon's commitment to her. After all, hadn't she given him the life he'd wanted? Hadn't he got to stay with the kids while she worked in a job she hated?

Everything was great at home, she told herself firmly. It was the Nest she had to worry about. Malena had asked how Florence and Lenore were. Alice had responded by saying Lenore was in bits about how the accident had happened, and the story had unfolded naturally from there. Malena had nodded, said she would need to talk to Beth and Georgie to confirm, and then the talk had turned to local gossip. Alice had tried to get away earlier, but she hadn't wanted to make it obvious she'd only been there to get Malena on board with the story as quickly as possible.

And thanks to her, they were in the clear.

Well, almost.

There was just one more thing. One thing that could ruin all of this; a slip of paper that could unravel the miracle she'd pulled off. She needed to find it – find it and destroy it before it destroyed her. Because it showed the accident wasn't Georgie's fault, like she had believed. It wasn't Beth's either. There was only one person to blame, and it was her.

Florence had got into the road because of her. Florence had been hit by the car because of *her*.

Alice gunned the engine and pulled away from Malena's house, anger surging inside. That bloody garden gate – the gate she'd known was broken and had forgotten to fix. It was such a stupid, small detail. She should have passed it on to Georgie, if only she hadn't been so caught up in that asbestos fiasco. But she hadn't, and now a child in their care had almost died.

She shook her head, remembering how the security company had come a few days earlier to do their regular review of the premises, ensuring all the security measures were working properly. A bright-eyed young man had inspected everything, telling her that the electric gate to the garden wasn't working properly – that it failed to latch once closed. He'd plopped the report on her desk, and she'd meant to give it to Georgie to make her aware and schedule a fix, but her phone had bleeped, and she'd pushed the report aside, going back to research how the hell she was going to get around this asbestos problem.

The gate had remained unrepaired. Georgie could have closed it a million times, and Florence still would have been able to get out. The garden hadn't been secure, and with it so close to the road, it put every child at risk. Worse, Alice had known about it, and she hadn't fixed it.

If news of her neglect spread, it wouldn't just mean facing the co-op members' fury, like if the asbestos was found, or being removed from the board. It could mean facing criminal charges of negligence. It would put an end to her law career... if she could call her work at the bottom echelon a 'career'. Worse still, she would never be able to work in the childcare industry again.

She slapped the steering wheel as she drove through the night. She had to find that report and get rid of it, but where the *hell* had she put it? She'd searched the office high and low before ducking out to Malena's, desperate to uncover it. *Leave the details to the little people,* her father had always told her. *Focus on the big ideas, the big picture. That's how you'll succeed.* She snorted, thinking how she'd tried to do just that. Funny how she'd ended up in a job where her whole role was checking details, and how a little detail could unravel the big picture she'd worked so hard to bring to reality.

No, she told herself. She wouldn't let it. She swivelled her neck, trying to ease the tension in her shoulders. Everything was fine. The big picture was intact. The Nest would remain a place of comfort, safety and caring. Everyone was on board, and Beth had been surprisingly easy to convince to betray Lenore, given that – from what Georgie had told her – Beth and Lenore were friends.

Underneath Beth's soft exterior, though, Alice had sensed something a little harder – a kind of steeliness that Alice admired. The Nest had given Beth an important foothold into the close community: immediate status and friendliness that other outsiders would have to work years to gain. That must be why she was so keen to preserve it, even at the expense of a budding friendship. And Georgie would never say a word, especially since she believed she was the one at fault. Alice would have her eternal gratitude for covering up what she thought she'd done.

Everything was going smoothly, but she needed to find that report. She turned into the car park, then slid her key into the lock and went to the office, resuming her search through the files in the corner. Usually, Georgie kept the office in tip-top shape, filing and tidying the trail of destruction and chaos Alice left behind. But she hadn't done anything for the past week, and the place was a disaster.

At least if she couldn't find it, no one else would be able to either. Not that she could take that risk, of course. Finally, just when she thought she'd never be able to retrieve it, she felt something sticking to the back of the folder she was going through. Holding her breath, she lifted it up. Bingo!

She held the paper in her hands, her heart beating fast. Rummaging in her drawer, she retrieved the matches she always kept there, along with a pack of cigarettes. She'd been a regular smoker in university, but when she'd started in the law firm in London, she'd noticed the people at the top never took breaks. She'd kicked the habit through sheer willpower and grit, hanging onto her final carton of cigarettes to show herself she was better than anything that might try to bring her down. She still had that carton here, a kind of talisman to her strength.

Alice lit a match and put the edge of the report into the

flame, watching it burn. She'd call the security company first thing tomorrow and have them fence off and gate the car park, under the guise of doing everything to help parents keep their children safe after pick-up. While they were here, she could have them 'upgrade' all the gates – nobody would spot they were actually fixing one. It would cost extra money, but no one would ever know that was how Florence had got into the road.

Alice stretched out her legs, her foot sending something rattling across the floor. She sat up. What was that? Georgie may have slumped on her paperwork duties, but having a random toy out of place was unheard of, especially in the office. She got up and scanned the space, eyebrows rising when she spotted a pill bottle. It was unmarked but half-full of small round pills stamped with 'OC' on one side. Alice tilted her head, thinking of her father. In the years before his death, his arthritis had been too severe to stay on his own after Alice's mother had left him. He'd moved into a care home not far from here, and the only thing that had helped him get through the day were pills exactly like these ones: OxyContin, an opioid she knew was prescription only.

What was a bottle of painkillers doing here – painkillers in an unmarked bottle? The only two people besides her who used the office were Georgie and Beth. In a million years, she knew Georgie would never take medication unless the doctor told her. So, maybe they belonged to Beth? Was that why Beth had been so willing to blame Lenore? She was worried about someone nosing around, finding out about her pill habit?

Alice gripped the bottle, fury shooting through her as she thought of how the reputation of the nursery could have been endangered if this got out. Nursery workers, taking unpre-scribed painkillers? Even if neither was responsible for the acci-dent, this could be disastrous... especially if anyone found out about the gate and tried to link the two. She froze as a thought hit. *Could* these drugs have been Georgie's? Was this why she'd thought she must not have closed the gate properly, because she'd been so out of it that she couldn't remember?

Alice took a big breath in, trying to keep her anger under control. To be honest, she couldn't picture either Georgie or Beth taking these pills. They both worked hard and were utterly committed to the Nest. But the bottle had got here somehow. It belonged to someone. If these were Georgie's, she deserved to believe she'd caused the accident. And if they were Beth's, then it made sense why she'd been so keen to shift the police away from investigating.

Alice slid the bottle of pills into her pocket. Whoever they belonged to, they were leverage to use if Beth or Georgie ever felt like talking.

Finally, a detail that could work in her favour.

FIFTEEN
LENORE

The first rays of sun slanted through the blinds of the waiting room, and Lenore glanced at the clock on the wall. Seven a.m., and the nursery would be opening in an hour. Though every bit of her ached with exhaustion, she propelled herself to her feet, glancing down at James who was dozing on the chair beside her.

In sleep, his face was soft and open, the lines of worry eased out. Her heart shifted as she thought that this was the person she remembered; the man she loved: tender, caring, gentle. Not the ever-present warden living on the edge, fearful his wife would hurt herself or their daughter.

She drew in a breath, remembering how he'd first blamed her for what happened to Florence. She couldn't go back to that; couldn't live with the feeling that she couldn't be trusted with the person she held dearest. She didn't want James to have to carry her any longer... she didn't need him to. She'd proved that to herself, despite only being on her own a short time. He had to keep believing in her and keep that fragile trust she'd earned growing.

'James,' she whispered, and he jerked awake.

'Florence?' he said, eyes widening in fear.

'She's fine,' Lenore said quickly. The night nurse had popped in not long ago to tell her that Florence had had a good night, and that for the next few days there wouldn't be much news to deliver as they kept her sedated. 'I'm going to the Nest,' she said, rubbing her eyes. 'I'm going to find out what happened.'

James reached for her hand. 'Listen, why don't you let me go? They're probably still trying to figure out what went wrong anyway. Get some sleep, and I'll have a word.'

Lenore shook her head. 'I want to talk to them.'

'Okay. But come back fast, all right? And whatever they say, we'll get through this together. I'll be here for you.' He yawned and his eyes closed again.

She nodded, thankful for his support after yesterday's harsh words. Thankful, too, that he believed in her enough to confront the nursery and find the truth of what had happened to their daughter. It was hard to shake off the past. She understood that, but she couldn't let it envelop them again.

The air outside the hospital smelled like wet leaves and earth, and she breathed in as she waited for a taxi to take her to the Nest. This time yesterday, she'd been on her way to the nursery with Florence. She'd been happy, and for the first time in ages, she'd felt settled. She'd actually been excited for the future. Twenty-four hours later, that life and her dream were destroyed. Her daughter was lying in a hospital bed, and someone she'd trusted with her darkest secret had betrayed her in the worst way possible. James was right: whoever had caused this accident did deserve to be punished. Anger gripped her so strongly that she almost didn't feel tired any more. She couldn't wait to ask Beth in person what had happened. Surely, she wouldn't dare lie straight to her face.

The taxi pulled into the Nest's car park and Lenore climbed out, blinking into the misty morning sun at the building in front of her. The windows were still dark, and the car park empty except for—

She squinted, wondering if her mind was playing tricks on her. Was that her car, parked on the far side of the car park? She peered closer, remembering her earlier thought that maybe Beth had mistaken it for someone else's. But yes, it was definitely hers. What on earth was it doing here?

Lenore tilted her head, struggling to grab hold of memories through the haze of exhaustion. She'd driven here with Florence that morning. She'd left for the doctor's after lunch, ducking home for the paperwork she'd forgotten to bring with her in the morning rush. She'd been about to get back in the car, but it had been such a gorgeous day she'd walked to the nearby surgery, leaving the car in the drive at home.

Miraculously, she'd finished at the surgery in record time. She remembered standing in the waiting room, thinking that maybe she would head straight to the Nest on foot rather than pick up the car from home. Although they usually drove, Florence loved the short walk back to their place, pulling up weeds from the roadsides and sloshing through the little stream that ran alongside in her wellies.

Then her mobile had rung, and Lenore had struggled to get away from an over-enthusiastic cold caller. She'd left the surgery later than she'd wanted, and she could remember jangling the keys in her hands, debating whether to hurry home and get the car or still walk...

She stared at the car in front of her. She wasn't going crazy, right? She hadn't driven here. Had she? The answer to her question was right in front of her, and yet... and yet, she could remember none of the journey from the surgery to the Nest. All she could recall was Florence in the road. The car sucking her daughter under. The terror as she raced towards her, unsure if she was alive. The panic when the paramedic hadn't denied that her daughter might yet die. Everything else was buried in that haze of emotion.

But no one else had keys to the car. Nothing else could explain how it had got here. She *must* have been in the car park yesterday. She must have come to pick up Florence. So, why couldn't she remember?

And if she couldn't remember that, then what else was she missing?

She felt herself swaying as fear and panic washed over her. Pictures scrolled through her mind, narrated by Beth's voice telling the story. *You were bringing her out to the car when Georgie and I heard the scream. She must have got away from you somehow and run into the road. And then—*

No. Nausea rose and she sank to the step. Those weren't memories, she told herself. That didn't happen. She hadn't done anything wrong. There was nothing wrong with her either. So she didn't remember driving back here. So what? She'd had a huge shock and a sleepless night. And sometimes things got a little fuzzy when she was tired. That was normal.

Even as she told herself that, though, the fear and panic still pressed down on her. She jerked to her feet and rushed to the car, as if it could protect her. She had to talk to Beth before James did, but she couldn't face her like this. She knew she hadn't caused the accident. She did trust herself – trust that she wouldn't have let Florence run into the road. But...

She gripped the steering wheel, thinking how right she'd been that the past was hard to shake off. Because although she knew it wasn't her fault, the ever-present doubt that had been fading was gathering once more, joining with the fear and panic, pressing stronger on the thin layer of belief she'd worked hard to build. She could feel it shaking; feel it creaking under the weight of emotion. And she couldn't risk letting cracks form. Not now. Not before she'd faced Beth.

She needed to get back to her daughter, she thought, fastening her seat belt. That was the only thing that would make her feel strong again and remind her of how far she'd come. She'd sit beside her for a bit; maybe get some sleep. Then things would be clearer.

Then she'd be ready – ready to face any accusations and lies.

Ready to find the truth.

SIXTEEN
ALICE

Alice sat up before the alarm went off, quietly rolling out of bed to avoid waking Simon. He'd been asleep when she got home last night, and although the last thing she wanted to do was talk about the terrible day, she missed when she would slide into bed and cuddle up against him, feeling as if he was a safe place where she could finally relax. She'd lain there and listened to him breathing, the space between them like miles, tossing and turning until she finally drifted off to sleep.

She stepped into her sharply tailored black suit and scraped her hair into a tight bun at the nape of her neck. Yesterday had been horrendous, but she had managed to get everything under control. No one would know the gate had been faulty. No one would know she or anyone at the Nest was to blame. She would station herself at the front door of the nursery this morning to reassure everyone that it was a tragic case of parental inattention. Later today, the security team would arrive to upgrade everything, and the parents would be so grateful. With Georgie and Beth flanking her, they would present a united front no one would question. And if either of her team did feel like talking, she always had that pill bottle.

Alice glanced at her mobile, wincing when she saw the column of unread emails from the office. Today was the day her team would present a big brief at the court, and she needed to be there to hand over the part she'd been responsible for. Actually, she should have been at the office all night with the rest of them, fine-tuning the arguments and deciding if 'if' or 'and' was the better word choice, even if she wasn't high enough on the totem pole to accompany the team to court. The Nest came first, though. She'd deal with everything else later. They probably wouldn't notice she was missing.

She pulled into the car park at the nursery, blinking in surprise that Lenore's car was gone. When had she come to collect it? Alice wondered. Florence must be okay if Lenore had left her side. The fact that it was gone made Alice more relaxed. Lenore had been here, and she hadn't caused any trouble. She'd be with her daughter now, away from here. They could put all of this behind them.

Alice unlocked the door to the Nest and went inside, breathing in the quiet and serene surroundings.

'Oh, you're here!' Georgie burst through the door just after her and Alice sighed. Peacefulness over; she'd have to use all her energy to make sure her manager didn't break down in tears or self-flagellation. They needed to avoid anything that might make them appear vaguely guilty, and Georgie looked downright awful. Her face was white and drawn, and she was so jumpy her own shadow might scare her. Alice stared hard at her, wondering once more if those drugs could be hers. Surely not, though. The thought was laughable.

'Have you...' Georgie seemed almost afraid to ask. 'Have you heard anything about Florence?'

Alice shook her head. 'No, not since yesterday. But Lenore's car is gone, so she must be doing okay.'

'Hi, all.' Beth came in, and Alice raised her eyebrows at her tired and haggard appearance. God, her staff really needed to pull themselves together. They couldn't face the morning drop-off like death warmed over. Forcing a smile, Alice dug in her handbag for some foundation and blush. It might not be the right shade for Beth, but at least it would make her look alive.

'Here.' She handed the make-up to Beth. 'Slap some on – it will make you feel better.' But Beth only stared at the make-up in her hand, as if Alice was offering her something crazy. 'Come on, put it on. We—Oh, good morning!' She forced her smile bigger as the first of the parents showed up with three of her children in tow. 'Are you dropping off, or are you on the rota for the day? So nice to see you!'

For the next fifteen minutes, Alice was swamped as women huddled around her, pouring out sympathy and explaining in a low, serious tone exactly what had happened to lead Florence out into the road, how she was going to install a fence for the car park and upgrade everything, and the possibility of starting a GoFundMe page for Lenore and Florence, to help them out while Florence was in hospital.

None of the women questioned whether what had happened could be the fault of the Nest, and Alice was finally able to slip out of the nursery and catch the train to the office. She was going to be spectacularly late, but hopefully the team would be so busy getting ready for the afternoon that they wouldn't notice. She was almost as invisible at work as she was at home, she thought to herself.

Sadly, despite her efforts to sneak down the corridor to her tiny office, Pritesh spotted her through the glass of the conference room. He got up and poked his head out.

'Where have you been?' He looked at her disapprovingly. 'We've been waiting hours for you. We need that brief you were working on – the one you said you put on my desk? The one that's not actually there?' He raised his eyebrows. 'We're leaving for court in half an hour. Didn't you get my messages?'

'Here you go,' she said smoothly, hauling it out of her bag, then brushing past him into her office. She slid out the phone, relieved to see no new messages. The quieter, the better.

She glanced up at the sound of the door closing behind her, not bothering to hide her irritation as Pritesh came into her office.

'Yes?' she asked. 'I thought you had to go.' These millennials really did struggle with time management, didn't they?

But Pritesh wasn't leaving. Instead, he was standing his ground. And he wasn't alone – he was accompanied by Jenny, their HR, who looked supremely uncomfortable. She and Jenny had joined the firm at the same time; Jenny had been the one to soften the blow when, review after review, Alice failed to make partner, citing her 'lack of commitment and attention to detail'.

What was Jenny doing here? Surely, she wasn't going to give her another warning. It was getting embarrassing – for the firm, not Alice.

'Sit down, please,' Jenny said, and her voice wasn't the usual warm tone that Alice had come to know. Alice shook her head. Whatever warning she was here to deliver – because it obviously wasn't good news – Alice wasn't going to lower herself while they towered over her.

'I have tried my best to work with you,' Pritesh began. 'I really have. The team has all tried to work with you. But you're consistently late and you leave early. We needed that brief today, and you weren't here.' He took a breath. 'We simply cannot allow you to damage this firm's reputation.' The words fell like a hammer, and Alice felt shock go through her. They weren't going to *fire* her, were they?

'We have given you three warnings,' Pritesh was continuing. Alice opened her mouth to protest that surely those couldn't have been *official* warnings, but Pritesh held up a hand. 'Jenny has them on record,' he said, and Alice closed her mouth as Jenny nodded.

'You've had ample time to make changes. To be frank, in my

opinion, you're lucky the firm has retained you this long. When I came on board, I was assured that despite your clear lack of attention, you were a valuable team member.' Jenny shifted, and Alice could see the words had come from her. 'But I only see someone who simply can't be bothered to put the work in. If I'm being honest, all you have done is drag us down. We needed that brief yesterday, not now.'

Alice pursed her lips, her mind spinning. She had to admit that she hadn't been at the top of her game lately – for a while, actually. It was just, well... details were for the people at the bottom of the chain. And she shouldn't still be at the bottom of the chain, simple as that. The work they kept giving her was beneath her. She might have tried harder if they'd assigned her something more intellectually stimulating.

But she wasn't going to let anyone fire her, for God's sake. She wouldn't give them the satisfaction. She'd resign, and she'd make it clear to all she was leaving on her own terms. She would be in control, and no one else.

'I'm happy to work out my notice period,' she said, drawing herself to her full height on her heels. She wasn't going to miss wearing those every day. 'But I'd like to tender my resignation as of today.' She should have done this years ago. Perhaps she *would* have done this years ago if it hadn't been for Simon staying home... and that unshakeable sense of letting her father down. But he wouldn't want her to stay somewhere she wasn't valued, she told herself. And it was more than clear that she was anything but valued here.

Jenny gasped and covered her mouth, and Alice only just stopped herself from rolling her eyes. So dramatic.

But Pritesh didn't look fazed or even shocked, and Alice felt something stir inside. She'd been here for years. Surely, she deserved some kind of response; some pleading to stay. But then, given what he'd just said, she was hardly in his good books.

'Don't worry about working out your notice period,' he said, his voice hard. 'You can get your things and go.'

Alice's mouth fell open. Go? No goodbye party, no speeches about how much they'd miss her? No chance to do the rounds of the office and say how much she would miss everyone, though she knew she wouldn't? Instead, she was being dismissed as if she had been fired, clearing out her desk and doing the walk of shame with the cardboard box like some lowly intern. All these years in this place, and she would have nothing to take away.

But what did it matter? She didn't want to take anything from here anyway. If she was being honest, all she really cared about was the Nest. And now she had what she'd always wanted: more time to focus, to invest, to come up with the big ideas she was famous for. The firm would still be paying her for the next three months, and she might be able to get a good income from the Nest if she changed the co-op structure to a proper private business. She could expand, starting up new nurseries in other villages around the area. In a time when people were screaming out for childcare, it wouldn't be hard to fill the places. Okay, so nurseries weren't known for being cash cows, but if he needed to, Simon could stop wasting time on the internet and find a job.

And maybe... she tilted her head as a seed of hope sprouted. Maybe it would finally create some space in the family for her.

She opened a drawer, shovelling the contents into her hand-bag. Jenny stood for a minute, then ushered Pritesh from the room and closed the door quietly behind her, leaving Alice alone in the office she'd always felt was more like a prison cell than anything else.

This was a good thing, she told herself. This was just what she needed to inspire her and give her a new focus. Give her an even more visible presence in the community... in the whole area. And the timing couldn't be better. The accident and

Lenore might be behind them, but she still had to deal with the asbestos issue. This would allow her to really put her mind to solving that problem. In fact, she'd head straight to the nursery instead of going home.

One door might have closed behind her – or, rather, she might have closed that door. But a whole new world – a better world – awaited.

And this time, nothing would stop her.

SEVENTEEN
LENORE

Lenore sat beside her daughter's bed, listening to the beeping of the machines as her daughter slept. She knew Florence didn't realise she was there, but being close to her was having the effect she'd hoped: making the doubt lift; clearing the confusion, the panic and the fear away. Maybe she had driven her car to the nursery. Maybe she didn't remember because of the shock that had followed. But that didn't mean she'd caused the accident, no matter what Beth tried to tell her. She would never hurt her child again. She knew that much for sure, and she was ready to fight anyone who would suggest it.

'Hey.' James came in and sat down beside her. 'I didn't know you were back.' He'd been sleeping when she'd returned, stretched across several seats in the waiting room, his chest rising and falling in a steady rhythm. 'How is she?'

'The same.' Despite the nurses saying there'd be little change for a day or two, Lenore couldn't help hoping that, against all odds, Florence would wake up, smile her cheeky smile, and ask for some 'chocca', her word for the chocolate Lenore sometimes slipped her when James wasn't looking. 'I went to the Nest, but no one was there,' she said. 'It might be a good thing, actually. I'll go back later. More time to talk after the morning rush is over.'

'Lenore...' James leaned back in his chair. 'Look, we need to talk,' he said in the soft, gentle tone she knew so well from the past. She winced, thinking she hadn't heard that for a while. Why was he speaking to her this way? 'I don't want to upset you – I know you've been under a lot of strain lately. But I think it's best if you stay away from the nursery.'

She raised her eyebrows. What? Didn't he want to find out what had happened?

'A police officer came by when you were out,' he explained, before she could ask. 'She dropped off some things they found on the road.' He held up a plastic bag with two small red shoes, and Lenore's gut squeezed at the thought of the car hitting her daughter so hard that her shoes had come off. 'She said she knew you, and she wanted to see how Florence was... how you were, after everything.'

Lenore swallowed. Oh, God. A police officer who knew her. It must have been Malena. How much did she know? Had Beth spread her story, and did she believe it? What exactly had she told James, and did *he* believe it? Her heart started pounding, and sweat broke out in a cold, clammy film on her body. Please let him not think she'd caused the accident. Please let him trust her; trust that she was a good mother. Trust that what he'd seen these past two weeks was the woman she was.

'I know you would never want to hurt Florence,' he said, breaking into her thoughts. She sagged with relief, but before she could say anything, his next words made fear shoot through her once more. 'Not on purpose anyway.'

She sucked in her breath. What did that mean? That he believed Malena? She had to tell him she wasn't to blame. He had to believe her.

'And I'm sorry I lashed out at you yesterday. I was just so scared of losing her.' He put a hand on her arm. 'I understand how it could put you on the defensive. But Lenore, you can tell me what really happened. I know you were there. The officer said your car was in the car park. Don't you remember?'

She flinched, knowing the significance of his question. When that first episode with Florence had happened, he'd asked her over and over if she could recall what she'd done, unable to understand how she couldn't. And now, once more she was missing memories. *Would* he believe her when she said it wasn't her? Could he trust that this wasn't an echo of the past? If he started doubting her, then he would believe whatever Malena had told him. And with Lenore's car at the Nest, the story was believable.

But it wasn't what happened, and she needed her husband to listen to her.

'Yes, I guess I was at the nursery,' she said, holding his gaze. 'I must have driven from the surgery after all. But James—'

'You guess?' He cut her off before she could say that she hadn't gone in to get Florence. She hadn't let her daughter run into the road, no matter what Malena might have said. 'I was afraid of that, Lenore. Afraid you'd start...' He tilted his head. 'Getting disoriented again. Forgetting things, like you did before.'

Lenore shook her head. No. No, no, no. She couldn't let him do this. She hadn't been disoriented. It wasn't the same as when Florence was born. Her daughter had had a terrible accident. Before the accident, she'd been doing fine. Great even. Despite James saying she'd been under a lot of strain, she hadn't forgotten anything.

Okay, yes, so maybe she'd had to go back for the surgery's paperwork yesterday. That was normal, though, when trying to corral a child through the morning routine. And then there'd been the night she hadn't locked the front door, but that was only because James had always done it. And— *I'm fine*, she told herself through gritted teeth.

'You are taking your medication, right? Maybe it's time to review the doses again. Maybe that's why you can't remember. Or maybe...' He gripped her hand as his words trailed off. 'I can bring you back to the doctor in London today. I know you don't like going there, but we've been through so much. If you need help, we have to get it for you. I couldn't bear it if something happened to you too. I remember what you were like when I found you in the bath, and...' He didn't finish his sentence, but he didn't have to. She'd never forget how he'd hauled her from the tub and wrapped a towel around her as she shook in his arms. They'd both been crying.

But she'd been in the grip of an illness then. She *had* hurt her daughter, although she hadn't meant to, and the guilt and pain were too much to bear. This wasn't the same – not even close. She wasn't responsible for what had happened this time.

'No.' She wasn't going to leave her daughter's side to go to a doctor when there was no reason. She didn't need help. Everything had been wonderful. She'd been happier than ever. 'Absolutely not.' She drew in a breath and turned to face him. He needed to hear her. 'I don't know exactly what Malena told you, but I didn't let Florence run into the road. You have to believe me.'

James's face twisted, and she could see that he was struggling. 'But you don't remember driving there. You don't remember—'

'Hello.' A nurse poked her head inside the room, and Lenore exhaled, thankful for the interruption. 'She's doing really well.' She smiled towards Florence on the bed. 'Would you like to bring in anything for her? Some familiar objects – soft toys, photos, maybe? It might be a comfort for her when she wakes up.'

Lenore nodded. 'Yes, that's a great idea.' Having a few of Florence's favourite things dotted around would make all of this seem less clinical. 'I'll bring some in as soon as I can.' She blinked, picturing Freddie, her daughter's favourite stuffed dog. Ever since they'd left London, she went everywhere with that thing, insisting on bringing it to nursery and back again – a comfort to her with all of the changes she'd been through. If she woke up and it wasn't here, there'd be hell to pay.

Come to think of it, where *was* Freddie? She jerked as a thought hit. Beth claimed that Florence had run off from the car park after Lenore took her out, and everyone believed her. But Florence would never leave without Freddie, so if Beth's story was true, she would have been carrying Freddie when she'd been hit. Either that or Lenore had put the soft toy in the car, because no way would they have left Freddie behind at the nursery.

But Lenore hadn't picked up Florence, and Freddie wasn't in the car. Florence hadn't been carrying it when she'd been hit, because she hadn't been intending to leave for the day. There was only one place the soft toy could be, and that was at the Nest.

Beth's story wasn't true, and Lenore had a chance to prove it: to the nursery, to Malena, to her husband. And with proof she'd never brought Florence out, Beth would have to say what had really happened. James would stop worrying about her and making comments about upping her meds. He would believe she'd done nothing wrong.

He would believe she *was* a good mother. The past would stay behind them, where it belonged.

She got to her feet. 'We can talk later, okay? I'll head home and get some things. I'll be back soon.'

The sooner, the better.

A few minutes later, she pulled up in front of the Nest, eyes widening at the workers installing a fence around the perimeter of the car park with what looked like an electronic gate. Was

Alice doing that because she knew something had gone wrong –
that Beth had let Florence get out? Or did she truly believe it
was Lenore's fault and this was simply to show how in tune the
Nest was with other parents' fears?

It didn't matter anyway. Lenore didn't care about the Nest.
All she cared about was her daughter and doing what she could
to keep moving forward. Energy and determination shot
through her, and she got out of the car and marched to the door.
She knew exactly where Freddie would be. Afraid he would get
dirty or lost, she'd made him his own cubbyhole where he hung
out during the day, ready to be plucked at the last minute when
they headed home. She had her key to the Nest. All she'd have
to do was go inside, get Freddie, and go from there.

She drew her key from her pocket and tried to fit it in the
lock, but the whole system seemed to have been changed. In
fact, there didn't seem to be a place to put the key any more.

'We're upgrading everything today,' a man from the security
company called from where he was pounding in a fence post.
'Sorry, I don't have the code for the door. You'll need to ring the
buzzer.'

Lenore's heart sank. Beth would know that Lenore didn't
believe her. Would she even let her in? Would Alice or Georgie
either? She tapped her foot, her mind racing. Freddie's cubbyhole was right by the children's coat hooks. She could say she
was looking for Florence's jacket, then grab Freddie too.

She pressed down hard on the buzzer and waited.

'Hello, come on in. Oh.' Alice's mouth gaped when she
spotted who it was. 'Lenore. I'm so glad you're here. We have all
been wondering how Florence is doing.'

Not enough to call, Lenore thought. The only one who had
rung was Beth, and that was to make sure she got her story
straight. Sadness and hurt needled Lenore that none of these
women really cared.

'She's sleeping, under heavy sedation,' Lenore said tightly, not wanting to waste time. 'I just came by to get her coat. I think she left it on the hanger.'

'Her coat?' Alice drew back, and Lenore had to admit it was a strange thing to think about when your child was lying in the ICU. 'I don't think she left anything here. Malena would have dropped it off with the rest of her things, if so.'

Lenore blinked at the thought of those small red shoes, and anger poured through her once more. She had to see if Freddie was here. She had to. 'Can I have a look? Please?'

Alice paused, then shrugged. 'Sure, of course.' Alice waved her in, and relief flooded over her. 'Beth and Georgie are out in the garden, otherwise I'm sure they'd love to send their best wishes to you and Florence.'

Lenore forced a smile, her heart pounding as she went down the corridor towards the coat hooks, then reached out to the cubbyhole. This was it. Soon, she'd have Freddie. Soon, she'd have proof she'd never got her daughter. She pulled open the drawer, excitement growing inside.

Her heart plummeted. The drawer was empty. Frantically, she scanned the small space, again and again. But nothing was there. Panic clutched at her, and she tore into the playroom, emptying out the toybox in the corner in case it was inside and upending the bin full of Lego. She raced into the nap room and peered into all the cots, one after another, praying to see Freddie's lopsided grinning face.

But still there was nothing.

'What on earth are you doing?' Alice appeared at her side, and she swung towards her.

'I need to see Beth.' The words burst out of her. 'I don't know what she told you. But what happened to Florence wasn't my fault. She got out of the Nest somehow and into the road, and I think it's because of Beth. She's trying to make it seem like me, though. And it wasn't. It wasn't, and I can prove it.' Or she thought she could anyway.

'Lenore.' Alice put a hand on her arm. 'Calm down. Please.' Her voice was soft, but her grip strong. She tried to propel her back towards the reception, but Lenore refused to budge. 'We all support you,' she said. 'We all understand how hard this must be. How you'd want to do anything to prove it wasn't you. We are with you, and we will do whatever we can to help.' She kept trying to move Lenore down the corridor, but still she refused.

'You know how you can support me?' Lenore drew herself up, anger spurting through her. 'You can get Beth to tell me what really happened. How my child almost *died* when she should have been safe here.'

Alice's gaze was sympathetic. 'I'm so sorry you're going through this. I wish things could be different for you. I know it can't be easy when you're battling mental health issues too.' She paused, and Lenore's anger grew into rage. What exactly had Beth said? How dare she spread something Lenore had told her in confidence? It felt like everyone was using that against her. 'But I can't have you come in here and attack my staff. Only you know what happened with your daughter because you'd already collected her. The Nest had nothing to do with it, and the police agree.' Lenore shook her head. Of course the police agreed. Half of them were on the co-op board here, including Malena.

'I think you should go. Go, be with your daughter.' She stared hard at Lenore. 'You need to leave, or I will call the police to escort you out.'

Lenore was shaking as Alice led her outside. For a second, she thought she might pass out; that the anger, pain and accusations were too much to bear. There was nothing wrong with her. She *hadn't* picked up Florence. And yet Freddie wasn't here – at least not in his usual place. So, where else could he be?

Could he be at home, maybe? Had they somehow forgotten

to bring him in that day? No. No way. Florence never would have left him.

Could... She swallowed as the thought entered her head. Could Beth have been clever enough to hide him somewhere? Or destroy him? She knew Florence loved the soft toy and brought him with her every day. She *knew* Florence would never leave without it.

Bitterness billowed inside. How could Beth do this to her? To Florence? And now she had to go back and face James. He'd heard the story. He'd heard she was to blame. He believed she was, and she still couldn't prove otherwise. He was already talking about how worried he was; how he wanted her to review her meds. If he thought she wasn't well, how would he ever trust what she said? Her face twisted as she recalled Alice saying how it must be hard with her 'mental health issues', along with an expression of derision and triumph, like she'd found a trump card.

'I'm not going to stop,' she blurted, though she had no idea what she could do. Break in, tear the nursery apart and pray that Freddie was there somehow? Ransack Beth's place to find him? People really would think there was something wrong with her then.

'You can say what you want, but I'm not going anywhere. Something went wrong here. Something that almost killed my daughter. Maybe you know, maybe you don't, but I'm going to find out. If the police don't want to investigate, I can hire my own investigator. I know everyone in this village looks up to you, respects you. But I can spread stories too. And even if they aren't true, they might just stick.'

Then, heart pounding, she pushed out of the door of the Nest and got into the car, gravel flying as she spun away.

EIGHTEEN
BETH

'Would you like more rice?' Beth hovered over a little girl with pigtails who was devouring her lunch. The girl nodded, then grabbed the rice Beth served her with one hand and shoved it into her mouth. Beth sighed and tried to pry some out. The last thing they needed was for a child to choke the day after the accident. She glanced at Georgie, who looked as pale and tired as she felt. They'd somehow managed to get through the hours, but they both resembled zombies.

Thank God Alice had been here to fend off Lenore. Beth and Georgie had been with the children in the garden when they'd seen Lenore pull into the car park. Beth had wanted to give her a huge hug and say she was there for her. But then fear had gripped her. What if Lenore wasn't going to give up and believe she was at fault, like Alice had said? What if she'd come to insist Beth tell the truth? What if this whole thing didn't go away? So Beth had stayed in the garden with Georgie, terrified that this time karma really had come calling. Because even if she'd had nothing to do with this, she *had* done something awful in the past.

The strange tightening in her abdomen made that feeling

yet more intense. She'd told herself it was only stress and tried not to worry, but the ache continued to come and go throughout the day. She folded herself into a chair and took deep breaths, attempting to stay calm for the baby who was trying to grow inside. This wasn't karma, she told herself. It wasn't. She deserved a life. She deserved a baby... no matter what had happened on a day she would never, ever forget.

It had been a lovely sunny July day after an endless stream of rainy weather, and she'd taken to the tiny patch of scrubby grass in the back garden to get some sun to look half-alive. If she closed her eyes and focused only on the heat and the coconut scent of the suntan lotion, she could almost forget that she was surrounded by a broken sofa on one side and a row of rubbish bins on the other. But that had only lasted a few minutes before her boyfriend Curtis grabbed her arm and told her to get dressed – that he needed her help keeping an eye out while he picked up a stash. As the biggest drugs supplier in south London, someone was always challenging his turf. Beth hated being a part of it, but naively she'd told herself he was just giving people what they would have got elsewhere. And if she only acted as a lookout, then she wasn't really involved, right?

She'd long since learned that any argument resulted in a heavy backhand, so she'd grabbed her clothes, got dressed and hurried out to join him in the car he was already waiting in. She hated these runs, and each time vowed it would be her last, but she ended up doing it again and again. She watched the London streets out the window as people flocked to the park, smelled the scent of BBQ and heard kids playing outside, and for the millionth time, she wished that she could have that life instead of this one. Some day she would, she told herself. Somehow.

Curtis turned onto a street that she wouldn't have dared send her worst enemy down, then swung towards her. 'Stay here and keep an eye out,' he said in his gruff tone. 'You see anything, you call.' He slammed out of the car and disappeared into a block of flats that looked like a maze. She scanned the street, up and down, looking and listening for any sign of movement, not just the police but anyone else who might want to ambush Curtis and steal the stash of drugs. Lately, Curtis had been ranting about a gang who'd been trying to take over his patch, and sometimes he'd work himself up into a frenzy. She'd try her best to calm him down, but the only thing that helped was when he took a hit of his own drugs.

She held her breath and prayed nothing would happen, every inch of her vibrating with tension. She peered as something came around the corner, gripping the phone tightly, then relaxed when she saw it was just a baby in a pram being wheeled by his mum. They came down the street, the mum puffing away on a fag, and Beth grimaced. When she was a mum, she'd never smoke near her baby. She was going to do everything she could to give it the best life... the life she'd never had.

She was so engrossed in the vision of her child that she didn't spot two men duck through the door of the block of flats. She only saw them as they burst out again and raced down the pavement, knocking into the mother and sending the baby's pram flying as Curtis chased after them. The mother was screaming, and Beth dashed from the car and over towards them, her heart in her throat as she saw the baby lying, motionless, on the grubby cement forecourt in front of the building.

'Oh, no,' she muttered over and over. 'Oh, God. Please be okay. *Please.*' She put a hand on the baby's chest and thought it was still moving, but she couldn't be sure. Without thinking, she used her mobile to dial 999. The mother was still screaming, her eyes wide and her face pale, and Beth crouched down beside her. 'An ambulance is coming,' she said, her voice low. 'It will be here soon. And—'

'What the fuck?' Curtis gripped her arm and yanked her away, frogmarching her back to the car. 'What do you think you're doing? Why weren't you watching? Do you know...' She tuned him out as a string of expletives came from his mouth, her heart beating fast as they passed an ambulance with siren wailing. Was the baby going to be okay? Had Curtis *killed* the baby? He grabbed the mobile from her and threw it from the car window, his rage almost palpable in the small space. She would pay for it when they got home, but she couldn't keep quiet.

'Curtis, the baby... it could be dead.'

'What do you care?' he sneered. 'Forget the baby. We need to make sure no one messes with us again.' He got on his mobile and punched in some numbers, and she turned back to the window while he made plans for retaliation. How could he not care? She winced, picturing the tiny body on the hard pavement.

She'd searched the papers for days after the incident, wondering if the baby had died. But there was nothing, and even if it had died, Beth knew that people didn't talk in that part of the city. The mother would keep her mouth shut, afraid of repercussions, knowing she'd played no part in anything but silently sharing the blame.

How could she stay with someone like him, she'd asked herself. Yes, he gave her protection – a place to live and a shield behind which she could hide, since no one would touch her as long as she was his girlfriend. But... she'd known then that she had to leave. Somehow, she had to find a way out.

That way out had come sooner than she'd thought, when the police had busted into their place, threatening to charge her along with Curtis when they found his supply. At the station, they'd offered her a minor demeanour in exchange for her testimony against Curtis, and she'd told them all they wanted to know. It was a chance to escape this life, and despite the fact that she'd been shaking with fear, she'd grabbed on to it with all she was worth.

Curtis was in prison, thanks to her. He couldn't ruin her life now, but if anyone went digging around, it would be easy enough to find that she hadn't always been the squeaky-clean village mum she was pretending to be... hoping to be anyway.

She opened her eyes in surprise as Alice's voice drifted towards her. Thank goodness she was here, Beth thought, wincing as another cramp hit. Maybe she could duck out early and go home to lie down.

Alice came into the room, motioning Georgie and Beth towards her. 'Lenore came by looking for something. She said it was Florence's coat, but unless she keeps the coat in a cubby-hole, I don't think that was it. Anyway, she didn't find anything, and she left.'

Beth sucked in a breath. It must be Freddie. Florence did love that thing. She never would have gone home without it. The very day of the accident, she'd brought it into the garden with her, Beth remembered. She'd been a little tearful and missing her mum, and Beth had retrieved it from its cubbyhole to comfort her. She hadn't seen it since. Florence must have taken it with her when Lenore picked her up, as always – more proof that she'd been here.

If Florence had taken it with her, though, why was Lenore looking for it?

'But she's not going to give up.' Alice sat down at a table, and they both followed suit. 'Beth, she believes you're the one responsible, and that you're making up the story that we've all bought into.'

Beth felt the colour drain from her face.

'She's determined to get to the bottom of it, saying she might hire an investigator. And I can tell you, she'll have no problem sharing anything she might find.'

Oh, God. This kept getting worse and worse.

'We have to get her out of here,' Alice said. 'Away from the Nest; away from the village. Then she can try to spread stories all she likes, but we'll already have the truth of what really happened out there. And who do you think they're going to believe?

'Anyway, this is in all our best interests,' Alice continued, her words swirling around them. 'It's better for Lenore to leave too. She certainly won't be back to work here, and a place in Guildford closer to the hospital makes more sense.'

Beth nodded slowly, though she still wasn't sure what Alice had in mind. She wanted this to end too. But how did you prompt someone to move? 'Maybe we can get the co-op to donate funds to rent a place for her in Guildford?' she said. A cramp hit and she flinched. This was getting too much. She just wanted to go home and lie down.

Alice tilted her head. 'We could, but given how she feels about the Nest, I really don't think she'd accept that.' Silence fell, and Beth tried to keep breathing through the pain. 'Malena says there's been a rash of break-ins around the village,' Alice said finally. 'Some new gang from Guildford targeting the area. Maybe we can use that to our advantage. I don't know, break some windows, damage some things, and that might scare her away. It won't look like it has anything to do with us – just rotten luck for Lenore.'

Beth drew back. *What?* Alice couldn't be serious. Could she? Did she really want them to scare off Lenore? Beside her, Georgie looked just as incredulous.

'But...' Georgie shook her head. 'How are we going to organise that? You can't just ring up someone and ask them to smash some windows. And is that going to be enough? What if she stays? And then starts investigating *that*?'

Georgie leaned forward, eagerly awaiting Alice's answer, and Beth stared. Was Georgie actually considering this? She couldn't be serious. Then again, Beth thought, Georgie lived for the Nest. It was her world, and she'd do anything to keep its reputation unsullied.

'Well, that's where you two come in,' Alice said smoothly,

taking something out of her blazer pocket. Beth and Georgie squinted at it. Was that... was that a pill bottle? It wasn't labelled, and it was half-full. What did that have to do with them?

'I found this under the desk in the office last night,' Alice said, setting it onto the table. 'It's OxyContin. There's no label on it, so it doesn't look like prescription.'

Beth's eyes bulged. Oxy. It was an opioid that had been getting popular when she'd sent Curtis to jail. It was highly addictive, and Curtis loved it when people first started on it, since he knew they'd always be back for more. He'd start them off with a low price to get them hooked. But why would those pills be here, in an unlabelled bottle, under the desk?

And who on earth could they belong to?

Beth turned to look at Georgie, stunned into silence beside her. She seemed just as shocked to see the bottle. It couldn't be hers, surely. She'd never jeopardise the kids here. Anyway, Beth would know if someone was on Oxy. Wouldn't she?

And where would you get it around here? This place was hardly an estate in London. It must be one of the volunteers – or maybe some of the secondary school kids they'd had in a few weeks ago on work experience. The bottle could have been under the desk for months.

'I don't know why someone would have drugs in a nursery, but I'm happy to investigate further. Since you two are here daily, it wouldn't be too hard to say it belonged to either one of you.'

Her words drilled into Beth, and she stiffened as fear poured through her. She couldn't have that. Because it wouldn't just be a bottle of pills. Her whole history could be revealed, and once her connection to drugs was uncovered, then it wouldn't be much of a leap to think she might still be involved... out of a nursery, no less. She let out a strangled cry. Oh, God. Beside her, Georgie had gone white, and Beth reached out to put a hand on her colleague's. This bottle could have serious implications for everyone, whether it was theirs or not.

She met Alice's steady gaze, and a thought hit. Could it be *hers*? Could she be using her own stash to blackmail the two of them? After all, she had a lot to lose if Lenore didn't back down too. Beth wouldn't put it past her. But then Alice didn't seem the type to allow herself near an addictive substance, let alone OxyContin.

'Beth, I think you should take charge of organising... whatever it is you decide to do to get Lenore to leave. I don't need to know the finer details, but Georgie is right. It might have to be more than some broken windows. The last thing we need is for this to backfire.'

'Me?' Beth's voice rose in a squeak. 'Why me?' She shook her head. 'No, I can't do that. I don't want to do that.'

Alice raised the bottle in the air, lifting her eyebrows, and fear shot through her. 'We're all in this together, Beth. You need to. Anyway, you're the perfect person.'

Beth met Alice's eyes. What? Did she somehow know about Beth's past? 'What do you mean?'

'Well, you're Lenore's friend, aren't you?' Alice responded, and Beth felt the air leave her body. She didn't know, of course. No one did. 'If someone spots you on her street or around her house, it will make sense. More sense than Georgie being on the scene anyway.'

Beth couldn't speak. She didn't want to. She couldn't agree to this, not in a million years. But if she didn't... she blinked, staring at the bottle. If she didn't, then things could be even worse for her.

'And you're the one she believes is responsible,' Alice was continuing. 'You're the one who'll be worst off when she starts spreading her own version of events.'

Beth listened silently. She couldn't argue with that. Alice had no idea.

'So get her to leave,' Alice said, sliding the bottle back into her pocket. 'Get all of this to go away, and we can get on with our lives.' She stalked from the room, and Beth and Georgie exchanged glances.

Maybe they could get on with their lives, but Beth feared things would never be the same again.

NINETEEN
GEORGIE

Georgie watched Alice leave the room. Her heart was racing, and she could barely breathe. Alice had found the pills. Alice had found *her* pills. Georgie had tried to get here as early as she could to search the office, but to her surprise, Alice had already arrived. Georgie had been shaking as she waited for her boss to say something, but then she'd left for London, and Georgie had slumped in relief. She'd searched the office and come up with nothing, and calm slid over her. Maybe she'd dropped the bottle somewhere else. She must have dropped it somewhere else. She was safe.

But now Alice had found them. Granted, she didn't know for sure that they belonged to Georgie, but if she connected their presence with the fact that Georgie couldn't remember if she'd closed the gate or not, then Georgie was certain she'd come to the right conclusion eventually. And Beth must know, too, since they obviously weren't hers. She'd seemed absolutely shocked, not that Georgie could blame her.

Beth began clearing the children's plates without a word, and Georgie leaned back, shame and guilt flooding through her. She'd tried so hard to keep the drugs from everyone. And now not only did her colleague and boss know, but they'd very likely realise that was the reason for the accident. That it hadn't just been a moment of distraction. That she'd been taking opioids, and that she'd put the children in danger.

She should be scaring Lenore away, not Beth. She should be the one taking the risk. But as usual, she'd been too weak to do anything. She'd been so relieved that Alice wasn't going to the police – yet – that she'd barely been able to breathe.

Georgie let out a cry, her legs twitching. She needed a pill. She needed one so badly, to deal with all of this. She thought longingly of the bottle in Alice's blazer, and for one brief moment, she thought of trying to get it from there. But she couldn't, of course. She couldn't show Alice how desperate she was. Sweat broke out on her brow. She hadn't gone so long without having a pill for ages. Was this what she'd have to deal with when she finally stopped?

She put her forehead to her knees, folding her body almost in two on the tiny children's chair. If she continued taking the drugs, then she would continue endangering children. But if she went cold turkey and tried to cope with withdrawal while working, she'd be endangering them too. There was only one solution: she had to quit the Nest. She had to leave, before another child got hurt. After what had happened with Florence, she could barely live with herself as it was.

She stood, trying to stop the shaking, and wiped her face. Then she went down the corridor to where Alice was in the office.

'I can't keep working here any more,' she said, desperate to get it out quickly.

Alice's head snapped up. 'It's normal to feel that way,' she responded. 'After all, the accident is your fault. And if those drugs are yours...' She raised her eyebrows as her voice trailed off, and Georgie swayed as the guilt hit her once more.

'But there's no need to make such a drastic decision,' Alice continued. 'You know how much we need you here. You know how it would look for the Nest if you did leave. That's why I didn't want to get rid of you when you first explained what happened, even if you may not have told me the whole story.' Her face hardened.

Georgie dropped her eyes. 'You don't need me like this, Alice. I... I can't.' A tear spilled down her cheek, and she swiped it away. 'Today will be my last day. Lots of co-op members will leap to help, I'm sure. And Beth knows how everything works inside out.'

'You can't quit,' Alice said in a low voice. 'If you don't care about the Nest, then think about what it looks like for *you*. If you leave, people will be asking why a woman who's been at a place for years – who's been happy at a place for years – would suddenly go, just after an accident.'

Her words rang loudly in the room, and Georgie felt her shoulders droop. 'She wouldn't, unless there was a reason,' Alice said firmly. 'That's what everyone will think, and they'd be right. You'll give way more fuel to Lenore's fire – the very fire I've been trying so hard to put out. Put out for *you*.'

'I know.' Georgie wiped another tear, her heart aching. She would look like she'd been at fault, but she *was* at fault. Drugs or not, she had left the gate open. She had caused the accident. Maybe she should just admit that. It might dent the Nest a little, but it would placate Lenore. There'd be no need to scare her away. At least that was something Georgie could do right. 'I know and I appreciate it, but—'

'You're not going anywhere, Georgie.' Alice drew herself up, looking taller than ever. 'You'll stay right here,' she continued. 'And you won't do anything more to put this place in jeopardy. You'll get on with your job, happy and cheerful, like always. And if you do slip up again – with *anything* – I'll make sure the full weight of the law comes down on you. You can be certain of that. Yes?'

'Okay.' The word came out as a whisper and Georgie nodded, despair flowing through her. She was trapped. She was trapped in this prison – a prison of her own making – and she had no idea how she'd ever escape.

She struggled to her feet, almost unable to bear the weight of the chain of events her mistake had unlocked. Not only had Lenore almost lost her daughter and had the blame shunted upon her, but her life here was going to be destroyed too. Georgie didn't know what Beth was planning, but Lenore would be forced from her home at a time when she needed comfort more than ever.

Nothing she could do would make up for all of this. She knew that. But there had to be something... anything... to ease the pain; to shift the guilt, even if just a little. She racked her brain in desperation, relief filtering in as an idea hit. Alice had said that Lenore was here looking for Freddie, Florence's stuffed dog. Florence loved that thing and was never without it. Georgie was certain that amid the horror and chaos of the accident, she'd seen that soft toy somewhere. If she could find it and bring it to the hospital, at least that would be something. She closed her eyes, willing herself to remember, but everything was fuzzy. It wasn't inside, or Lenore would have found it. Could it be by the road still?

Forcing herself to cheerily call out to Beth and the volunteers that she was checking something outside, she went to the gravelled car park. After nodding to the security workers installing the fence, she crossed to the side of the road and started combing through the long grass inch by inch. Where was it? Desperation grew as the minutes passed. She had to find it. She had to do something. Finally, she kicked aside a plastic bag, and there, wedged underneath it, was the soft toy. It must have got knocked out of Florence's arms when she'd been hit, and Georgie winced at the thought of the impact. She clutched Freddie in her arms, tears streaming down her cheeks.

She'd duck out to the hospital under the guise of picking up the load of fresh fruit they needed for the late-afternoon snack. She wasn't brave enough to face Lenore, but she'd drop Freddie at the nurses' station. It couldn't change what had gone wrong, but by bringing this to the family, maybe she could give them some small comfort.

Maybe it would give her some small comfort too.

TWENTY
LENORE

Lenore drove to the hospital, then sat for a while in the car park, her mind whirring. She'd been so sure she'd find Freddie at the Nest, certain that would give her the proof she needed. What was she going to tell James? She'd meant what she'd said about doing all she could – hiring whoever she could – to uncover the truth, but how was anyone going to help if *she* couldn't remember things clearly herself?

She closed her eyes, desperately trying to bring the events before the accident into focus. But all she could recall was Florence standing in the road, and then the car swallowing her whole. The scream that pierced the silence, and then somehow kneeling by her daughter's side.

Where had Florence run from? How had she got out? Had anyone been chasing her? Georgie had been the first on the scene. Could it have been her? Had Lenore parked first, or had she entered the car park later? Maybe she'd still been on the road when the accident occurred.

Lenore hit the steering wheel in frustration. Why couldn't she remember? Was it really just shock, or was James right that she needed to see a doctor? And then the darker thought loomed once more... if James was right, *could* she be sure she hadn't let Florence run into the road?

The same doubt she'd felt earlier hovered over, expanding to fill the small space in the car. She breathed out, telling herself over and over that she was fine. She *was* different. This wasn't the past, and she hadn't caused the accident. But even as she thought that, the barrage of words she'd faced from Beth, James and then Alice all slid towards her, crashing into her like a physical blow, and she could feel the cracks she'd been so afraid of begin to form.

She needed to see Florence again, she thought as she scrambled from the car and hurried towards the hospital. That had worked before, when she'd felt this way. Just being beside her daughter had righted her and made the doubt dissipate. It would work again. It had to.

Desperation growing, she raced down the corridor towards Florence's room, peering into the waiting room as she passed. James was there, sprawled out on some chairs, tapping away on his phone.

'Hi,' he said. 'Come wait with me. They're just changing some of Florence's bandages, so they ordered me out.' He glanced at her empty hands, eyebrows rising in surprise. 'I thought you were getting some toys for her?'

She plopped down beside him, praying the nurses finished soon. She had to see her daughter. 'I was looking for one of her favourites, but I couldn't find it.' She still couldn't believe Freddie hadn't been at the Nest.

'That's okay,' James said. 'She's got something with her now anyway. One of the nurses said a woman from the nursery came by and dropped it off.'

'*What?*' Lenore's mouth dropped open. Could he mean Freddie? No, surely not. That would be way too much of a coincidence: that she'd gone to the nursery looking for Freddie as proof that she hadn't been involved in the accident, only for the soft toy to turn up in her daughter's room just minutes later. Or had it been dropped off earlier before she'd gone to find it?

James was giving her a strange look. 'Are you all right?'

Lenore didn't answer. She couldn't speak. She got to her feet, then hurried down the corridor to Florence's room. The door was half-closed, and nurses inside bustled around the bed, but she pushed the door open wider.

She blinked, unable to believe her eyes. There, on the bedside table beside her daughter, was Freddie. She took a few halting steps forward, reaching out to touch his matted ginger fur. A memory of Florence's chubby grin as she tied his ears together came into her mind, and her stomach twisted.

'When did the woman come by?' she asked, barely able to get the words out.

'I'm not really sure,' James said. 'I was getting something to eat downstairs. The nurse said it was found at the side of the road.'

The side of the road. Oh, God. That would mean her daughter had it when the car had hit. That would mean Lenore had picked her up. That she'd been with Florence when she'd been hit by the car. That she'd been responsible.

Or was that what the nursery wanted her to think? Had they brought Freddie here to use against her? To try to make her believe their version of events?

Which version was the truth?

She let out a cry and started rocking back and forth in anguish, the doubt that had hung over her and followed her to this room expanding like a dark cloud... a dark cloud enveloping not only her but also her daughter. She shook her head furiously, hoping to dispel it, but it swirled around, tainting everything black. She'd come here to make things clear, but instead... she looked at Freddie once more.

Instead, nothing was.

'Are you okay?' James was looking at her, and she realised

she was breathing hard, as if she was running a race. She turned to face him, struggling to form an answer.

'I don't know,' she managed to say. *Was* she okay? Or did she need help? She swayed as exhaustion and confusion overcame her, and James took her arm and manoeuvred her into a chair. She took in a few mouthfuls of air, trying to ease the dizziness.

'You're scaring me, honey.' James's face was pale. 'Look, I know this is a lot. I know you didn't mean to let Florence get hurt. It was an accident. I know you can't remember, and I think that's what scares me most of all.'

His voice dropped, and he put a hand on her arm. 'I wasn't going to talk to you about this for a while, but...' He sighed. 'I think it's best to get everything straight, so there aren't any unexpected surprises when Florence is released.'

She met his eyes. Unexpected surprises? What did he mean? She hadn't yet thought about what might happen once Florence was released. Her only hope had been that her daughter would recover as quickly as possible.

'You wanted to be on your own with Florence. You know I worried it might be too much.' James swallowed. 'I didn't want to say this earlier, but it's obvious that being alone with Florence *was* too much.' Lenore almost opened her mouth to refute his words, but she stopped. Was he right? She thought she'd been doing so well, but could she be sure that was true? 'And when Florence gets out of here, she's going to need a lot of physio, a lot of extra care. It's not going to be easy. I'm sure it will stretch *me* to the limit, and I'm so much...'

And I'm so much stronger than you, she finished in her head. She could hear the words almost as if he had said them. He was strong. She knew that he'd helped her so much in the past. It was just... she thought she'd been getting stronger too. Had she?

'So, why don't you come home?' James continued. 'When

Florence is released, you can both come back to me. My mum can help out, too, and I'll be around twenty-four seven. You can get the help you need and get stable again. And until then, someone will always be there. We will make sure Florence stays safe.'

Safe from *her*? Lenore stared, disbelief washing over her. Despite being at her lowest, James had still let her care for her daughter – albeit under his eye. Now it sounded like she wasn't even going to be able to do that. She'd be cut off from Florence, their growing bond fading despite the fact she was able and well.

'I'm not going to agree to that.' The words burst through the confusion still spinning around her. 'No. No way.'

James's face dropped, and he sighed. 'I was afraid of that.' Silence fell, and then he took one of her limp hands in his. 'I don't want to have to get lawyers involved here,' he said. 'But I need to do what's best for my daughter. If you can't see that, well...'

Lenore's mind worked frantically, trying to find something to say. What *could* she say? She knew what she wanted to tell him: that this time was nothing like when she'd tried to stop Florence's cries as a newborn. Then she hadn't seen herself as a mother, or Florence as her daughter. All she'd known was the darkness, the crying, the groping through the day without knowing what she was reaching for.

And now... she knew she was a mother. She *felt* it. Everything was different.

But when she opened her mouth, she couldn't push those words out.

'Please.' That was the only thing she could say. 'Please don't do this. Please don't take her away. I can't let that happen.'

James stared at her, and tears filled his eyes. Then he let out a low shuddery sigh, as if it came from the very depths of him.

'That's what you said the last time, too, remember? When I lifted her from your arms?'

Lenore felt the colour drain from her face. Because that was something she *did* remember, although she wanted more than anything to forget.

James got to his feet and left the room, and Lenore stared down at her daughter. She reached out and gripped Florence's fingers. 'I'm sorry,' she said, brushing away a tear. 'I'm so, so sorry.'

But she didn't know why she was apologising, other than for that same guilt and fear that had found her again. And she didn't know to whom: James, her daughter, or herself.

All she felt was the darkness around them, and that was enough.

TWENTY-ONE
BETH

Afternoon pick-up and tidying seemed endless as Beth went through the motions. The dull ache still pulled at her stomach, but she fixed a huge smile on her face for the parent volunteers. Behind the smile, though, all she could focus on was Alice's command to scare Lenore away. How the hell was she going to do that?

She bit her lip, memories of the past flooding into her head: how she'd crept into houses to steal cash or other valuables while the occupants were sitting there, laughing at some inane show on telly without a care in the world. She knew it was wrong, of course, but it seemed so unfair that she had such a terrible life when others were so comfortable. They probably wouldn't realise it was gone, she'd told herself as she'd grabbed it and left. And she needed it way more than they did. She needed it to survive.

She'd done that for a year or so, then met Curtis. She'd been so grateful to have someone to lean on that she'd barely noticed that she was nothing more than a decoy for him. He didn't love her.

She sighed and got into the car, his face looming into her

mind yet again; his vengeful words ringing in her head. He didn't need to threaten her, she thought. Her past was enough of a threat, and now it was coming back into her present.

Somehow, she had to find a way to get Lenore to leave. And Georgie was right: simply breaking a few windows might not be enough. She'd need to get inside and make sure the place was ruined, maybe turn on some taps or smash things up. The very thought of that was ridiculous. There was no way she could risk getting caught with a baby on the way. But if she didn't...

She grimaced as the dull cramps she'd been feeling earlier flared into sharp pains. Panic raced through her. She knew what that felt like. She'd felt it before... before she'd lost her babies. Tears came to her eyes and she inhaled slowly, trying to slow her pulse as yet another pain hit with greater intensity. Everything would be okay, she told herself, though she knew it might not be. This baby was a strong one. This one was meant to be.

But even as she told herself that, she could hardly move for the fear. She had to get to the hospital and make sure everything was fine. As she hobbled from the car park to the hospital entrance, she prayed not to feel the telltale wetness of blood between her legs. So far, so good, she thought, although her stomach was still twisting like someone wringing out a wet cloth.

Finally, after what felt like forever in the waiting room and then an interminable wait in a tiny hot cubicle, the doctor came into the room. 'The midwife says you've had some cramping and discomfort? And you're coming up to ten weeks?'

Beth nodded, her heart beating fast. Please let their baby be okay. Please. She'd do anything. *Anything.*

The doctor was wheeling over the ultrasound machine. 'Let's have a quick look, then, and see what's happening. Have you had a scan yet?'

Beth shook her head. She'd wanted to, and as a high-risk pregnancy after two miscarriages, everything she'd read had said that she should. But she'd been so worried about finding something wrong that she hadn't been able to bear it, telling herself to hold out till the usual three-month scan. And here she was. Her heart was beating so fast that she felt like she was going to pass out.

The doctor squeezed some cold gel over her stomach and moved the probe across her still-flat belly, and Beth closed her eyes.

'Okay...' The doctor's voice filled the small room, and Beth squeezed her eyes shut even further. What was happening? Was everything all right? God, this was torture. 'Right.' She felt something like kitchen towel being shoved into her hand, and she wiped off her belly and pulled down her top.

'Is everything okay?' Her voice trembled with fear.

'Everything looks perfect.' A whoosh of relief went through her, and her eyes flew open to see the doctor smiling down at her.

'Really?' Her voice emerged as a squeak. She couldn't believe it. She hadn't let herself dare believe it.

'Yes. Your baby is developing just as it should.'

'So, what caused the cramps?' Beth asked. She almost didn't want to know, but if the doctor had said all was okay, then she didn't have to worry.

'I can't see anything that could be causing it,' the doctor said. 'It could simply be your body adjusting to the baby – making way to accommodate something new in your body.' He eyed her closely. 'Have you been under any stress recently?'

Beth nodded slowly.

'Well, that could be it,' the doctor said. 'Remember, whatever upsets you has an impact on the baby. I don't want you to worry about that, mind,' he added. 'But generally, the calmer and more relaxed you are – the better you take care of yourself – the easier the pregnancy will be for both you and your child. Okay?'

Beth slid off the table, her hand moving to her stomach. Everything was fine. She still couldn't believe it.

The doctor handed her a piece of paper. 'I printed off a few scans for you.' Beth tucked it into her pocket. She wanted to keep it safe, next to her, as if by protecting that, she could protect her baby.

Beth climbed into the car to drive home, her mind whirling. *The calmer and more relaxed you are – the better you take care of yourself – the easier the pregnancy will be for both you and your baby.* If the notion of her breaking into Lenore's was ridiculous before, now it was downright dangerous. She wasn't just risking her and her baby's future; she was risking her baby's life.

Maybe... maybe she could find someone to do it for her. It might take a bit longer to organise, but she did know lots of people who'd find breaking in and smashing up a place child's play – well, she *had* known lots of people anyway, and they shouldn't be too hard to find again.

But that would mean reaching out to her past, opening up that part of her life once more. And what would they want in return? Money? She chewed her lip. She could give them that, at least. She'd been saving for a new car if the baby came, but this was more important.

She'd promised to do anything to keep this baby safe. Although connecting with her past was the last thing she wanted, she would. She'd find someone who could do what the Nest needed, and then she'd focus all she had on this child.

After what felt like forever, the house was silent, and Rich's steady breathing filled the room. Beth had been waiting all evening for him to go to sleep so she could make this call. The sooner she got this over with, the better.

Thank God her cramps had stopped. She slid the ultrasound photo from her pocket, where she'd been keeping it close.

She still couldn't believe she was having a baby, and she wanted to be happy. She *was* happy, but she hated that this thing was looming over her – hated that it had touched one of the best moments of her life.

One call, she told herself. One call, and then she could forget everything from the past and focus on the future. The number was engrained into her mind, though they hadn't spoken for years. She and Jess had been like sisters after meeting in one of the many foster homes they'd been shunted to. Jess hadn't lasted long there – she'd got kicked out for smoking marijuana in the bathroom – and Beth hadn't been far behind her. But during those few months they'd formed a bond that came from being the only people in each other's world. When they'd graduated from the care system, Jess had tried to help her as much as she could. In fact, she'd been the one to introduce Beth to Curtis.

Beth bit her lip, thinking how she hadn't talked to Jess since she'd told police all she could about Curtis. She'd said her piece, then cut off all ties. She'd had to – not just for her own safety, but for her future. She'd missed Jess and her cutting humour, but then she'd started at college and her new life had taken over. What would Jess say to her now? Would she want to talk to her; to find someone to help her?

And if Beth opened up this door to the past, would she ever be able to close it again?

She had to, she thought, sliding from the bed. Jess would understand. She might actually be happy for her. Heart beating fast, she eased from the room and went downstairs. She punched in the number, then waited as it rang.

Someone picked up, but the line remained silent. 'Jess, is that you? It's Beth. I know it's been ages.' She forced a laugh. It came out sounding tense and tight as she waited for Jess to answer.

'How are things in London? I'm just outside Guildford,

working in a nursery, if you can believe that. I'm sorry I didn't get in touch sooner. I wanted to,' she babbled, keen to fill the awkward silence. She needed Jess's help. 'I—'

'It's not Jess,' a male voice said, and Beth let out her breath.

'Oh, I'm sorry. I must have the wrong number.' She was about to hang up when the voice started talking again.

'It's not Jess, but I am glad you called.'

She drew back, almost dropping the phone in shock. It wasn't Jess's voice, but it was another voice from her past – a voice she would never, ever forget.

Curtis.

He'd been released from prison? How hadn't she known that? And how had he got this phone? Had Jess given it to him? Had he taken her mobile in a bid to track down Beth, hoping she'd call? Was Jess okay?

She hung up as quickly as she could, then leaned over and took deep breaths, trying to right herself; to right her world. Hearing that voice had put her back in a dark fearful place. An image of how Curtis had looked at her with such hatred flashed into her mind, and she started shaking. She nearly jumped out of her skin when the phone rang, Jess's number flashing up on the screen. Oh, God. He was calling back.

She turned off the mobile as fast as she could, barely able to breathe through the fear pummelling her. What exactly had she told him? Had she given him enough detail that he'd be able to find her?

Would he hurt her? Hurt her *baby*? She'd thought she'd been doing this to keep her child safe. Now she might have threatened it even more.

Fury ripped through her – fury that after everything, in this moment when she should be celebrating – she had to face this fear once more. She didn't need this. She didn't deserve this... did she?

She swallowed back the questions and got to her feet. She

couldn't afford to crack open that door again. She shouldn't have in the first place. She was strong – her baby was strong despite the scare she'd had. The doctor had said so. She would do this thing to Lenore herself. She would be careful, and if anyone saw her, she'd say Lenore had given her a key or something. She'd always been good at making up stories.

She shrugged on her coat and prepared to finish this, for once and for all.

She just hoped Curtis was finished with her too.

TWENTY-TWO
LENORE

Lenore dragged herself from the car to her house, feeling like she couldn't move another inch. She'd spent the day at Florence's side, praying for some improvement in her condition. But she remained exactly the same: locked in slumber by the sedatives they'd given her. Lenore couldn't even hug her daughter to provide some comfort.

What was she thinking, Lenore had wondered as she pushed back a strand of Florence's hair from her bruised cheek? Was she dreaming, watching the car speed towards her before feeling that final thud? Had she sensed that, or had she been knocked unconscious before she'd hit the pavement? Lenore prayed she hadn't felt a thing.

But more than that – in the midst of those questions pounding her – one overpowered them all: what was she going to do? Could she go back to living with her husband, an arm's length from her child? What if James did hire a lawyer? She tilted her head, remembering her threat to Alice to hire an investigator. Could she prove she hadn't been at fault? The dark cloud pressed around her, and she shivered as a thought came to mind. What if she *was* to blame?

The house seemed emptier than ever as she went inside, wincing at the cool draught swirling through. She went up the stairs and peeked into Florence's room at the end of the corridor, tears filling her eyes as she took in the fluffy bears lining the tiny cot, the pink furniture and the pink curtains plus matching duvet – Florence's favourite colour, despite Lenore trying to sway her more towards the greens and yellows she favoured.

A tear streaked down her cheek as she remembered how she'd been so full of hope as she'd set up Florence's new bedroom, picturing their life ahead in this wonderful place with laughter, fun and friends. Now the bedroom was as empty as the rest of the house. Was this how she'd feel every night if James had their daughter? God, she couldn't stand that. She needed Florence, and Florence needed her.

She had to think of something.

She went into the bathroom and started getting ready for bed, then crawled under the cold duvet and turned out the light. But no matter how exhausted she was after last night and today at Florence's bedside, she couldn't sleep. It reminded her of the time after Florence had been born when they'd come home from hospital. James had propelled her to the bedroom, saying she should rest when Florence did. She'd tossed and turned in the dimly lit room, her mind racing, trying to adjust to the new reality of motherhood. How could anyone sleep when so much had changed?

She hadn't slept the first week at all – or the second or the third. Finally, she'd gone to the GP in desperation, and he'd prescribed mild sleeping tablets, telling her with a laugh that she should be falling asleep standing up.

'My wife almost did once!' He'd chuckled fondly, and she'd forced a smile, a sinking feeling inside that she was doing something wrong. That she wasn't a mother at all, and she never should have tried in the first place. The next week was when she'd almost hurt Florence, as if it was a confirmation of her very fears.

She still had some of those tablets left, she thought, sitting up slowly in the dark cold room. She hadn't taken any for months – she hadn't needed to – but she'd hung onto them as a kind of safety blanket, despite telling herself she'd never be in that dark place again. But now... she shook her head. She just needed to rest, that was all.

She crawled from the covers and went into the bathroom, rifling through the medicine cabinet until she found the bottle. Then she swallowed one down and went back to bed, closing her eyes and waiting for sleep to take her.

TWENTY-THREE
GEORGIE

'Morning.' Georgie forced a smile at Kasper as he came into the room. The sun was streaming through the window and the birds were chirping like crazy. Georgie usually loved this time of year, when everything was so green and fresh after the dull drab winter. At the moment, though, all she could think about was the Nest. What she'd done to Florence, and what she might do if she stayed. It had been ages since she'd had a pill, and she was shaking and nauseated. What would she be like as the day wore on? She could barely concentrate as it was, and it was bound to get worse.

'Molly okay?' she asked as she tugged on the Nest's polka-dot top. It was the first question they asked each other every morning, and the last thing they talked about every night.

Kasper sighed. 'She's very down this morning, actually.' Georgie glanced over at him, surprised at his downcast tone. He always managed to sound so upbeat and optimistic, no matter the challenges they faced. 'I haven't been able to get her up yet. I tried to get her out of bed, but she said she didn't want to go to school today.' He ran a hand over his face, and she could feel his exhaustion as palpably as if it was her own.

Georgie's heart contracted in her chest as she took in his words and his anguished expression. He needed her. He needed her to be strong; to say something to lift him up. But in the haze clouding her, she couldn't grasp on to anything that might help.

'I have to go,' she croaked, grabbing her keys and rushing down the stairs. She sat in the car for a moment, her stomach spinning. God, what a failure she was. Her family needed her, and she'd run out. She'd already let down the nursery; already made a brutal mistake. And now, she was worse than ever.

She needed to get more pills. That was the only answer – the only thing that could keep the situation under control. Yes, they might make her a little off her game, but a little was better than completely. And if she was careful and took them only when she absolutely needed them, she should be okay. Anything was better than the way she was feeling.

But where to get them? She could hardly march into her doctor's office and ask for OxyContin. He'd probably give her antidepressants or something, but that wasn't what she wanted; what she craved.

Shaking, she remembered how Malena had given a presentation to parents at the secondary school on the growing drugs problem in the area. What was it she had said? Georgie tilted her head, trying to remember. There was an estate in nearby Guildford where drugs were rife, and parents were warned to make sure their children kept well away from it.

She looked at her watch. She had plenty of time before she needed to be at work. She could nip over to Guilford first. But would anyone on the estate be up this early?

She'd go see, she told herself, starting the engine. If everything went well, she could be there and home again in an hour. She'd hide the pills at the back of the medicine cabinet; no way would she risk having the bottle at the nursery.

A short drive later, she pulled into the estate, her heart

sinking when she noticed how quiet it was. Nothing stirred in the early-morning sun, the place looking tired and dingy. She slowed and pulled over to the side of the road, turned off the engine, and waited.

She sat there, feeling like an idiot. What had she expected? A blinking sign advertising illegal drugs? Maybe she should come back later, when more people would be around. But she'd made the journey, and she didn't have time later. Even as she told herself that, though, she knew it wasn't the real reason. She needed those pills, and she needed them now. They were the only thing keeping her sane.

Well, maybe if someone saw her, they'd come out. She got out of the car and started towards a huge block of flats. She was standing in front of a scarred metal door wondering what to do when a burly man pushed out, almost knocking her over.

'What do you want?' he asked, his voice gruff.

Georgie shoved her hair behind her ears. 'I'm looking for... for some pills?' Her voice was thready, her heart beating fast. This was the stupidest thing she had ever done. How the hell had she ended up here? She didn't know this man. He could be an undercover police officer or something. Never again, she told herself. This was the last time she was coming here.

The man scanned her from top to bottom, as if assessing if she was a real customer or not. 'What kind of pills?' he asked, stepping out and closing the door behind him. 'Codeine, morphine, oxy? Take your pick.'

Georgie felt relief wash over her. Oh, thank God. 'Oxy, please.'

He beckoned to someone behind him, and then two boys appeared. They couldn't have been in secondary school yet. 'You work at a nursery?' he asked, nodding towards her polka-dot shirt with 'The Nest' embroidered on the pocket. Georgie cursed herself once more. What an idiot she was, turning up in her uniform.

'How much?' Her voice wavered.

The man told her an exorbitant amount, and she nearly fell over. 'I don't have that much on me,' she said. 'But I can nip to a cashpoint and come right back.'

'Don't bother.' The man's voice was harsh. 'Give me the cash you have, and I'll give you the pills. *If* you tell me what I want.'

Georgie drew back. Tell him what he wanted? What kind of information could he need that she could give him?

'I'm looking for a woman,' he said. 'She'd be a few years younger than you, dark hair, and I know she's in the area. She works with kids too.' His eyes lasered into her. 'Her name is Beth Maloney.'

Georgie froze. *Beth?* Could he mean the Beth at the Nest? Her surname wasn't Maloney, but that could have been her maiden name. What would someone like this want with her, though? How would someone like him know Beth?

'Um, why?' Georgie squeaked out.

The man smiled. 'Oh, we're old friends. We go way back. We just lost touch.' He leaned closer, and a shiver went through her. 'I know she'd be delighted to hear from me.' The formal words sounded odd in his rough and ready accent, and despite what he said, somehow Georgie felt the opposite.

'I don't think I've heard of her,' Georgie responded, her voice shaking. She just wanted those drugs and to get out of here.

'Really?' The man tilted his head. 'It looked like you recognised the name when I said it.'

Georgie swallowed.

'And if you want these pills, you need to talk.'

Oh, God. Fear and panic spurted through her as the three of them drew closer. They wouldn't hurt her, would they? Not here, in broad daylight. She glanced around, but the place was still deserted. She should just tell them she knew someone called Beth. Maybe it wasn't the same one he was looking for anyway. She couldn't imagine it was. And even if it was, hadn't he said they were old friends? Who was she to suspect any different?

'Actually, now that you mention it, the name does ring a bell. I have a colleague called Beth, but I'm sure it's not the same one. She's been there for years, and she's married, and—'

'A colleague?' The man sneered. 'You work with her? At... the Nest?' His hard stare went right through her, and she nodded, her heart pounding. 'Take it and go.' He shoved the bottle at her, and she almost fell over in her haste to get back to the car. She locked the doors and pulled away, feeling his gaze following her.

Trembling, she pulled over to the side of the road a few minutes later, fumbled with the bottle, and took a pill. She leaned her head forward on the wheel and waited for the effects to kick in, still unable to believe what had just happened.

Had she really told that man Beth worked at the Nest? What had she been thinking? What if he came to find Beth there... what if he told Beth that he'd found out she worked there from Georgie? Found out because she'd bought drugs from him?

Should she *tell* Beth what she'd done? Warn her, maybe, that someone might come looking for her?

No, she couldn't. Alice had said she couldn't mess up. And she'd gone to buy drugs in her bloody uniform from the Nest, no less. What had she been thinking? If she told the story to Beth, then she was risking Beth saying something to Alice. And Georgie couldn't take that risk. Not when Molly needed her so much.

Anyway, it wasn't the same Beth. The man would probably realise that before he thought about tracking her down here.

Georgie waited for the pill to make everything okay; to blur everything over. She had learned her lesson. This was the last time she was going to come back here.

Somehow, she had to find another way to get through all of this.

Just not today.

TWENTY-FOUR
LENORE

Sun was streaming through the gap in the curtains when Lenore opened her eyes. She sat up and looked at the clock: it was almost eight, and she'd finally slept. Slept like the dead, actually. Usually she was a light sleeper, twitching at every movement, but last night she hadn't even got up to use the bathroom. Thank God she'd hung on to those sleeping pills.

She pulled her robe around her and went down the corridor towards the toilet, stopping in her tracks. What was that noise, like water running? Had she left the tap on last night, or maybe the toilet was broken? She hurried inside the bathroom, gasping when she spotted water pouring over the edge of the bath. One of the taps was on full force, and she sloshed across the floor and turned it off. How on earth had that happened? She'd been tired last night, but surely, she couldn't have been that careless. She didn't want to think of the state of the floor below, where all of that water would be draining.

Dread dogging every step, she made her way downstairs and into the lounge, groaning at the damage in front of her. A huge stain spread across the ceiling, with water streaming from the centre straight onto the sofa. Brown water dripped from the blanket Florence had curled up on as a baby. Bits of plaster had begun to fall already, and it looked like it was only a matter of time before the whole thing caved in. The sofa had absorbed as much water as it possibly could, and the floor was covered in at least an inch. The whole room looked like a bomb had hit it... a very wet bomb.

And it didn't stop with the lounge. The water had somehow made its way through the ceiling into the light fixture in the kitchen, pouring in a steady stream from there and onto the newly laid countertops.

Her friend was going to *kill* her. Lenore was supposed to be taking care of her home while she was gone, not destroying it. She laughed in disbelief as she looked around the lounge. This was more than just damage. This was absolute destruction. The whole thing would need to be dried out, replastered, and God knew what else. Frustration swarmed over her. She couldn't stay here, clearly. But where on earth was she going to go? This was the last thing she needed to think about!

First things first, she had to get dressed. Then she'd call her friend and try to explain. Walking carefully so she didn't slip, she went up to the bedroom and threw on jeans and a T-shirt. She ran a brush through her hair and gazed in the mirror.

God, she looked a mess. Dark circles ringed her eyes, stress had made the spots she'd thought she'd banished as a teen return to her chin, and the once-glossy bob was dull and greasy. An image of herself after Florence was born flashed into her mind, her face superimposed onto the one she saw in front of her, sliding into place on top of it in a perfect match. She blinked and it disappeared, but the vision clung to her.

The ringing doorbell cut into her thoughts, and she ran down the stairs. Who could that be?

'Oh!' Her eyebrows shot up when she spotted James on the step.

'I hope you don't mind me coming by like this,' he said, 'but

I was worried about you. And I brought breakfast.' He held up a bag, and despite his threat to take Florence hanging over them, the tempting aroma of freshly baked croissants was too much to resist. 'I brought some raspberry jam too,' he added.

Her favourite. She could never say no to raspberry jam, and he obviously remembered that. That one small detail brought a memory of the connection they used to have; how they'd laugh over breakfast and look forward to a day of perfection together. They *had* been perfect, until it had all fallen apart when Florence had been born.

And now he wanted to shield their own daughter from her. Now he believed she was a danger, so much so he was willing to hire a lawyer to keep her at bay. Was that why he was here? Because he was worried about how she'd taken the conversation yesterday?

'Well, how could I say no to that?' she said, shaking her head as she ushered him in. She was starving, and there was no food in the house. Besides, they needed to talk. Maybe he didn't really mean what he'd said. Maybe—

'Wow.' He interrupted her thoughts as he saw the damage in the lounge. 'Oh my God. I was right to be worried then,' he said. 'I knew it. I knew something was wrong when you rang me last night.'

Lenore drew back. *What?* 'I didn't ring you last night. Did I?'

He nodded. 'It was around midnight. You... you didn't sound well.' He let out a breath, and she could see how much her call had affected him.

'I don't remember,' she said slowly. 'I'd taken a sleeping pill. I don't take them any more – I hadn't had one for ages – but I couldn't sleep. What did I say?'

'I couldn't really catch the words. You were slurring a bit, talking fast, saying how sorry you were. Something like that.' His face twisted. 'I heard the water going in the bath, and it...'

He dropped his gaze. 'It made me remember. That day I found you lying there, with the tub overflowing. When you said you were sorry about what you'd almost done to Florence and how you... How you couldn't bear it.' He paused. 'I was terrified, so I called the police. I would have come myself, but I'd gone back to London, and I thought they could get here quicker.'

'Right.' Lenore felt light-headed, as if the ground had dropped out from underneath her. Snatched memories came back to her, like someone firing poison arrows. Crawling from the bed. The water gushing from the tap. The feeling that all she wanted was to get into it and sink down... *I'm sorry. I didn't mean to.*

But no. No! That wasn't last night. Lenore shook her head so hard it hurt. Maybe she couldn't remember everything. Maybe the doubt had invaded once more, sinking in to where the cracks had appeared. And maybe the darkness was swirling around her, but she hadn't succumbed. Not this time. She would never do that to her family again.

She could hear the words in her head, though. She could see the water dripping. And – she grabbed her mobile, scrolling to the call log. She had called James after midnight, like he'd said.

She locked onto her husband, the one thing keeping her steady as the room spun around her. She didn't know what was happening. There was so much she couldn't make sense of. The car at the nursery. Freddie on the side of the road. What Beth, the one person who'd been her friend, had told her. What everyone believed. Her phone call to James, and the tap. The fact that she couldn't remember.

She stood stock still as everything inside her began to crumble. She tried to hold herself up, tried to keep breathing, but she couldn't bear the weight of the guilt and pain pressing down on her. Images flashed through her mind: James's horrified face, and how the nurse had looked at her when she'd screamed. The car bearing down on Florence, and the doctor, not denying Florence might die. Her daughter lying so still and pale, Freddie watching by her side. How she'd knelt by Florence just yesterday, echoing those very words.

I'm sorry.

She had caused the accident. She couldn't deny it any longer.

She couldn't trust herself with her daughter.

She couldn't trust *herself.*

James took her arm as she slid to the ground. 'I'm here for you, Lenore. I'm always here for you.' He cradled her in his arms, and tears slipped down her cheeks. He'd seen her at her worst, then and now, and he hadn't let go. Instead, she'd been the one who wanted space; who'd wanted to be on her own.

But being on her own was the last thing she wanted. She needed him by her side, like he used to be. Making sure to keep their daughter safe. Making sure to keep *her* safe.

But did he still want to be with her? Would he reject her; ask only for Florence?

'Do you...' Her voice caught, and she gripped onto him to steady herself. 'Do you still want to be a family? The three of us, together?'

James squeezed tighter. 'Of course I want to be with you,' he said, and relief poured through her. 'We belong together. And Florence belongs with us.' He wiped the tears from her face. 'Everything will be okay, you'll see. I'll make sure of that.'

And though Lenore knew there was no way James could control the future, she desperately wanted to believe he could make everything better. If anyone could, it would be him. She was tired – so, so tired. And if he could carry her, carry Florence again, then it was time to let him.

TWENTY-FIVE
ALICE

Alice couldn't hide her smile when she breezed into the Nest that morning. Everything was going to plan. Malena had rung to say something had happened at Lenore's house, and it looked like half the builders in town were there. Word was the house would be unhabitable while the damage was repaired. After the destruction she'd apparently caused, Lenore would have trouble finding another place. Rental properties in Mapplestow were few and far between anyway.

Alice shook her head, thinking she couldn't have asked for a better result. Beth had gone above and beyond by not just scaring Lenore but making sure she'd be out for good. Lenore would be leaving and this whole mess would be behind them.

Now Alice could focus on what was really important: the Nest and her future plans. With Lenore gone, she'd have to find another member of staff quickly – maybe two, if possible. There was still the problem of the asbestos to solve, but with all the extra time she had, she was sure she'd think of something. And once that was out of the way and there was nothing more to hide in any paperwork, she would think about commissioning a few case studies and using those to leverage the media ahead of expanding in other cities. God, she was excited just thinking about it.

Smiling, she let herself drift into a daydream where she was at the head of a network of co-op nurseries across the country, a new style of childcare that everyone was embracing. She'd won Woman Entrepreneur of the Year Award – no, sod that – simply *Entrepreneur* of the Year – and she was being interviewed on BBC Breakfast, explaining what a joy it was to help women around the country access affordable childcare, knowing their children were safe with people they trust. Simon would smile over at her, and she'd take his hand and squeeze it, her grin growing bigger when she pictured all those people in the law firm who'd thought she wasn't capable. She was bigger than them. They would never have her recognition or success.

Of course she'd have to tell Simon that she was leaving her law career, but she had a few months before the firm stopped paying her – more than enough to sort out the asbestos and make sure the Nest was secure. She tilted her head, wondering what he would think. It was a change that could potentially affect their family in a big way if he did have to go back to work. Would he wonder why she hadn't spoken to him first? But then, when did she ever? He'd never seemed too bothered, bobbing along in whatever course she'd set for them. For a second, she wished he *was* bothered... or at least interested. But hadn't that been what she'd wanted? Someone to let her set the pace?

'Everything okay?' She popped inside the playroom, where the kids were busy making something unfathomable out of toilet paper rolls. Beth and Georgie looked at her and nodded, though they seemed anything but. But she didn't care; as long as they kept their mouths shut, everything would be fine.

God, imagine Georgie thinking she could leave! Thank goodness Alice had nipped that in the bud. If Georgie quit, that would be disastrous. Even if she did take responsibility, there would be more questions and inspections checking their safeguarding. The crack in the wall might be discovered, which meant the asbestos would be too. There was no way Alice could risk it, especially since the Nest was more important to her future than ever.

Alice peered closely at Georgie, thinking she did look slightly strung out. *Could* those pills have been hers? She still couldn't imagine it, but it didn't really matter who they belonged to. She wasn't going to look a gift horse in the mouth, because that's exactly what that bottle had been. *Focus on the big picture.*

'Alice...' Beth came over to her side, looking as if she wanted to fill her in on last night. But Alice put a finger to her lips and motioned towards the kids. It wasn't so much that she didn't want the kids to hear. *She* didn't want to hear. The less she knew about what Beth had done, the better. 'Sorry, no time to chat,' she said, and Beth backed away.

Alice went into the office, eager to think about the future. She gazed out the window, squinting at a car that slowed to a snail's pace as it passed the nursery. Two men peered out, then sped away. The car disappeared around the bend, then reappeared minutes later, the men still staring.

That was odd, she thought. She didn't recognise them – and with their shaved heads, they definitely weren't fathers of any kids here. She pursed her lips, remembering what Malena had told her about burglaries in the area. Could they be casing the place? Honestly, a burglary was the last thing they needed.

She kept staring as the car slid out of sight, training her eyes on the road in case it came back again, but it didn't. She'd call the security company, she decided, and get them to return. The car park and all the gates were completely secure, but anyone could come round the side where the windows were and get in that way, if they really wanted. She'd get them wired up and an alarm fitted too.

She was about to make the call when she heard the buzzer at reception ringing. She went to the door, eyebrows rising when she spotted the dark car parked across the road and one of the men who'd been peering from the car at her door. A shot of fear went through her, but she pushed it down. This man with his stocky build, thick neck and – she grimaced – tattoos down his arm might not be her ideal customer, but surely if he was going to do anything nefarious, he wouldn't turn up in the middle of the day.

'Can I help you?' she asked smoothly, pasting on her best professional expression.

'Yeah, hope so. I'm an old friend of Beth's. She here today?'

'Oh, Beth.' Alice's eyebrows flew up in surprise. 'Yes, she's here, but she's busy at the moment. If you'd like to leave your name and number...' She turned to grab a piece of paper, not wanting him any further inside the Nest. Maybe he wasn't a burglar, but he looked far from innocent. How on earth did Beth know him?

She slammed straight into Georgie as she turned. To her surprise, Georgie was staring at the man as if *she* recognised him. What was going on? Georgie's cheeks were turning a startling shade of red, and she was slowly moving away, as if the man was poison.

Alice swivelled back around. What the hell? Who was this man, and how did her staff know him? 'So, how do you know Beth?' Alice asked, keeping the smile nailed on to her face.

'We go way back,' the man responded, but his eyes looked anything but friendly. In fact, something about the way he was glancing around the place made the hairs on Alice's neck stand up. Maybe he *was* here for something nefarious, though she couldn't imagine Beth embroiled in anything unsavoury. But then... she tilted her head. Could those drugs be hers? 'Look, I need to talk to her. You said she was here. Get her.'

'Um, Beth just went out on her break,' Georgie mumbled, not looking at the man or at Alice, for that matter. What was wrong with her?

'Why don't you leave your name and number, and I'll make sure she gets in touch,' Alice said once more, holding up the pen and notepad. She'd get Malena to run a check on him too.

'That's fine. I'd rather see her in person. It's been way too long for just a phone call.' He looked around the place, and once again Alice felt that uncomfortable feeling stirring inside. Without saying more, he turned and left.

'What was that...' Her voice faded as she realised Georgie had already ducked back to the children.

Alice shook her head and picked up the mobile again to call the security company, telling them she needed them here urgently to alarm the windows and doors. The man who answered bleated out that they'd come as soon as they could, and she hung up and smiled. Maybe she was overreacting, but something about that man had unnerved her, and she wasn't going to take any chances this time. A stellar future awaited her, and nothing would stop her. She caught sight of herself in the gold-framed mirror behind the desk, her hair tugged back into its usual low ponytail. Her cheeks were flushed, and her eyes twinkled, and she grabbed the knot and yanked, her hair tumbling out around her shoulders.

It was time for a new style, she thought, examining herself. Everything was under control here, and finally she had the chance for some 'me time'. Maybe a nice, layered cut with high-lights would do the trick. Something that wasn't too severe; something that screamed 'yummy mummy'. She wasn't a hard-nosed corporate lawyer any longer. She was a successful wife, mum and founder of the best nursery for miles. Everyone would not simply admire her, but they'd want to be her friend too.

She'd swing by the stylist's, and by lunchtime, she'd be a new woman.

No, not a new woman.

An even better one.

TWENTY-SIX
BETH

Beth handed the little boy a glue stick and smiled, tiredness washing over her as the child babbled. She had no idea what the toddler was trying to tell her, and she hadn't the energy to figure it out. She'd been awake all last night after coming back from Lenore's, desperately praying no one had seen her. Red-and-blue police lights had cut through the night as they'd slowly cruised by the house, and Beth wondered if someone had reported her lurking around. After the spate of burglaries in the area, everyone was on high alert. She'd plastered herself against a bush at the side of the house, hoping she was invisible. Thankfully, the police had passed by, and she'd got into her car and driven home, shaking. She didn't care what Alice wanted, she would never do this again. She'd thought she'd been lucky this time. Until...

She swallowed. Until she'd got up this morning and gone to put on her coat. She'd reached into the pocket to find the ultrasound photo of her baby. She needed a reminder of all that was good in this life... of everything she was striving to protect and keep safe; of all that awaited her and Rich and their family in the future.

Her fingers had fumbled through the lining of the pocket, eyebrows rising when it was empty. Maybe she'd put it in the other pocket? No, that one was empty too.

Shit. She'd sat back, fear and panic building inside. She knew she'd had it in her coat, and the only place she'd gone to was Lenore's. It must have fallen out somewhere along the way. Maybe in the car?

Please God, let the photo be in the car, she'd prayed. *Please.* Heart racing, she'd torn outside and opened the car door, scanning the interior, but it was nowhere to be seen. She'd collapsed in the seat, telling herself to calm down. It could have fallen out anywhere. And even if it had, a random ultrasound photo proved nothing.

Still, it did have her name on it. And if Lenore found it, she would have questions. Questions Beth did not want to face.

The shrill ring of the buzzer from reception cut through the laughter of the children as they made a disaster scene from the mountain of toilet paper rolls in the corner of the room. Neither she nor Georgie had the energy to try to turn this into a 'learning activity' – when push came to shove, they'd just say it was a child-initiated task, i.e., a mess. Beth cast a glance at her manager, thinking she looked worse than usual today and that she seemed a million bloody miles away too.

'I'll see who that is,' Beth said, since Georgie hadn't seemed to clock that the buzzer had sounded.

'No, no.' Georgie waved a hand in the air. 'Keep going. I'll check.'

Beth turned back to the child, gently removing the glue stick from his sticky grip. She was just taking him to the sink by the open door when she heard a voice that cut straight through her.

Curtis was here. He was here, just down the corridor, only a few feet away.

How had he found her?

Her heart was beating so fast that she felt like she was going to pass out, and though she wanted to run, she couldn't move a muscle. The boy was staring at her in fascination.

'Okay?' he asked, prodding at her arm. 'Miss Beth? Okay?'

But she couldn't answer. She couldn't do anything.

'Beth?' Georgie's voice cut through the fear and panic that gripped her. 'There was a man here to see you. He said he's an old friend?'

'No.' The word came out as a whisper. She could hardly speak, but she had to. It was survival. She couldn't see Curtis. She couldn't. God knows what he would do to her – do to this place – in revenge. 'He's not a friend. He—' She paused, wondering again what he had done to Jess to get her phone. Was she okay? 'Is he still here?'

'He's gone,' Georgie answered, and Beth sagged onto the floor beside the boy, who was merrily splashing water everywhere. But she didn't care. She didn't care about anything other than keeping Curtis away from her... away from her baby. 'Alice asked if he wanted to leave his name and number so you could call, but he said he'd see you later.' Beth could see all the questions spinning in her colleague's mind.

'Oh my God.' *See you later.* Would he come back? Did he know where she lived? Would he follow her until he found out? She bent over, her stomach twisting and nausea rising as she realised that she would never be safe here. That everything – the life she had built, her job, her marriage, the future she'd so been looking forward to – was about to come crumbling down. The past had caught up. It had found her. And it would destroy everything.

'I've got to get out of here,' she said, struggling to her feet. 'I've got to leave before he comes back. I can't believe he found me.' She could barely stand, her legs were shaking so much, and fear poured through her once more as she stared at Georgie's stricken face.

'What's wrong?' she asked, taking Georgie's hand. She looked as if she was in pain. 'Are you okay? Did he hurt you? What did he do to you?' Curtis was a monster. She wouldn't put anything past him.

But Georgie was shaking her head, pulling away from Beth's grip, as if she couldn't stand to be touched. 'I'm sorry.' Her voice was a whisper.

'Sorry?' Beth's brow furrowed. Why was Georgie apologising?

'It's because of me,' Georgie said, slumping over. 'It's all because of me. I brought that man here.'

'What?' Beth's mouth dropped open. How the *hell* had Georgie connected with Curtis? It wasn't like they frequented the same drug dens or anything... Her mind spun wildly, landing on an image of the pill bottle in Alice's hand. The OxyContin that she'd told herself could never belong to Georgie. Could it have been hers? Could she somehow have got it from Curtis? Oh, God.

'I didn't know he was dangerous.' Georgie's voice emerged in an anguished croak. 'I just went to get some pills to get me through. He was there, and I was wearing my uniform, and he asked if I knew a Beth who worked at a nearby nursery. I was scared, so I gave him your name. I'm so sorry, Beth.'

Beth stared. How could this be happening?

'I wanted to stop taking them,' Georgie was babbling, as if she had to get everything inside her out. 'I knew I wasn't doing a good job here. After the accident, I asked Alice if I could quit, so I could stay at home and get better. But she wouldn't let me. She said it would just show everyone I'd done something wrong, and I, well... I felt so guilty that I wanted to help.'

Silence fell as Beth tried to digest the words. *After the accident. Show everyone I'd done something wrong.* Did Georgie mean the drugs? Or was there something else? A thought was ballooning in her head, growing bigger and bigger. Georgie had been completely out of it the day of the accident. Beth had thought she'd been tired. And when she'd asked Georgie later what had happened, Georgie hadn't known. It was only later that the whole story about Lenore had come out – a story Lenore thoroughly rejected.

What if Lenore hadn't left with her daughter after all? What if Georgie had something to do with the accident? An accident that had happened because she'd been on drugs? Anger was tumbling over her, a waterfall covering everything in fury. Beth might be able to understand simply leaving the gate open by mistake, but Georgie hadn't just made a mistake. She'd made a mistake because she'd been addicted to drugs. Drugs that the man who'd made Beth's life hell had given to her. Drugs that had meant he'd been able to find Beth.

She thought she'd been so safe here, in this place of innocence and calm. But nothing was safe. She never had been, and she never would be.

'It was you, wasn't it?' she said slowly, focusing on Georgie. 'You're the reason Florence got onto the road. The accident happened because of you.' Seconds seemed like years until Georgie nodded, and the anger kept flowing – quickly followed by guilt as she remembered how she'd hammered home the story with Lenore while her daughter lay on an operating table. *God.*

'I didn't mean to leave the gate open,' Georgie said, tears streaking down her face. 'I'll never forgive myself. But please don't tell anyone, Beth. Please.'

Beth shook her head. 'I believed Alice when she said Lenore had come to pick up Florence.' She bit her lip, thinking once more that she hadn't seen Lenore – and she knew Florence had been with her in the garden. So, why had she been so eager to believe the story?

She drew in a breath as the answer filtered in. She'd been so

eager because it was easier – for her, and for the Nest. She'd
bought into the lie because she'd wanted to, and she'd hit
Lenore with it at a time when her friend needed her most.
Lenore had worked so hard to understand that what had
happened after Florence's birth hadn't been her fault. She'd
come for a fresh start, but yet again she'd faced a wall of blame,
a whole community saying she'd almost killed her daughter
through her inattention. In reality, it hadn't been her at all.

There was only one thing Beth could do – one thing that
could make up, just a little, for the pain she'd caused.

She met Georgie's wide eyes. 'Lenore deserves to hear the
truth. The truth about everything. Not just the gate, but the
drugs too. And if you don't want to say it, then I will.'

'No.' Georgie's face went from scarlet to white so quickly
that Beth wondered if she was going to pass out. 'Please.' She
gripped onto Beth's arm, and Beth jerked away. She didn't care
if Georgie *was* going to pass out. She didn't want to be touched
by her. 'You don't understand. My daughter needs me. She
needs me, and I—'

'You know what?' Beth drew back, her heart pounding so
hard she was afraid the vibrations would hurt the baby. 'My
family needs me too. Until you brought Curtis to my door, we
had a good life. And now...' She sighed. 'And Florence needs
her mum as well. She needs a mother who knows what a good
parent she is, not one constantly being told she's at fault. I can't
be the person to take that away from her. I won't be that person.'

And before she said or did anything she might regret –
regret more – she turned and walked away, sadness weighing on
her like a stone. Her life here was over. Her marriage was over.
It had to be, because if Curtis tracked her down to her home, no
one there would be safe.

She had to tell Rich she was leaving – make up some excuse,
grab her things, and try to find somewhere safe. And

then... then, when she was far away where nothing could reach her, she'd tell Lenore the truth about what had happened at the Nest that day.

TWENTY-SEVEN
GEORGIE

Georgie slowly got to her feet, blinking to keep everything in focus. She had to shake off this film surrounding her – the film she'd wanted around her, to block out everything. She didn't want that any longer, though. She had to think clearly. She had to act, before Beth told everyone what had happened was her fault... and why.

If it came out that she'd been using drugs at the Nest and that was why the gate had been left open, she could be found criminally negligent. She might even go to prison, at a time when Molly needed her more than ever. Navigating the teen years with a degenerative disease was bad enough, but doing that with your mother in prison? Georgie couldn't begin to imagine.

She couldn't let that happen. Where had Beth gone? Back home? To Lenore's? To Malena, to talk to her first? Georgie's mind spun in a million directions. She had to tell Alice. Alice would know what to do. She would have a plan to stop Beth. She'd get everything sorted out.

Georgie grabbed the two volunteers in the storeroom and asked if they could watch the children for a minute, then ducked into the office to talk to Alice. Her heart dropped when she noticed the empty chair. Where had she got to? A note on the desk caught her eye, her heart dropping when it said only that the security company was coming today to set some alarms. Well, wherever Alice was, she couldn't have got too far, Georgie thought, sliding her mobile from her pocket.

She waited, listening as the phone rang out and voicemail kicked in. Then she dialled again and again. Still nothing. Unsure what to do, Georgie sat down at the desk. Alice always answered her phone. Why wasn't she picking up at the moment when Georgie needed her most? At the moment when the Nest needed her most? If they didn't do something fast, everything would be destroyed.

Georgie tapped her fingers on the desk, trying to get her mind in gear. Where would Alice be? She must be going to the office – maybe that was why she wasn't answering, because she was driving to the station to catch the commuter train. Georgie looked at her watch. Alice had been here ten minutes earlier. If Georgie left soon, she might be able to catch her before she got the train. But she couldn't leave the nursery with just two volunteers. They couldn't take the risk of anything happening, especially now.

They'd have to close for the rest of the day, she decided, frantically trying to think of a reason. Alice wouldn't like it, but she would understand once Georgie explained the survival of the Nest depended on it. Maybe she could say there was some kind of viral outbreak – that always sent parents scurrying to collect their children. There weren't too many kids here today anyway, so if they started ringing around, it wouldn't take long to clear the place. She'd get the volunteers started, and then duck out. Hopefully, she'd be back with Alice by the time the security company arrived. If not, the volunteers could stick around.

A few minutes later, she grabbed her handbag and rushed

out to the car. She sat for a minute, blinking to get a grip, before starting the engine and easing carefully onto the road. The last thing she needed was an accident. Thankfully, she made it to the station without incident, then parked up and raced in. The next train to London was in five minutes, and Alice... she glanced up and down the platform. Alice was nowhere to be seen. Had she already left? Trains only came every half hour or so, but she might have made the one before. She might be at Waterloo, or on the Underground where her phone wouldn't work.

Georgie took the mobile phone from her back pocket to try calling again, her eyebrows rising in surprise when she saw five missed calls from Kasper. He must have rung when she was driving – she'd had the phone on silent at the nursery, so she hadn't realised. She made a face. Well, he hadn't left a voice-mail, so it couldn't have been too important. Maybe he'd pocket-dialled her. She'd told him over and over to make sure his phone was locked, but he always forgot.

She was about to try Alice once more when her phone started ringing. Oh, thank God. Finally, Alice was calling. 'Where have you been? I—'

'Georgie.'

It wasn't Alice. It was Kasper. And something in his voice made everything inside her brace for a coming blow. Beth must have talked to him. Beth had told him what had happened, and her whole world was about to collapse.

'Kasper, I'm so sorry. I never meant to leave the gate open like that. I—'

'I don't know what you're talking about. It's not that.'

Georgie jerked. He didn't know? Beth hadn't told him? But why did he sound like this, then? So... frantic. So upset.

'I've been trying to call you,' he continued. 'Where the hell have you been?'

Georgie struggled to find words. How could she begin to

explain when she didn't know what was going on herself? 'Is everything okay?' Everything was so far from okay that it didn't bear asking, but he couldn't know any of it. Not yet anyway.

'No, everything is not okay.' His voice broke, and fear charged through her. What on earth had happened? 'It's Molly.'

'Molly?' Georgie could barely get out the name. 'What's happened? Where are you?'

'I'm at the hospital,' Kasper said, and her heart beat so quickly that she thought her chest might explode. 'Molly... oh, God.'

'What?' Georgie felt herself sway, and she reached out to steady herself. But the ground still felt like it was moving beneath her; like no matter what she did, nothing would be solid until she heard that Molly was all right. 'Molly *what?*'

'Molly overdosed,' Kasper said, his voice breaking.

Georgie froze. She'd been prepared for so many things: to hear that Molly had come home from school, that she'd fallen, that some strange symptom of her illness had descended. But an overdose?

'I think she was trying to... kill herself.' Kasper's voice cracked on the words. 'I found her...' He paused, and she could imagine him rubbing his eyes like he did when he was tired or sad. 'I found her on the bathroom floor, with a bottle of pills beside her. I don't know how long she was there. I had to break the door down to get in. Thank goodness she was still alive.'

Still alive. Her daughter hadn't died. Georgie did sink to the ground now, her legs giving way.

'The bottle wasn't labelled,' Kasper continued. 'I don't know what the pills were, or where she got them. I can't begin to imagine.'

Georgie let out a cry as the words sunk in. An unlabelled bottle, full of dangerous pills, that somehow her daughter had got her hands on. She put her hands to her head, as if she could keep the thought out, but she knew it had to be hers. Her daughter had tried to kill herself using pills she had hidden.

'The doctors are still trying to work out what they are so they know what best to give her to counteract their effects. Once they do that, they think she'll be okay.'

'OxyContin.' Georgie's voice was a whisper, and she cleared her throat. 'They're OxyContin.'

'What?' She could picture Kasper's confusion, and every bit of her wanted to run from what she was going to tell him, but this wasn't about her life any more. This was about her daughter's. 'But how do you know?'

'The pills.' She took in a deep breath. 'They're mine.'

'But they didn't have a name or prescription on them. They weren't labelled or anything.'

'I know. I didn't get them from the doctor.'

'Then where did you get them?'

She shook her head, wondering where on earth to start. All she could think was that her daughter needed her.

'Georgie, I...' Kasper's voice faded away. She waited as silence echoed between them, bracing herself for his onslaught. She deserved every little bit of it. 'I don't know what to say,' he said finally, in an incredulous tone. 'I can't talk about this. I need to get back to Molly.'

And with that, he hung up, leaving her all alone on the empty platform. She stared at the train tracks in front of her, her eyes filling with tears. She let her vision slide out of focus, trying to draw the film around her once again. But it couldn't protect her from what was happening; couldn't keep those terrible consequences away.

Because of her, a child had almost died. Two children now: one of them her own.

How could she have left that bottle in the medicine cabinet? She knew how down Molly had been. Why hadn't she stopped to think what could happen? She leaned her head forward onto her knees. She'd been thinking of nothing but her daughter, but she'd never imagined Molly might use the drugs herself. She'd only been thinking of how to get through the day so she could be there.

She'd been trying so hard to hide her mistakes – her weakness – from her family in order to keep them together, but after all of this... maybe she didn't deserve to have a family.

She didn't deserve to have anyone.

TWENTY-EIGHT
LENORE

Lenore sat back and looked at the empty room. The boxes she'd unpacked only a few weeks earlier were filled again with belongings. The time that had stretched ahead, bursting with possibilities for her and Florence, would never be. As much as she hated to admit it, James was right. She wasn't ready to be on her own. How could she be, when not only had she harmed her daughter, but she'd also tried to harm herself?

Thank God for her husband, she thought, watching as he carefully packed away the last few items in the lounge. He was the one thing in her life that had remained steady. No matter what happened, he'd always been there to support her. She let out a breath, thinking how she must have hurt him so much when she'd said she needed space. How much he must have loved her to let her and Florence go like that; to give her a chance. Thank goodness he still wanted her in his and Florence's lives. She would try her best to make it all up to him.

'Right. I'll take this out to the car, and then we only have a few more boxes.' James went over to her and put his arms around her, and she breathed in the warmth of his body. 'If we move fast, we can be back at the hospital to see Florence, then head straight from there to London. You never have to come to Mapplestow again.'

She nodded. She never should have come here in the first place. Tears filled her eyes as she remembered thinking, that first day she'd left, that it was one thing to test your strength alone, but when someone you loved with all your heart depended on you, could you risk them? She hadn't meant to, she thought, swiping the tear from her cheek. She'd thought she was strong enough; that she could pass the test. But now that she knew differently, she had to keep her daughter safe.

James hefted the boxes and went outside to the car, and Lenore took a final walk through the rooms to see if they'd missed anything. She shivered in the cold spring breeze that was curling through the air, making the place feel emptier. It had been unseasonably warm these past few days, but it seemed to have returned to winter. The wind shook a windowpane at the side of the house, and she went to make sure it was closed properly.

Hmm, that was strange, she thought as she stared at it. The latch at the top was open, and a tiny gap at the bottom meant anyone could slide the sash window up and down from the outside. Had it been like that the whole time she'd lived here? She'd never noticed. Well, it didn't matter. The whole house was going to be gutted. A latch on the window was the least of their worries.

But just as she was about to turn away, something fluttering in the wind caught her attention. She stared at the piece of paper, caught on the bare branches of the bush outside the window.

What was that? Just some rubbish? It seemed a random place for it, though.

Curious, she opened the window again and reached out to lift it from the bush, oblivious to the cold rushing in around her. The paper was thin and filmy, and her eyes opened wide as she drew it closer. It was an ultrasound. A baby, in the very early stages. And... oh my God. Her mouth dropped open as she stared at the tiny print at the top.

It belonged to Beth, and – she squinted at the date – it had been taken yesterday.

She leaned against the wall, her hands gripping the paper, staring at the name as her mind spun. Beth had been here. She must have dropped this by accident, and it had blown into the bush. But why had she come by? After all Lenore had said to her, she must be the last person on earth Beth would want to visit.

Lenore winced, thinking of how she'd accused Beth of letting Florence run onto the road. Beth was the one person she'd connected with – the only one who'd really known her and her past. She'd tried to tell Lenore what had happened, but Lenore had been so keen to believe she was well that she hadn't taken in the words. She'd simply rejected the whole thing, and she hadn't spoken to Beth since.

But now, Lenore was prepared to hear it. She needed to hear it, from the person who was there and who'd seen every-thing. She wanted to know every little detail of that day, to see what she might be able to finally remember. The guilt and pain would be unbearable – she knew that from past experience – but remembering would be the only way she could ever move past it. If she didn't, it would always be a dark spot pulling her back in. She needed Beth's help more than ever.

Lenore blinked down at the photo of the tiny baby. She remembered when she'd first held her own ultrasound photo in her hands, full of joy and delight that it had finally happened for her and James. They hadn't been able to take their eyes off it. They'd gone to the café across the street from the hospital for lunch afterwards, and James had proudly shown the waitress the photo too. She'd rolled her eyes, and although Lenore knew she and James were behaving like the only two people to ever have children in the world, she couldn't care less. She was way too excited, and she couldn't wait for the future ahead.

Maybe her own future had turned out miles from what she'd expected, but for Beth, this pregnancy would be the start of everything: a life, a family she'd always wanted. This photo was a record of that, something she'd always treasure. It was irreplaceable, invaluable.

It was the least Lenore could offer in exchange for the truth.

'I'll be back in a minute,' she said to James, brushing by him as he came inside. She climbed into the car, starting the journey to the Nest one last time.

TWENTY-NINE
BETH

'Hey, honey. What are you doing home?' Rich dropped a kiss on her forehead, then drew back. 'What's the matter? Everything okay?'

Beth gazed into the face of the man she loved – the man who had given her another life, far from the kind she'd grown up in. This home had been a dream to her, and it was going to be destroyed. And as much as she wanted to blame Georgie, she knew it was really all down to her. If she'd been honest about her past, then she wouldn't have been so scared about the police – and she wouldn't have been so quick to believe Alice's lies.

She wouldn't have thought about breaking into Lenore's house.

She wouldn't have rung her old friend to see if she knew anyone who would do it.

And, most importantly of all, she wouldn't have talked to Curtis.

She shivered, thinking about her ex-boyfriend inside the Nest. She'd crept out to her car and driven home shaking, in a feverish combination of fear, anger and disbelief. She'd watched in the rear-view mirror to see if anyone was following her, and she'd run into the house like someone was watching. Rich had been out on a job and she'd been too afraid to turn on the lights, so she'd sat here in the dimness of the kitchen, waiting for him to come home. It was as if all the old fear, all the old tricks and strategies she'd used in her childhood to keep safe had come flooding back, like they were lying dormant, knowing she'd need them again one day.

She'd need them more than ever once she left here. How would she keep her baby safe, knowing Curtis could be behind her every step of the way?

'No,' she said slowly, still looking into his eyes. 'It's not okay.' Tears threatened, but she refused to let them fall. She wasn't going to cry. She had to be strong – stronger than ever.

'Is it that girl, the one who got hit by the car?' Rich went to put his arms around her, but she stepped back. 'Oh, love. You know that wasn't your fault. Whatever has happened, you couldn't have done anything.'

'Maybe I couldn't have done anything differently about the accident, but...' Beth took a breath in. 'Rich, I'm leaving.'

Rich tilted his head. 'What do you mean? Leaving where? The Nest? But honey, you love that place.'

Oh, God. Pain went through her, but she forced it away. She had to get this out, and then she had to go. 'No, you don't understand. I'm leaving you.'

'What?' Rich's eyes were wide, his face tight with shock and disbelief, but she forced herself to carry on. There wasn't time to waste. She had to close this door to keep them safe – fast.

'I'm sorry,' she said, hardening her tone and her face, instantly channelling the person she used to be... the person who pushed everything away in order to survive. Only she wasn't doing this for herself any longer. She was doing it for her family. 'But I've never been happy here. This town, this place, it's suffocating me.' Never had words been more of a lie. 'I need to get out of here.'

Rich's face was white. 'Is it what happened at work? With that girl? If it is, then I can understand, babe. Of course you need to get away. Look, why don't I take the next few days off? The kids can stay at my sister's. You and I can take a mini-break somewhere.'

Beth stared at the man she loved, feeling her heart break into a million pieces. Oh, how she wished she could do that. But she hardened herself again. 'No. That's not what I mean. I am sorry, but it's not work. It's not just the town either.' She stared straight at him, needing him to let her go. If this took any longer, she might just break.

'It's you, Rich. This isn't working. And I don't want to make this any more difficult for you or the kids, so I'm going to leave.' Just the thought of their faces when they came home and found her gone made her want to howl. It had been such a difficult adjustment for them to get used to her in the first place. She knew she had never replaced their mother in their hearts, and she wouldn't have wanted to. But she'd been a friend, a confidant, another presence in the house that had lifted them to a new place from the grief that had lingered. How would they feel when they learned another person they loved had been ripped from their life? She couldn't bear to think of it.

'You're leaving *now*?' Rich shook his head. 'You can't go! What will I tell them? You can't leave us, Beth. You can't.' He reached out to her, but she spun away from his grip. If he touched her, she might collapse.

'I'll... I'll be back to get my things,' she said, moving towards the door. She was so close. All she had to do was get there, then shut it behind her. She'd been planning to take a bag with her, but she couldn't prolong this any more; couldn't bear to see Rich's hurt and confused face. She wouldn't be back, but he wouldn't know that.

'And Rich...' She breathed out. 'If anyone comes asking, just tell them I've gone, okay? For good.' She didn't want to say more. It was best for them if they stayed ignorant. Curtis would sniff out a lie in a heartbeat – he always could.

Before Rich could respond, she hurried out the door and into the car. The connection between them was severed, and Beth felt the loss as keenly as if she'd lost one of her own limbs. For the past seven years, this man had been her lifeblood. He'd enfolded her into his world and his family. He'd given her a new life – and a life that was growing within her. And now, she was leaving.

She started the engine and backed out of the drive. Pain shot through her as she realised the image she'd held so close to her heart – telling Rich they were finally having a baby – would never come true. Their child would grow up without a father; without family... without the birthday parties surrounded by loving faces; the tiny village school where all the kids went and the mums headed out to the café for a quick cuppa after drop-off. None of that would happen.

But her child would be safe, she reminded herself, wiping away a rogue tear that had somehow managed to escape. Her child would be safe, and it would have her: a loving mother, something Beth herself had never had. And Beth would do all she could to make sure her baby had the best life possible.

She could make a new life, somehow. She *would* make a new life, for her child, if not for her.

She'd go to London, she decided, driving down the deserted village street. She'd check into a hotel and think about what she could do to start a life there. In such a big place, it would be easier to disappear than another small village. Anyway, she couldn't bear to try to live the idyllic life she'd had. It could never be replaced.

She turned onto the road towards the city, following the bends and curves. The Nest came into view, and Beth was about to turn away when she spotted Lenore's car in the car park. She blinked, wondering what she was doing there. Only a few lights were on inside. Most, if not all, of the children would have gone by this time, and Georgie and the volunteers would be tidying up.

A quick scan around showed no strange cars or vehicles. Wherever Curtis was, he wasn't here. Probably out scouring the streets or asking more people around town where she lived. In a place this size, it wouldn't take long. Thank goodness she hadn't told Rich anything. He might find out from Curtis who she'd been, but he wouldn't know where she'd gone.

Her stomach twisted at the thought of Rich uncovering her past, but perhaps it was for the best. Once he found out who she'd truly been, he wouldn't want anything to do with her. The door to their wonderful life would be closed for good.

She bit her lip, her mind whirling. Maybe she could talk to Lenore now, and then she really could put all this behind her. It wouldn't take long. It was perfect that Georgie was here as well. She might try to deny what had happened, but could she persist in Lenore's face, once Beth was there too? Beth didn't think so.

One last thing to do in this village, and then she and her baby would be gone.

THIRTY
LENORE

Lenore jiggled her leg impatiently as she sat in her car outside the Nest. Where on earth was Beth? Or Georgie, for that matter? When she'd arrived a few minutes earlier, a volunteer had answered the door, saying that the Nest was closed for the day due to a viral outbreak, and that both women had left on urgent business. Lenore's heart had sunk when the volunteer had told her she wasn't sure if Beth would be back today. She could leave the ultrasound, but she really needed to talk to Beth too. Whatever Beth told her, she could accept it this time. Lenore had got back into her car, thinking maybe she'd wait for a bit and see if Beth did return. And here she was, still waiting.

She sighed, taking in the new security gate and extra fencing ringing the car park. If only that had been in place earlier, Florence never would have got into the road. She couldn't blame the Nest, though. Whatever had happened hadn't been their fault. She needed to accept it, and hopefully hearing the details would help.

After what felt like forever, Beth's car pulled into the car park. Beth emerged, and relief flooded through her. She wrenched open her door and hurried to meet Beth on the step.

Her mind flashed back to the moment a few weeks ago, when she'd come here with Florence to find Freddie, and Beth had let them in. So much had changed since then – and so little. She was right back where she'd begun. Actually, no. She was worse.

'I need to talk to you,' Lenore said. She slid the ultrasound from her pocket and held it up. Beth's eyes widened as she took it, colour draining from her face. 'I found this on the bush outside my window.'

The remaining volunteers inside bustled past them to their cars, telling Beth that the children had gone and they were going home too. Beth beckoned Lenore into the empty reception area, closing the door behind them.

'Lenore, I need to talk to you too. I—'

Lenore held up a hand. She didn't want to wait. She couldn't wait. She had to know. 'I'm sorry I blamed you. I just, well... I was sure I hadn't been here, but obviously I was wrong. My car was here, Florence had Freddie...' She caught her breath, thinking of the running water and the words she'd said to James on the phone. 'Please, can you tell me exactly what went on that day? I need to hear it.'

Beth nodded, her eyes burning. 'I will tell you everything. The truth of what happened – what really happened.' She drew herself up. 'Because it wasn't your fault. None of it was.'

What? Hope flashed through her before she realised that Beth was probably only trying to soften the blow by saying it was a mistake anyone could make; that she'd only turned away for an instant.

'Beth, you don't have to worry about me. I can take it. You told me once what happened. Just tell me again – everything this time, from start to finish. I... I need to hear you say it again, now that the shock has worn off.'

'You were right: you hadn't picked up Florence yet,' Beth continued, as if she hadn't heard Lenore. 'You must have driven into the car park just after Florence got out of the garden. She was in Georgie's group, and Georgie hadn't closed the gate properly.' The words poured from her. 'She wasn't watching, not like she should have been. She has some issues of her own, and she was abusing pills.' Lenore's mouth dropped open as she struggled to take in what Beth was saying. *Georgie?* On pills? 'Florence ran into the road. That's when she got hit.'

Lenore shook her head. The words swirled around her, but she couldn't grasp them. She was almost afraid to grasp onto them – afraid to believe it hadn't been her. But that fleeting hope was growing and growing, and she couldn't stop it.

'I'm so sorry, Lenore.' Beth sighed. 'I didn't know the truth until earlier today. Georgie obviously didn't want it to get out, and Alice was concerned about the nursery's reputation, as always. And I...' She dropped her eyes. 'I had my own past to protect. I should have known you'd never do anything that might harm Florence, but it was better for me to believe what Alice was saying.' She glanced up. 'I'm sorry I wasn't there for you. I'm sorry we – I – tried to make you think it was you. It wasn't, Lenore. It never was.'

Lenore stared, unable to move as relief washed over her. She hadn't almost caused her daughter's death. It wasn't her fault. This time, it *was* different. But... was she? There was still so much she didn't remember; so much that didn't make sense.

'What about Freddie, then?' Lenore asked when she could finally speak. 'The nurse at the hospital told me he was found at the side of the road. Was that made up?'

Beth's eyebrows rose. 'Freddie? I don't know who brought him to you, but I did let Florence have him in the garden that day. She was feeling a bit unsettled without you.' Beth paused, reaching out to grip Lenore's hand. 'It wasn't your fault, Lenore.'

Lenore jerked her hand away, anger mixing with the relief. Beth might not have known the truth until now, but she still hadn't acted as a friend – far from it. And as for Georgie and

Alice, well... that anger turned to rage. They'd known the real reason, and yet they'd chosen to protect themselves and the Nest. *Anyone who works at the Nest is a member of the family.* How could Alice have betrayed her if she thought that?

But she never had been family, Lenore realised. She'd wanted to believe she'd belonged here, but the very fact that she was an outsider had let the community accept she was at fault for the accident. It wasn't her fault, though, and for that she would be eternally grateful. Knowing the truth would go a long way in helping her get through the difficult time ahead... helping her trust in herself once more. Because even if she wasn't to blame for the accident, the confusion still clogging her mind made her scared to be with Florence on her own. The way she didn't remember driving to the nursery; the words she'd said to James last night when she'd called; the water flooding from the tap... She swallowed. Cracks had formed, and until she could close them up, she couldn't trust herself again. She wasn't going to take the risk this time.

But she hadn't played a hand in the accident. And that... that was huge.

Her mobile started ringing, and she drew it out of her pocket. 'Hello?'

'Where are you?' James's voice was puzzled and slightly irritated. 'I have everything packed and ready to go.'

Oh, God. He hated when she was late, but this... well, this was a good thing. She'd found out the truth. She hadn't hurt their daughter. Knowing that would help them get to a place where they could *both* trust her sooner. James would be furious at the nursery, but at least he wouldn't have to help her carry the guilt.

'I'm at the Nest,' she said, the words bursting out of her. 'And I know what caused the accident. I know how Florence got hit by the car.'

'What? How? Actually, don't say any more,' he responded,

before she could explain. 'Come here, and we can talk. You can tell me everything then.'

'Okay.' Lenore hung up. He was right. This wasn't something she wanted to say over the phone. She still had so many questions, but all she needed was for him to realise that she hadn't been responsible. While she may not have been ready to be on her own, at least she hadn't hurt Florence. Not this time.

She glanced at Beth, who was staring down at the ultrasound as if her whole life was contained in that one photo. They'd first connected over Beth's pregnancy, when Lenore had said that whatever fear and uncertainty she felt, her child would be worth it. Lenore didn't know what in Beth's past might have prompted her to believe Alice so readily, but she could understand wanting to do anything to keep her family safe.

Beth was right: she should have been there for Lenore, and she'd never forget the pain of being told she was to blame while her child was lying in intensive care. But Lenore couldn't summon the anger she'd had before. No matter her reasons, Beth had believed it was the truth. And in the end, Beth had set her free from the guilt that could have crushed her.

'Good luck,' she said, and Beth looked up to meet her eyes. 'You're going to be a great mother.'

Then she got in the car, thoughts swirling through her mind. Maybe she had a long way to go, but she hadn't let down her daughter. She *was* a good mother. And with James by her side, hopefully she would be a great one too.

THIRTY-ONE

BETH

Beth watched Lenore leave, the sound of her car fading away. She still didn't know everything, but at least she knew that the accident wasn't her fault. She could choose to do what she wanted with that information. She glanced around the empty place, wondering the real reason why Georgie had closed for the day. Maybe it had all been too much for her. Maybe she'd gone to get more drugs, Beth thought, her gut twisting.

A pounding at the door made her jump. Had Lenore got in touch with the police already? Were they coming to investigate? She strode to the door and was about to open it when it began to jerk back and forth, like someone was trying to force it open.

'Beth! Are you in there? I know you are. Open the door!'

Curtis. A cold sweat broke over her, and her legs began to shake. He was here. The secret she was running from – the secret she'd been trying to bury, and that had risen to the surface, destroying her life, destroying her future.

Was he about to destroy her too?

No, she thought. No, she wouldn't let him. She had to protect her baby.

'Beth!' A furious pounding shook the door again, and she

took her phone from her pocket, punched in 999, and quickly relayed their location and what was happening. Meanwhile, Curtis had rounded the building to the side, where a large window looked out into the fields beyond. He locked eyes with Beth, and she shuddered. He was as terrifying as ever: shaved head, thick neck and piercing eyes. How had she ever been with him? How could she ever have helped him? She knew now that it was more out of fear and longing for someone to protect her than anything else, but it still seemed like a different person.

She had been a different person, she thought, as he tried to jimmy the window open. It might be her past, but she wasn't that young girl who'd latched onto anyone if they gave her a moment of safety. She was stronger. *She* was the one making sure her child stayed safe.

No sooner had she thought that than Curtis raised a heavy stick and smashed it hard into the window. With a terrible noise, the glass shattered, and Curtis stepped in. He was here. Her past was here. And as much as she wanted to escape, she knew she had to face it.

Face *him*.

The police were on their way. This was her chance to finally contain him – to have him locked away, so she and her baby could be safe. So Rich and the kids could be safe. If she could just keep him calm until they got here...

Curtis hit the window again and smashed out the remaining glass. As the jagged bits fell to the floor, Beth thought of how her world was like that now: sharp shards of a picture-perfect life, in pieces.

Curtis put his hands on his hips, his presence so incongruous against the pastel backdrop of the Nest. 'You didn't make that easy, did you?' he said, his rough voice cutting through the shrill sound of the alarm.

'Did you hurt them? Did you hurt my family?' she asked. She had to know if they were okay.

'Your family.' Curtis spat out the words, edging closer. 'Bunch of poncy people living in the middle of nowhere. I got no interest in them.'

Beth let out a breath. At least they were safe.

'And they aren't your family. You aren't like them, Beth.' He tilted his head, and a shiver went through her. 'You've forgotten that I know you. I know what you're like. I know what you did.' His eyes darkened. 'I know what you did to me. Jess knows, too, and she doesn't like a snitch. That's why she let me have her phone in case you ever called again.'

He stepped closer, and she backed away. Somehow, she had to find a way to stall him until the police came. She couldn't hear anything over the bloody alarm shrieking, and she prayed they were on their way.

'You're right,' she said in a shaking voice, sliding her hand down to her stomach in a protective gesture. 'You're so right. I don't belong here. I never did.' Her mind raced as she clutched at the right words to say. Curtis may not ever have loved her, but her betrayal would have hit his ego hard. 'I never should have done that to you,' she continued, praying he bought her act; that the words sounded genuine. 'I didn't want to. The police forced me to, and by the time I realised how they turned my words against me to arrest you, it was too late.' Her eyes raked his face to see if he believed her or not, but his expression was stony.

'They made me testify, and then they wouldn't tell me where you were. I couldn't come visit. I was all alone, and I was terrified.' She forced herself to step towards him. 'I'm sorry. I'm so sorry. And...' She took another step. 'I'd love to be with you again,' she said. 'Let me come with you. We were a great team, right? We can be one again.' Oh, God, she thought, as she saw his expression shift slightly, as if he was thinking about it. Please let the police come soon. *Please*.

'And the police trust me,' she continued, trying to think of anything to keep him talking; keep him from hurting her.

'They'll think they can turn me against you again, but I can feed them useless bits of information to throw them off what you're doing. I can be a valuable asset.' What the hell was she saying? 'What do you think?' she asked, tilting her head.

'Come on, then.' Curtis grabbed her arm, and she wanted to jerk from the touch, but she smiled up at him. Revulsion went through her as his eyes pierced into her, but she kept the smile etched on her face as fear gripped her insides, making the nausea rise. Her stomach clenched, and she winced before straightening out her face again.

I'm sorry, baby, she said in her head, thinking her stress would almost certainly be felt by the child within her. *I'm sorry, but I'm doing this for us.*

Where on earth were the bloody police?

She forced her smile wider as she looked up at Curtis. 'Let's go.'

THIRTY-TWO
ALICE

Alice hummed as she got into the car, glancing in the rear-view mirror and fluffing up her hair. It rested softly on her shoulders, framing her face, the choppy fringe making her look years younger. Definitely more yummy mummy than corporate slave – exactly what she wanted. She pulled the mobile from her pocket, grimacing when she noticed several missed calls from Georgie but no voicemail. Alice tried to ring her back, but the phone rang out, and she put it into her pocket. Probably just called to report the security team had alarmed the windows, like she'd asked. If it was something major, then Georgie would have kept ringing – or at least she would have answered. The poor woman was so afraid of making a mistake these days that she called if someone spilled a drop of milk on the floor, for goodness' sake. As annoying as it was, though, she had Georgie exactly where she wanted her.

Alice drove home quickly, thinking maybe she'd surprise Simon. It had been ages since she'd been home during the day... ages since they'd actually had a conversation longer than a minute. They'd never been one of those couples who would chat for hours, but they had enjoyed meeting for lunch each day back when Simon worked a few streets away from her office in London. Alice had loved the chance to flee the firm for an hour to see Simon's loving, admiring face before heading back for the hours-long slog.

She missed those days, she thought. She missed the way he used to look at her, but maybe now that she had more time, they could start having those lunch dates again. If she was going to be a wholesome mumpreneur, she needed him by her side as a loyal partner. She *wanted* him by her side as a loyal partner. Somehow, they needed to find a way to bridge the distance that had crept between them.

She bit her lip, trying to remember when they'd last had sex. Then her face flooded red as a memory came into focus. She'd returned home late after drinks at work, unsteady on her feet and a little dishevelled. She'd clomped up the stairs, not caring about the amount of noise she was making, and burst into the bedroom. Simon had sat up in alarm, and she'd planted a huge kiss on his lips, wrapping her arms around him. *Is it a bad sign I only want him after drinking a bottle of wine?* she'd asked herself drunkenly. It didn't matter. She'd deal with that later.

'Maybe you should have a shower,' he'd said, angling away from her. She'd clambered off the bed and into the bathroom, where she'd stood under the water for ages and wondered why his words hurt so much. She *did* stink of booze, she told herself. She probably would have acted the same if he'd done that to her. Nevertheless, it had stung. It still did. And they hadn't had sex since.

They just needed to reconnect, she told herself. Maybe... maybe they could have sex today. That would be sure to jump-start things, and then they could have a nice lunch out. It would be good for everyone to see how solid she and Simon were before she presented her ideas for expansion. She didn't want anything – personal or professional – to detract from that.

She went inside and crept up the stairs to the bathroom for

a quick shower first. No way would she suffer a repeat of the last rejection. She was about to climb under the spray when she decided on a bath. A long, luxurious soak was just what she needed to shake off the day and gear up for the future.

Alice lay in the tub for what felt like hours, taking the time to shave her legs with precision rather than the usual rush job she did in the shower, which usually resulted in several spots oozing blood. She padded into the bedroom and opened a drawer, scrounging in the back for the one set of lingerie she owned. It was a simple lacy black affair, but she loved how it felt against her creamy skin, and how the high-cut briefs made her legs look endless. The last time she'd worn this – years ago – Simon's eyes had almost popped from his head. It still fit her perfectly. She would never be one of those women who let herself go. She fluffed out her hair and spritzed on perfume, pushing his last rejection from her head. It would be a distant memory after today.

Downstairs, she could hear the clacking of the computer keyboard, and she crept towards the study and stood motionless in the door, arranging herself in a sexy pose.

'Hello,' she purred, and Simon almost fell from his chair in surprise.

'Jesus!' he said, righting himself. 'You nearly gave me a heart attack. What are you doing home?' Finally, he seemed to take in what she was wearing. 'And why are you dressed like that?'

She'd been hoping for a slightly more encouraging response – and maybe a compliment on her new hair – but at least she'd got his attention away from the screen. She edged closer in what she hoped was a sexy non-threatening manner, but how he moved away made her think it was more of the latter. She wasn't going to let that put her off, though. It had been so long, each of them had just forgotten how sexy the other was.

But... she stared at her husband, trying to conjure up a flicker of fire. Registering his baggy T-shirt, cargo shorts and long hair that was badly in need of a cut, she saw more of an overgrown teen than a man she wanted to have sex with. She'd feel more desire once they got started, she told herself, creeping closer.

She raised her hands to put them around her husband, but before she could touch him, he leaned back. She tried to pull him towards her, but he took her arms and held her in place.

'What are you doing?' she asked, struggling to get free. He was holding on so tightly that she couldn't, and she stared at him in puzzlement. Was this some kind of strange foreplay? He couldn't not want her so badly that he'd stop her from touching him, could he?

'Stop, Alice,' he said, as she continued to struggle. 'Please, *stop*.'

She jerked back, finally yanking her hands away. 'Simon. It's been ages. Come on. We need to do this.'

He shook his head. 'Why? Because it's something you want?'

The tone of his voice made her take another step back. 'Well, yes.' She paused. 'Don't you?'

Simon sighed. 'Alice... I'm sorry, but no. I don't.'

Hurt flashed through her, but she refused to let it show on her face. He was just busy. Or tired. Or something. 'Okay. Maybe later?' They could go for lunch, talk, and then come back here.

But Simon was shaking his head again. 'I don't think so. No.'

Alice blinked. He must not mean that. He couldn't. Maybe the distance had grown between them, but surely it hadn't got to the point where he was point-blank refusing sex now or in the future. 'Look, I know we haven't exactly been on the same page lately,' she started. 'But I want to change that.' She tilted her head, thinking it might not be the time to tell him about her big plans for her future – *their* future. 'I want us to reconnect.'

'Reconnect?' Simon sighed. 'Alice, let's be honest. We never connected in the first place. Not really.'

She raised her eyebrows in surprise. *What?* Of course they'd connected. They'd got married, hadn't they?

'You were always one step ahead of me. When we first met, I loved that.' Simon's eyes softened. 'I'd never met someone so strong, who knew exactly what they wanted. I was a little in awe of you, and I was happy to follow you. I thought it was what I wanted too.' He swiped a hand across his face. 'But then...'

Alice blinked, remembering the hesitation she'd noticed on their wedding day. But he *had* said yes. They'd been together for years. So, where on earth was all of this coming from?

'Then I started feeling like you'd forgotten I was there – that your family was there. That in all of your forging ahead, there were people waiting for you to turn and notice them. Don't get me wrong: I wanted to stay home with the kids. But between the office and the Nest, there wasn't much of you left for us. Sure, you tried for a while to come home for supper, but the kids can't eat at eight. It's way too late, and you know it.'

She swallowed. If she'd thought about it, he was right. There hadn't been time to think, though. 'But I was doing it all for you and the kids,' she cried, stung by his words. She hadn't wanted to stick at the firm. For him to throw that at her...

'I don't believe that for a second,' he said calmly. 'Being a lawyer was all you ever wanted. That office has been your world for years – you spend hours there. And as for the Nest, well, I know it gives you the admiration and the respect of the community. I can see how that buoys you up. You may have done some of it for us, but most of it was for you.'

She bit her lip. He was right about the Nest, but how could she begin to explain the truth about the firm; to tell him that she actually detested something he thought was such a big part of her for years? The distance between them yawned further, and she felt panic grow. They'd built a whole life together. A wonderful life. They could make this work. They had to.

Simon sighed, his face sad. 'I've given this a lot of thought, and it's time for me to make my own path. To step out from behind you and your career. It's taken me a while to get here, but I'm finally ready.'

'Of course you can make your own path!' she said, forgetting for a minute that she'd been planning for him to join her on hers. 'I'd love that. I'd never stand in your way – I can help. What do you think you'd like to do?' She forced enthusiasm into her voice, but it came out far from genuine.

'Like to do?' Simon raised an eyebrow. 'What do you think I do all day?'

'Surf the net?' She hadn't meant to say that, but it was too late to take it back, and the reality was she really had no idea. She could see by the way his face twisted that the words had wounded him.

'Right.' Anger replaced the hurt. 'Of course you think that. You never once asked how my course is going, or what my module is like. I bet you don't even know the name of the degree I've been working on these past few years.'

Oh, shit. Guilt flashed through her. She'd forgotten he'd been retraining to do something in computers. No way could she recall the name. Had he told her? She had to admit that she probably wouldn't have remembered if he had.

He was right: she'd been so busy trying to keep things on track that she hadn't made much space for the people she loved. It wasn't that she didn't care. It was just that Simon was the one who was always there. It had been so easy to overlook him.

But it wasn't only her to blame. On the rare occasion she had tried to be a part of the family, Simon hadn't made space either. When was the last time he'd asked about her work? About the Nest? With all that had gone on recently, he'd never once tried to talk to her about the accident. And then there was that half-term holiday she'd wanted to go on with them...

'I'm sorry I haven't been there,' she said. 'I really am. But I meant what I said earlier. I'd love to help you however I can. I promise I'll be around more. For you and the kids.' The children were still at home for a few more years. Without her job at the firm, she'd have time to make that connection; to be a presence in their lives. To go to the concerts and football matches and everything else she'd missed. Desire grew inside, and she realised with surprise how much she really did want to be around more for Simon and the kids – to reclaim her place and be a family unit once again.

'Do you think... Do you think you can let me? Let me be with the kids again and go on trips with you all, like at half-term?' She wrapped her arms around herself, feeling bare and exposed. 'I did want to go, you know. But you didn't think to ask.'

But Simon was still shaking his head, and that panicky feeling was growing. 'I'm sorry about that trip, Alice. I really didn't think you'd be free, because you never are. It didn't occur to me that you'd *want* to go. And the fact that I didn't think to ask – and that the children didn't even ask me about you, well...' He met her eyes. 'Look, I wasn't going to tell you this until the weekend, when we might have more time to talk about it.'

Alice caught her breath. 'Talk about what?' A flash of fear went through her. He wouldn't actually leave her, would he? She may not have said it as much as she should have, but she did love him. His steady presence in the background was what had let her make a success of the Nest. She'd been able to forge ahead because she knew he was there, always supporting her. But with a sinking heart, she realised that she hadn't felt he was there for a long, long time.

She could fix this, though. It wasn't too late. She just

needed time. Time to show him she could be around and that she did know how to be with someone, right by their side.

Simon faced her, his eyes solemn. 'You know I'm almost finished with my degree.' He sighed. 'Well, maybe you don't know that, but I am. And I've been interviewing for jobs.'

She nodded slowly, wondering where this was heading. He was right: she hadn't known. She hadn't realised he'd wanted to go back to work full-time. That was great news, though. That would take the pressure off her and the Nest, plus it would give her a chance to be with the kids without him there. This could be just what they needed to start again.

'That's wonderful,' she said, injecting as much excitement as she could into those words. 'I'm really proud of you.'

Simon didn't acknowledge her praise. 'I got a great job offer in Birmingham,' he said. 'At a start-up doing some amazing things in AI. It's my perfect job, really, and they're offering a brilliant salary. I want to take it.'

Alice blinked. 'In *Birmingham*? You want to take a job in Birmingham? But... but what about the kids? What about us?' Her mind spun, frantically trying to find a solution. She couldn't let him go like this. Not before they had a chance to work things out. And what would the village think when they heard Simon had left? She could hardly be the woman who had everything if she'd lost her husband.

'Maybe the kids and I could come with you,' she said slowly, her brain still slotting things into place. She'd been looking to expand. Birmingham was as good a place as any to begin. She could keep the Nest running here with someone solid at the helm and start to build her empire in the Midlands.

'You? Come with me?' Simon's eyebrows rose.

'Yes.' A fresh start, not just for her company but for her and Simon too. It would be completely different: no longer would he be sitting at home, glued to the computer. He'd be going out to the office, helping to build the future. The beginnings of attraction stirred inside of her.

'But... but what about your job?' Simon asked. 'I know how much it means to you. You practically live there. And the Nest? You'd leave that behind?' He wiped a hand over his face as he stared at her in amazement.

'Yes. I'd do that for us.' She cringed inside, thinking he still didn't know the truth about the office or her business plans. But she was excited to see what they could make of a new life. This time, they would forge the path together.

She started moving towards him, ready to throw her arms around him, but he was backing away, shaking his head.

'I appreciate that,' he said, his words oddly formal as he faced her. 'I do, but it's too late.'

She stared hard at him, her pulse racing. 'It's never too late, Simon. Come on. We have the kids to think about.'

He raised an eyebrow, and she knew exactly what he was thinking. Where had she been all those years if she really had been interested in the kids?

'We can talk to the kids,' Simon said. 'We can have a conversation about whether they'd like to live with me or stay with you.'

'Well, I think we know how that will go.' Bitterness tainted her voice. The kids had always been more attached to Simon, likely because he was the one who was always there.

'A year or two in a city might be good for them,' Simon said. 'They've grown up in this small place. It's great, but it's so sheltered. It's not the real world. And they seem excited.'

'You've already talked to them?' Her voice rose. How could he ambush her like this?

'I wasn't planning to, but Sophie overheard one of my calls with the company. And I didn't want to lie.' He held her gaze. 'Look, the salary is enough that I can fly the kids back to

London every weekend, every holiday. Anyway, you barely see them through the week as it is.'

So much for reconnecting with her family, Alice thought, turning things over in her head. Anger and pain twisted her gut as she pictured coming home to an empty house, with her children miles away. And forget losing her husband: what would the village think when they heard her whole family had upped sticks and moved to Birmingham, leaving her behind? The wholesome mumpreneur image would be gone in one fell swoop.

'Is there someone else?' she asked, throwing that out like a grenade, mainly to hurt him. She knew Simon, inside out. He would never cheat on her, as much as he might want to leave their marriage. He was open and honest to a fault.

'No, there isn't,' he said, and she nodded. She knew it. 'But I have to say, I did think about it over the years. I just didn't think I could live with myself if I did that.'

She winced, pain needling her at his words. He couldn't live with himself, not live with what that might have done to hurt her. She stared at her husband, and she could see that he'd made his mind up. Their marriage was over. He was leaving, and the children would go with him. And she'd be left here. God, the village would have a field day.

She would get through it, she told herself, taking deep breaths to expel the pain. She always did. And maybe... maybe it was for the best. Maybe they *were* just too far apart. Maybe they always had been, and trying to stay beside him would only slow her down. The last thing she wanted was to go all the way to Birmingham only for them to separate anyway. She would miss him – miss the life they'd had, even if she hadn't really been a part of it. And she'd miss the kids dreadfully, but perhaps their relationship would get better if they spent some dedicated time together when they visited, rather than a few brief interactions here and there. They could still have a connection. She could have a place in their lives, albeit not the one she'd envisioned.

And as for the village, well... Alice could deal with that. She would show everyone how strong she was after her husband left her. She would be the epitome of resilience, garnering admiration. This wasn't a failure, a breakdown... this was an opportunity. Still, despite telling herself that, pain circled inside as she thought of her husband leaving – of her children leaving. How could they do this? How could they go?

She pushed it away. *Not a failure. An opportunity.* She'd have more time to focus on the Nest and on building up the business. She'd have all the time in the world.

'All right,' she said, taking a step back. God, she couldn't wait to put her clothes on. Actually, she couldn't wait to get out of here. All of a sudden, this place felt dark and oppressive, a weight pressing down on her.

'Okay.' She could see the relief on his face. 'Look, we can sort out all the paperwork and everything later, whenever you feel ready.'

'The sooner, the better,' Alice said, her words sounding more bitter than she'd meant. Simon flinched, and part of her felt pleased that at least he was feeling something.

'All right. Well, I'll—'

'I don't have time to chat,' Alice said, backing away. God, she had to leave here. 'I need to do something at the Nest.'

'Right.' Simon turned away. She fled up the stairs and into the bedroom, throwing on some clothes. There was nothing urgent she needed to do, of course, but the Nest was the one safe place that remained. Unlike her marriage, she'd kept it from falling apart – so far anyway. And now...

Now it was her future.

It was the only thing left that *could* be her future, and she'd do whatever she needed to protect it.

THIRTY-THREE
GEORGIE

Georgie stood on the platform for what felt like hours, watching the trains speed by. She had to get to the hospital to see her daughter. She had to see if Molly was okay, but she couldn't move. She couldn't face staring down at her daughter, knowing she'd done this. Knowing her *weakness* had done this. If she'd never had those pills, Molly wouldn't have used them to— She tried to push away the thought, but it ricocheted through her like a bullet. To try to kill herself. If Kasper was right, her little girl had wanted to die.

Why hadn't she talked to them? Why hadn't she told them exactly how she was feeling?

Georgie bit her lip. She hadn't talked to anyone or told them how she was feeling either, had she? She hadn't said how overwhelmed she was, how upset, how worried and scared for her daughter's future. She'd tried to follow Kasper's example – how stoic and strong he'd been, how steadfastly he'd held the family together – not wanting to be the one to let them all down; wanting to show that she was strong. Instead, she'd turned to pills.

Her daughter had done exactly the same.

Georgie cried out, the guilt ripping through her. She'd tried to be there for her family. But everything had crumbled around her. She stepped closer to the platform edge. She wasn't lifting anyone up. Instead, she was dragging them down. She—

'What are you doing?' She gasped as arms encircled her and hauled her back from the edge, bundling her to the safety of the waiting room. She twisted in the grip, surprised to see Malena in full uniform. Had Beth been in touch with her already? Was she here to take Georgie away?

'Someone rang emergency services saying there was a woman who'd been on the platform for ages, and who looked as if she might do something to harm herself,' Malena said, her kind eyes staring into Georgie. 'You weren't, were you?'

Georgie didn't think she was going to... was she? She thought of stepping into the air, of the sharp rush of the train spinning past, of the darkness that would follow.

'No,' she answered. She'd messed up so much, but leaving her family behind like that would be devastating. She wouldn't do that to them, but she couldn't carry on like this: trying to pretend that everything was okay. It wasn't. It was so far from okay it was laughable, and no amount of drugs or delusion could erase that. But maybe... maybe being strong didn't mean pretending. Maybe real strength was found in saying the truth; how you really felt.

In facing the outcome, whatever it might be.

She thought of Florence in hospital, and of her own daughter. She'd been so worried about the consequences of her actions, but nothing could be worse than the guilt of what she'd already caused. And while she may not ever be able to make up for what she'd done – to her family, Lenore, or to the Nest – she could be strong enough to tell the truth – or own up to her part, if Beth had already said it. To say she had been weak, that she'd needed the drugs, and that she'd left the gate open because of it.

Alice would be furious, of course, but the Nest would survive. Alice would make sure of it.

'Has Beth... has Beth talked to you yet?' Georgie asked, unsure what Malena might already know.

'No. Why?'

'The accident at the Nest.' She drew in a breath. 'We all... we lied. It wasn't because Lenore got distracted and let Florence run into the road. Lenore hadn't come in to get her yet.'

'What?' Malena jerked back. 'What do you mean?'

'I mean...' Georgie drew in a breath. 'Florence got out into the road because of me. She was in the garden, and I didn't close the gate properly.' She dropped her head. 'I've been taking some pills to help me deal with my daughter's diagnosis of MS, and they, well, they have an effect on me. Make me a bit hazy.' Truthfully, she still couldn't remember much about that time in the garden at all.

'A bit hazy?' Malena shook her head. 'So everything Alice told me about Lenore picking up her daughter was a lie? *Shit.*' Anger crossed her face. 'But—' She shifted on the bench. 'But Lenore's car was there that day. I saw it. It was part of what made me so certain that what Alice was saying was true. Along with you and Beth backing her up.' She paused. 'And if what Alice was saying wasn't true, then why didn't Lenore tell me that?'

Guilt gripped Georgie once more as she thought of how they'd all worked together to gaslight Lenore. 'We all decided we'd tell her she was to blame. She'd had such a shock that she couldn't remember much about it. And she'd had a few mental health issues in the past, so...' Her voice trailed off. She couldn't bear to think of how Lenore must have felt. Pain hit as she realised she didn't have to think about it. She knew it. Hadn't she almost caused her own daughter to die?

Malena sat for a minute, taking in everything as the trains

rumbled by them. 'Right, well, I suppose I'd better talk to Alice. Beth will corroborate everything you say?'

'Yes, she will.'

'Okay. I'll need to talk to you again, too, probably down at the station. Get everything on record.' Malena sighed. 'Thank you for telling me. I appreciate it can't have been easy. I don't know where all this will go from here, but officers will be in touch. I would suggest that you get yourself a lawyer. And in the meantime, it goes without saying that you won't be working at the Nest any more. The board will send through all the paperwork.'

Georgie nodded, a tiny shred of self-respect creeping into her despite her fear of the future consequences. It hadn't been easy, and though she should have done it sooner, she *had* done it.

'Why don't I drop you at home,' Malena said. 'It's on the way to the station anyway, right?'

'Actually, I was going to head to the hospital.' Her heart flipped again as she thought of Molly downing her pills. Please God, let her be okay. 'My daughter is there.'

'I'll give you a lift. Come on.'

'Thank you.' Georgie gazed gratefully at Malena.

They left the train station and climbed into Malena's squad car. They'd just pulled out of the car park when Malena's radio squawked.

'Intruder at the Nest nursery on London Road. Any units in the area, please respond.'

Georgie's eyes widened. 'There's a break-in at the Nest?' What kind of person would target a nursery, of all places? Maybe it was just a false alarm set off by the security company as they installed the new system. Unless... fear jolted through her. Unless Curtis had come back to make trouble. Oh God. Oh, *God.*

'Malena, there's a chance it might be someone who wants to

hurt Beth,' Georgie said, the fear building inside. She couldn't take it if someone else got hurt. 'It's a drug dealer, someone she used to know,' she said. He knows she works there, and he called round earlier today. He might have come back again. I don't think Beth's there, though.'

'Okay.' Malena's jaw clenched, but her tone was calm. 'I'll check it out since we're so close. There's also been a rash of burglaries around the area, so it could be related to that. Let's hope it is.'

She sped along the road, and a few minutes later, the Nest came into view. Georgie sucked in a breath. Beth's car was there, alongside a darker one with the windows shaded. Her heart lurched.

Malena swung into the car park. 'Right. You need to stay here and not move an inch,' she said, surveying the front of the building. Everything looked okay, but... Malena got out of the car and crept around the side of the nursery, and Georgie held her breath. A few minutes later, a scream pierced the silence, and her heart started pounding. Someone in there was in trouble, and she was the one who had brought the wolf to the den. She couldn't sit back and let things happen; let someone get hurt. She had to help.

She was more scared than she'd ever been, but she followed Malena's trail, peering around the corner and into the large bay window. Shards of glass littered the ground outside, and inside... she stifled a gasp.

Malena was lying on the floor, unconscious. And Curtis had Beth by the neck, pinned up against the wall. She was struggling to get away, her legs kicking as she twisted and turned, but her face was turning red as Curtis continued to grip her. His face was contorted into an angry mask, his eyes bulging and the muscles in his arms taut. Georgie could almost feel the anger and fury radiating off him in a dark cloud. For an instant, she froze at the horrific tableau in front of her.

Then anger and determination spurred her on. She couldn't let this happen. She *wouldn't* let this happen. Before she knew what she was doing, she grabbed a shard of glass from the ground and climbed through the window.

'Let her go,' she said to Curtis, brandishing the glass. She didn't know if she could use it, but she had to act fast. Beth was slowly fading, and Curtis still had her by the neck.

Curtis spun around in surprise, thankfully dropping Beth, who crashed to the floor, gasping. 'Well, hello there,' he said in a sneering tone. 'Want some more pills? You threaten me again, and I can promise you you'll never get them from anywhere.'

Georgie shrugged. She didn't care. She was never going to have those pills again anyway. 'Look, just go, okay?' She tried to sound firm, but her voice was shaking. Still, she held the piece of glass tightly, glinting in the light above her. She wasn't going to step back. She was going to stand strong.

Curtis laughed. 'With pleasure. And I'm taking Beth with me.' He reached down and grabbed her arm, starting to drag her across the floor. She let out a cry of protest but was too weak to do otherwise.

'No.' Georgie held the shard of glass higher. '*No*.' She took a step closer, still not sure what she was going to, when Curtis suddenly dropped to his knees and fell to the floor with a grunt. Georgie jerked back in surprise.

'Well, that should do him.' Malena slid her baton into her belt and knelt down. She rolled Curtis onto his back, then put his hands behind him and clicked on handcuffs. 'What a nasty piece of work.'

'Are you okay?' Georgie asked. She hadn't heard her stirring.

'I'm fine. Just a knock on the head. He grabbed Beth when he saw me come in and tried to use her as leverage to let him go. When I wouldn't, he hit me with the chair.' She gestured at the broken wooden chair in the corner of the room. 'I called for backup, but God knows when they'll arrive.' She looked at Georgie. 'I told you to stay in the car. It could have gone very wrong for you... for all of us. But...' She held Georgie's gaze. 'Thank you.'

Georgie nodded, feeling for the first time in a very long while that she'd finally done something right.

Together they knelt beside Beth, who was still lying on the floor. 'Beth?' Georgie said softly. 'Are you okay?'

Beth groaned, and she and Malena helped her sit up slowly. 'My baby,' she said, sliding a hand down to her stomach. 'I need to make sure my baby is okay.'

Malena met Georgie's eyes over the top of Beth's head, and surprise jolted through her. She hadn't known Beth was pregnant; Beth had never said a word. Like Georgie, she'd had so many secrets, and she'd tried so hard to protect them... protect herself. But secrets had a way of tumbling out, sometimes in the worst way imaginable, and with the worst possible consequences. Georgie had learned that the hard way herself, and she prayed that Beth wouldn't have to learn it too.

'A backup unit is on the way,' Malena said. 'They can take you to hospital, okay? In the meantime, I'm going to take him in and make sure he stays in prison for a long, long time.'

'Are you okay with him on your own?' Georgie asked, looking down at Curtis groaning on the floor. Now that he'd been defeated, he didn't seem as scary as before.

'I'll be fine,' Malena answered. 'Thank you again for your help. I'll be in touch.'

'What the *hell* is going on?' All three of them looked up in surprise as Alice came through the front door.

'This man broke in and assaulted Beth,' Malena said. 'He knocked me out and was about to take her away. Thank God for Georgie.'

'For Georgie?' Alice's eyes bulged.

Malena nodded, her face hard. 'She managed to distract

Curtis, so he let Beth go. Without her, I don't know what might have happened.'

'Right.' Georgie could tell by Alice's tone that she didn't believe it. All these years, Georgie realised, and Alice had never once said anything nice to her. But they hadn't actually been friends, she thought. Real friends knew each other; supported each other. She'd looked up to Alice, but that had been about it.

'Right, I'm going to get him to the station.' Malena tugged on the handcuffs, and Curtis groaned. 'Beth, backup should be here soon, okay? They can take you to hospital – it will be faster than calling an ambulance. I hope everything will be all right with the baby. Please let me know.' Her gaze swept over Alice once more.

'And Alice, you need to have a word with the officers. Not about this. About the accident. About why you lied.' And then with one final yank of the handcuffs, she was gone, leaving the three of them standing amongst the sharp shards of glass in the Nest.

Alice drew in deep breaths, telling herself it would be okay as she stood in the reception. A chill wind blew through the shattered window and right into her, making her feel as if her very protection had been taken away. She told herself not to be silly. It was just a window, and that could be easily fixed. The broken chair could be replaced, and the walls repainted, if necessary. Thankfully, for a reason she had yet to uncover, no children seemed to be here. Everything would be fine.

Except... what had Malena meant when she'd said she needed to talk to Alice about how she'd lied? Alice looked over at Beth, hunched in the corner, eyes glazed and gripping her stomach, then swung her gaze to Georgie. Which one of them had spilled? They were both in deep, and she still had that pill bottle. Would they risk their futures like that?

'I told her,' Georgie said, as if she could hear Alice's thoughts. 'I had to say what really happened. I couldn't keep it hidden any longer.' Her voice was loud and clear, and Alice thought that she almost sounded like a different person. 'And if you're thinking you might use the drugs against me or Beth, I told Malena about that too.' Her voice was triumphant despite

the consequences it would have for her. 'I'm sorry for what that
means for the Nest, but I'm sure you'll find a way to succeed.
You always do.'

Alice raised an eyebrow at her tone. It was almost bitter,
and so unlike anything she'd heard from Georgie before. A bit
of discomfort circled inside that she no longer had the admiration of the person who'd always looked up to her, but she shoved
that away. Georgie didn't matter. Alice still had the whole of the
community who admired her, and soon – if her plans came to
fruition – even more people would applaud her.

First, though, she had to stop Georgie's admission from
damaging her reputation. It wasn't like anyone knew the real
truth about what had happened, thank goodness. They didn't
know, and they would never find out.

She tilted her head, scrolling through solutions. She hadn't
been here when the accident happened. She could say that
Georgie had lied to her – that she hadn't known. She'd get Beth
to back her up: she'd offer her Georgie's job at the Nest to
sweeten the deal. They would lose some business – that was
inevitable   –   and   there   would   be   an   inspection.   The
asbestos... Alice chewed her lip. With Simon and the kids
moving to Birmingham, they wouldn't need the house any
longer. The market was hot, and their place would be snapped
up. The funds from that would go some way towards covering
the cost of removing the asbestos, sooner rather than later, and
before any inspection could take place.

'Beth, would you like to be the manager here?' she asked,
turning towards where Beth was huddled on the floor.
'Georgie's admitted what she did wrong, but you didn't do
anything – at least, not that you told me about,' she said,
thinking of the break-in she'd encouraged at Lenore's. Thank
God she'd told Beth to keep her mouth shut so she could claim
ignorance. 'In fact, Georgie didn't tell either of us anything, did
she?' Her eyes flashed as she dared either one of them to chal-

lenge her. 'The Nest can carry on. It can be more successful than ever.'

Beth raised her head, about to answer, when they heard a car pull up outside. There was a knock on the door – that must be the backup. She would send Beth and Georgie away, and then try her best to finesse the situation.

But when she opened the door, it was only one of the men from the security company, ready to alarm the windows. Talk about too little, too late.

'Is this your idea of urgent?' Alice shook her head. 'Maybe if you'd got the job done sooner, we could have scared off the intruder!'

'Intruder?' The man went white.

'The police took him away,' Alice said.

'Oh.' His face flooded with relief. 'Okay, then. Sorry we couldn't fit you in faster, but we've had a busy day. You'll have to get the window fixed before I can alarm it, but would you like me to check on anything else while I'm here? I can make sure that gate is still working properly. I'm so chuffed I was able to fix it. Saved you a costly replacement on that, I did.' He looked so proud and eager to please that the words tumbled out of him, and Alice froze. Oh, God. The gate. Please may Beth and Georgie not have heard.

But behind her, she felt them rustle, as if the words had ignited something inside of them.

'No need,' Alice said hurriedly, trying to shut the door. 'Thank you for coming. Have a lovely evening.'

But Georgie was having none of it. She managed to wedge herself in front of Alice and confront the man. 'Did you say something about a gate? A gate you fixed?' she asked. Alice felt everything inside her tighten, as if she was going to snap.

'No, no, he was just leaving,' Alice said, still trying to close the door.

'He *did* say something about a gate.' Beth's voice was low

and gravelly, and they all turned to face her. She was pale and red marks were ringing her neck, and it seemed as if every word was tearing her throat raw, but still she forced the words out. 'Where was it? When did you fix it?'

Bloody hell. Alice felt the panic rise inside. She had to contain this before it went any further.

Before it ruined everything.

Before it ruined her.

'Oh, it must have been weeks ago,' she said breezily, staring hard at the man and hoping he would somehow take the hint. 'I'm surprised you remember.'

'Oh, of course I remember, ma'am,' he said, and Alice bristled. Ma'am? 'I mean, it's been maybe a week since I put in the report that the garden gate was busted – that it didn't latch at all when you closed it. Only, I didn't fix it then.' He nodded, as if affirming his own words, and Alice felt her heart plummet. Oh, God. 'It was just fixed yesterday, when we came to put in the fence and upgrade all the other gates.' He grinned. 'You're becoming my favourite client.'

'Right.' Georgie's voice was incredulous, and Alice could only guess what she was thinking, where her mind was going. Alice's brain spun for something to say, for anything, but for once in her life, she came up blank.

'Thank you for your help,' she managed to dredge up lamely. 'Goodbye.'

This time, Georgie did let her close the door. Then she turned to face Alice, and Alice took a step back at the anger on her face. She'd never seen Georgie look like that. Beside her, despite the ordeal she'd been through, Beth's expression was thunderous.

Alice held up her hands, as if she could ward them off. 'Okay, so maybe the gate wasn't working properly that afternoon. But the children were still your responsibility. You should have been watching, not high on pills.'

But Georgie simply stared at her, as if she hadn't heard. 'I did close the gate that day,' she said, as if she was watching a film play in front of her. 'I *did*. I'm sure of it. I remember.'

'Right,' Alice scoffed. 'That's a likely story, now you know the gate wasn't working. Why didn't you say this before, if it's true? Why did you tell me you hadn't closed the gate?'

Georgie shook her head. 'I don't know. It was all so hazy, and when you said that Florence got out into the road, I thought it must have been because of me. I already felt like I was failing everyone by taking those pills. I guess it wasn't a big stretch to believe.' She stepped back from Alice. 'But it wasn't true. Yes, I should have been watching. But if that gate had been working, the accident never would have happened. Florence would have been safe in the garden, safe in the Nest, like she should have been.' Her chest was heaving, and Alice could see the anger growing.

She raked her brain for something to defuse the situation, but all she could do was stare at the women in front of her. She wanted to ask them – to beg them – not to say anything, scrabbling to think of any more leverage she could summon. But the power she might once have had was gone. Gone, leaving nothing but their contempt.

'And you knew that. You knew it hadn't been working – for more than a week, by the sounds of things,' Georgie continued. 'Yet you were only too happy to let me think I was to blame. If the police charged me, it could have ruined my life – and my family's. All to save yourself from looking bad.' Alice could almost feel the fury streaming off her. 'I know I said that you always find a way to succeed. But guess what? I'm going to make sure you don't this time.'

Beth blinked slowly at her. 'And I want you to know something. I would never, ever be manager of this place if it meant helping you,' she said. 'Because I *have* lost everything.' Her hand slid to her stomach. 'Well, almost. And maybe I deserve that for what I've done in the past; for the secrets I kept from the people I love. But you...' She looked around the reception, shivering in the cold breeze. 'Secrets do have a way of coming out... of making sure you get what you deserve, in the end.'

Just on time, as if they'd heard her, the police pulled into the car park. Alice froze, wondering if they were going to talk to her, but instead they turned to help Georgie get Beth to the car.

'We're taking this lady to hospital,' one of the officers said. 'But we'd like for you to come to the station this evening. We'll take your statement there.'

Alice nodded, thinking they'd be doing more than that by the time Georgie and Beth were done talking. And with that idiot from the security company only too happy to blab about fixing the broken gate, it would be all too clear who was really to blame for the accident: her.

She wandered into the office and sat down at the desk, staring out into the night. When the co-op board heard what had happened, she'd be kicked off. The Nest would no longer be her baby. Her reputation would be ruined. No one would trust her to open another nursery in the middle of nowhere, let alone spearhead a whole new chain of co-ops. The media would have a field day with this, too, once it got out.

When Lenore discovered the real reason for Florence's accident, she might file a claim of negligence against Alice. In all likelihood, the courts would agree. She could end up with a criminal record, for God's sake. Even if she'd wanted to go back to law, there was no way she could do it with a conviction.

There had to be a way out. Didn't there? A way to move forward, move ahead, forget this mistake and focus on the big picture, like always. She ran a hand through her hair, desperately trying to think of something. Maybe Malena? Could she continue to use that relationship to her advantage? But Malena knew now that she had lied – and got others to lie too.

No, Malena wouldn't cover for her any longer, that was certain.

Secrets do have a way of coming out... of making sure you get what you deserve, in the end. Beth's words echoed in her mind, and Alice let out a cry. No job. No marriage. No prospects, for the first time in her life. She did have the kids, but... she gave a bitter laugh. What kind of role model would she be to them? They might not ever have been as close to her as they had to their father, but they looked up to her. She knew that much. She'd seen it in their eyes. But once they found out what she'd done, all that would change.

She rummaged in her desk for the pack of cigarettes. She'd never felt the urge to smoke them. She'd always been stronger... until now. She took them out, turning them over in her palm. What the hell, she thought, ripping off the top of the packet and pulling one out. Why shouldn't she smoke? What was the good of staying strong and pressing forward if you ended up with nothing anyway?

Alice scrabbled in the drawer and found the box of matches, then lit the cigarette. She stared at it for a minute, watching the smoke as it curled higher and higher in the air, then disappeared. She felt like that, too, as if everything she'd built was fading away, dissipating into blackness. This place would be hers no longer. She, the person who had founded it and nurtured it, would be cut off from its future.

She put the cigarette to her lips and drew in a long breath, coughing as the smoke hit the back of her throat, sparks spraying from the end. Christ, it had been so long that she wasn't used to this any longer. Still holding the cigarette, she ducked to the kitchen to get a glass of water, gulping it down as she went back to the office.

'Oh my God.' Flames were shooting from the papers on the desk, growing higher and higher with every second. What the hell? Those sparks when she'd coughed must have landed on the files. She stood, horrified and mesmerised as the fire grew in intensity, the heat and light getting bigger and brighter. She knew she should grab her phone, get out of there and call 999, but her legs refused to move. She wouldn't run from this place. She wouldn't abandon it.

The Nest shouldn't continue without her. No one could carry it forward like she could. Without her at the helm, it was sure to fail. And she couldn't bear to see that. It – she – didn't deserve that.

The flames reached up, licking at the walls closing in around her. She wanted to urge them on, to cheer them forward. To engulf this place she'd coaxed into life and end it, once and for all.

She stood in the centre and waited for the light.

Lenore drove towards her house, happiness and relief swirling inside. She should be tired after the past two days, but instead energy surged through her. *It wasn't my fault.* What had happened to Florence had nothing to do with her. Finally, she could tell James something good – something that would lift him up too. Something that could help them move forward together.

As for Georgie and Alice, well... she still couldn't believe they'd tried to pin the accident on her. She was horrified at what had happened, but she didn't have time to think about what action she might take. All she wanted was to talk to her husband and to be with their daughter.

She pulled into her drive, eyebrows rising when she saw James standing on the front steps. What was going on? His face was tense as he rushed down the path. He opened the door of the driver's side. 'The hospital called. Florence crashed, and she's been taken into surgery again. Slide over, I'll drive.'

'Oh my God.' Lenore's heart beat fast as she scrambled over to the passenger seat, tugging on the seat belt. 'Did they say what was wrong? What happened?'

'I don't know.' James's face was grim as he backed out of the drive and sped down the street. 'They just said to get there as quickly as possible.'

Lenore gripped onto his leg, as if she could anchor herself. *Please be okay*, she chanted inside her head. *Please live*. Florence had to, now that her family would be together again. Beside her, James was clenching the wheel, driving faster than Lenore had ever seen him. But she didn't care how fast he went. It would never be enough. She had to see her daughter.

Trees and signs flashed by, and it felt like forever until the turn to the hospital came up. Instead of taking it, though, James kept going.

'James! You missed the exit!' God, he really was in a state. '*James*.'

He didn't respond. And he didn't turn around. He kept speeding, the speedometer rising more with every second.

'James! What the hell? We have to get to Florence!' Was he having some kind of breakdown? Lenore wondered. Were her words getting through to him?

'You said you know the truth about what happened to Florence,' he said finally, his voice sounding louder in the cocoon of the car. 'Does anyone else know?'

'James, we can talk about this later, okay?' Lenore drew in a breath at his strange expression, the shadows on his face making him look unfamiliar. 'We need to get to the hospital.'

'I said, does anyone else know?' His voice rose in a way that was so unlike his usually controlled tone. Unease filtered in, layering on top of the fear and panic. Why was he asking this?

She tried not to think about the car getting further and further from the hospital... further from Florence. 'Well, the women who work at the nursery, of course.'

'Of course.' A muscle in James's jaw twitched, and he gripped the steering wheel so tightly his knuckles went white.

The speedometer kept creeping upwards, the car juddering as it struggled to gain speed. What on earth was wrong with him?

'James, can you slow down, please? Can we turn around to go to the hospital? Florence needs us.' She stared hard at him, hoping to get through. 'She's strong. She is. She'll pull through.'

But James was shaking his head, writhing in the seat as if he was in agony. 'She might pull through, but I've still lost her. Because you're never going to let her see me after this, will you?'

Lenore jerked in surprise. What was he talking about?

'She wasn't supposed to get hit by a car. She was never supposed to get hurt. All I wanted was to have you both home again.'

Lenore stared, scrabbling for words through the shock reverberating inside of her. Did he realise what he was saying? What *was* he saying?

'You know I never wanted you to leave,' he began. 'I didn't want our family to be apart. What loving husband and father would?' He paused, his face twisting. 'I couldn't keep you both safe if you weren't here.'

'Okay,' Lenore said slowly. She could understand that, after all they had been through. She knew he'd found their absence hard. She felt terrible for hurting him more, but getting some space was the only way she could think of that would let them have a future. But what did this have to do with anything?

'I didn't think you were serious at first,' he said. 'Then when you rented the house, I thought, well, you won't last long. That you'd be back within a day or two – a week, tops. And after realising you can't do it alone, you'd never leave again.'

Lenore dropped her head, her gut twisting. It had been obvious that he'd never expected her to go through with it. She couldn't really blame him for thinking that way: he had always been there. But to believe she'd return only because she'd failed, and not because she'd proven she could cope? Had he only let her go to show she couldn't do it?

If he really believed she couldn't, how could he risk his daughter like that?

She must not have heard him properly, she told herself. She must be confused. James would never have let her go if he'd thought she was that bad. He'd never take that chance with Florence just to prove he was right.

'One week passed, then two, and you still weren't back. I knew you were struggling, but you wouldn't want to admit it. So, I thought I'd come talk to you. Tell you it was time to come home. That this couldn't carry on.' He glanced over at her. 'Because you need me. You know you do.'

Lenore fixed her eyes on him, taking in his words. He was right: she had needed him. She *did* need him, but she wasn't going home with him because of what he thought: that she'd let down their daughter. Maybe he was right that she had been struggling, but she hadn't caused the accident.

'I went out to the village that afternoon.'

'The day of the accident?' She stared at him, incredulous. He'd never said a word about being in Mapplestow.

He nodded. 'Yes. I thought you'd be finished for the day at the nursery. But when I got to your place, you weren't home. I rang the bell and waited, and I started getting more and more upset.' His lip curled. 'You and Florence should have been with me, not at a bloody *nursery*.'

Lenore stayed silent. She could hardly disagree. If Florence hadn't been at the Nest, the accident wouldn't have happened.

'I went inside the house. I didn't think you'd mind.' He shrugged. 'You never minded in the past, before we moved in together.'

She tilted her head, remembering how he used to come to her tiny studio flat to fix anything that had broken. She'd been on her own after her parents died, and she'd loved returning home from work to find yet one more thing had been fixed. She hadn't been quite as keen when he'd repainted the cheery yellow walls in stark white without asking her first, but his investment in her and her space made her feel warm and cosy inside. It had meant one fewer thing to do when it came time to sell the studio too. But that had been years ago, and... she blinked as a question filtered in.

'How did you get in?' Lenore asked. The faulty window came to mind, but surely, he couldn't squeeze through that?

'I had your key copied before you left,' he answered. Disbelief spilled through her as her mind whirled. She'd picked up the keys from her friend the week before they'd moved in. James would have had plenty of time to copy them. She'd known he liked to check everything and make sure she was safe, but it was one thing to give someone a key, and another for them to copy it without you realising.

But maybe he was right to do that, she told herself. After all, he hadn't thought she was fine. She *wasn't* fine if she couldn't remember things. Of course he'd want to make sure his family was okay.

'I was going to take out the rubbish, have a look around again, make sure everything was in order. But then I saw the calendar on the fridge. I saw that you were registering at the surgery. And I realised you weren't planning on coming home anytime soon – maybe not ever. You thought you could take my daughter away and have a life without me. After everything I've done for you. Everything you've put me through.'

Lenore's mouth dropped open. *What?* That hadn't been what she was thinking. She'd only wanted time to grow as a mother, and she couldn't do that with him around. It was true she'd loved it here, and that the thought of going back to London hadn't exactly thrilled her. She'd enjoyed the freedom and independence of making decisions all on her own, but she'd never once thought of leaving him. He must know that. He was just upset. 'James, I—'

'So, I decided I'd get Florence from the nursery and bring

her back to London,' he said, before she could tell him he was way off. 'Where she belongs. Where *you* belong. And where you should have stayed.' Dark shadows enveloped his face fully, and Lenore shivered as unease grew. She'd always liked that he was so protective of her, but this... This was something different. 'Your home is with me, and nowhere else. *You* might have forgotten that, but I didn't.' His tone softened as he put his hand on her leg, but his face remained shrouded in darkness. His touch had comforted her in the past, but it felt like he was claiming her, gripping onto her, and she shifted away. She'd always leaned into him, but now she felt the urge to put space between them.

'I knew where her nursery was, but I'd taken the train from London,' he continued. 'I still had my keys to your car, so I took it to the nursery and parked out front.'

Lenore breathed in as a piece of the puzzle slotted into place. The car. That was how it had got there. She hadn't blocked it out; hadn't been confused. She had been on foot after all.

'All the children were in the garden at the side,' James said. 'I went over and called Florence. She was in the corner away from the other kids, and she came running over with that soft toy.'

Freddie. Lenore let out a breath as the car raced down the motorway.

'I lifted her over the fence. I didn't need to get permission from your friends. She's my daughter, and the sooner I got her out of that place, the better.' He stared straight ahead into the darkness. 'I was planning to call you once I had her in the car; to tell you where she was and to get you to come back home to London. I knew once you were there, you wouldn't be able to leave again. But then...' His face twisted.

'But then?' Lenore almost didn't want to hear, but she had to.

James swiped a hand over his face, as if he could erase the horrific events from his mind. 'I put Florence down so I could get the keys from my pocket. It was only a second, I swear.' Lenore could see tears gathering in his eyes. 'And then she was in the road. I couldn't reach her in time. And...'

Lenore caught her breath as the terrible memory assaulted her. Florence, disappearing under the car. Florence, lying in the road. Georgie running towards her, leaning over her.

But what about Beth's confession? Why would Georgie say she'd left the gate open? And where had James disappeared to after Florence had been hit? He couldn't have left his daughter lying there... could he? She turned towards him with an incredulous stare, trying to find the man she thought she knew underneath the terrible story that was unfolding.

'I panicked,' James was continuing. 'I knew if you saw me – if I told you what I'd done – I would never get you back. I would never get Florence back. So, I hid in the bushes at the side of the road. One of the nursery workers was already there by then, and you were rushing towards her. There was nothing I could have done to help at that point.' He sounded like he was trying to convince himself, and Lenore couldn't begin to conjure up words. His daughter had been lying on the road, critically injured – possibly dead, as much as she hated to think that. And James had hidden by the side of the road and *watched*. What could she say to that?

'I ran all the way to the station. I don't know how I got there. Then I got a taxi to the hospital.' His chest heaved. 'It was the worst day of my life. I couldn't believe what had happened.'

'So... So you thought you'd try to make me believe *I* caused it?' Bile rose in her throat, and she swallowed it down. How could he have done this to their daughter? How could he have done this to *her*?

'There was no way I could tell you the truth,' James said. 'And when I spoke to the police officer at the hospital and she

told me what they thought happened – that it was your fault...'
He let out air. 'Well, it made sense, didn't it? And with what
happened in the past, it very well could have been. You weren't
ready, Lenore. You were stressed and unhappy without me.
Anyone could see that.'

Lenore shook her head, unable to believe he'd do that to her.

'But *you* didn't see that,' he carried on. 'You still couldn't
accept the obvious. You couldn't believe it was you, even though
your car was there.'

Lenore stared at him, replaying the events of the past few
days. He was right: despite everything, she'd struggled to accept
it. It wasn't until James had told her about the phone call, her
muffled words of seeming guilt, and how he'd been worried
about her – how she'd left the tap on – that she'd had no choice.

She jerked as a thought hit. *Had* she left those taps on? He
did have a key after all. He could have come in and done everything while she was knocked out by that sleeping pill. But
would he have gone that far? She knew the answer instantly.

'The taps... that wasn't me, was it?' She could barely
breathe, thinking about it. James knew she'd done that in the
past, when she'd been at her lowest. How could he use that to
manipulate her – to make her think she'd sunk that low once
more?

James shifted in the seat. 'No, it wasn't you. I came by to
talk, but you didn't hear the doorbell. You were completely out.
I took your phone and rang my number to make it look liked
you'd called. Then I turned the water on and left. I did call the
police to come by and do a welfare check. I wanted everyone to
see that you weren't fit. They just drove by, though.'

Lenore blinked, finally seeing through the shield of darkness to the man beside her – to the *real* man beside her. She'd
wanted to believe his protectiveness and vigilance for both her
and Florence was down to the strength of his love. She'd
thought he was her support; her rock to cling to when the

waters closed in. Instead, he was a heavy weight dragging her under as she churned in the dark, forcing her to clutch onto him as she gulped just enough air to keep breathing.

She had been well. She hadn't been under any strain. She'd been happier with her daughter in this new life than she had been for ages, gaining in confidence with each decision she made on her own. She'd realised that she *could* make decisions on her own, after years of relying first on her parents and then on James. She'd been looking forward to being an equal partner in her marriage for the first time.

But he didn't want that. Looking back, she could see that he never had, even before they'd had Florence. Lenore had been only too happy to let him take the lead, revelling in the fact that he cared enough to pick the guest list for the wedding or choose the area they'd live in. She hadn't protested; hadn't disagreed once. Maybe that should have been a red flag, but she'd told herself it signalled their compatibility. And the one time she had gone against his wishes, James couldn't accept it. He didn't want her to be strong, because that would mean she wouldn't have to clutch onto him so tightly.

She stared at James, her anger expanding. She hadn't caused the accident. It had been *him,* and their daughter might die. And now, he might have taken her very last chance to see Florence alive.

'James.' She almost choked on his name, her voice ringing with desperation. She had to think of something to say to make him turn around. She had to see her daughter, before it was too late. 'James, I—'

Her words ended with a scream as the car shot off the side of the road. Then everything went black.

Beth bent over, taking deep breaths as the police car sped towards the hospital. She prayed that her baby would be okay. Her neck ached, her throat burned, and her arms felt bruised and tender where Curtis had grabbed her. She didn't care about any of that, though. All she wanted was for her baby to be safe.

She took another breath, her mind scrolling through the horrific events just a short while ago. She'd been about to follow Curtis through the broken window when Malena had startled them both. Before she could blink, Curtis had grabbed her and told Malena to back off or he'd hurt her. Malena hadn't, though, and he'd knocked the police officer to the floor with a wooden chair. Beth had screamed, the sound coming from the very depths of her, as if it had been ripped from her soul and embodied all the terror, pain and horror she'd locked deep inside. Now those emotions were here. Now they were with her, and that scream had been a desperate attempt to expel them.

But it hadn't worked. It had only stirred something inside of Curtis because he'd turned towards her with that look she knew; the look she feared. He'd taken her by the throat and rammed her against the wall, and as she struggled to breathe, her only thought had been about her baby. She had to get away. She had to get him off her. She'd kicked and twisted, but Curtis had held her firm, and she could feel her energy fading.

I'm sorry, she'd said to her child. *I'm sorry you never had a chance to live. I'm sorry I couldn't protect you.*

Then, just as her world had been about to go black, Georgie had come through the window. She'd distracted Curtis with the glass. Malena had hit him, then slapped on the handcuffs and taken him away. Curtis was gone. The man who'd haunted her dreams – haunted her present once more – would be back behind bars for a very long time. He'd ruined her life, but had he destroyed the one thing she cared about most? If it hadn't been for Georgie, that answer would definitely be yes.

Beth glanced at the woman beside her. Georgie had come with them to the hospital, saying she needed to see her daughter there. Beth had wanted to ask if everything was okay, but she'd only been able to focus on breathing. She reached over and touched Georgie's arm, thinking how odd it was that they'd worked closely together for so long and yet they hadn't known each other at all. Beth never would have guessed in a million years that the woman who seemed so down to earth would be struggling with addiction. And she was sure that Georgie would never have imagined that her past could be so dark – or that she was pregnant.

Please God, let her baby be all right.

'Thank you,' she said to Georgie. She may have made mistakes in the past – they both had – but in the end, Georgie had saved her.

'It was the least I could do after everything,' Georgie responded. 'I'm so sorry that I brought him to your door. If I'd known...' A tear streaked down her cheek, and Beth squeezed her hand. If only they'd all known – so much. If only Alice could have admitted straight out that she'd made a mistake by not fixing the gate, then none of this terrible chain of events would have unfolded. Yes, Florence would still be lying injured in hospital – Beth prayed that she, too, would be okay. But Beth's life would be intact, and her child would be safe. Georgie would never have been sucked into this. The only one who'd take the hit would be Alice.

Anger surged through her as she thought of the woman. She might come across as strong and unyielding, but tonight Beth had seen who she really was: a selfish coward, trying to pin everything on a devoted colleague rather than taking the fall herself.

While everyone else had finally owned up to what they thought was the truth, Alice had continued to try to dodge it. For all they knew, she was still trying to find a way out of this. But this time, Beth knew that she and Georgie would make sure there wouldn't be a way out. They all knew what had really happened.

The police car pulled up to the hospital, and Georgie came around to help Beth out. Finally, they stood in the lobby, facing each other.

'I hope everything will be okay,' Georgie said, staring at Beth. 'Please let me know.'

Beth nodded. 'Let me know about Molly, too, all right?' How strange that after everything that had happened to both of them, here they were, hoping their children would be fine. In the end, that was all that mattered.

'Ready? I'll see you up to antenatal care.' The officer appeared at her side.

'Ready.' She reached out and gave Georgie a hug, realising that this was the first time they'd ever done that. Georgie squeezed back, then Beth stepped away and followed the officer into the lift.

In the antenatal unit, the waiting room was empty except for another couple huddled in the corner. Beth lowered herself into a chair. God, she wished Rich was here, she thought as she trained her gaze on the clock above her, focusing on the hands moving. If only she could be in his arms at this moment, safe and protected. Minutes passed and time slowed as she waited, praying all would be fine.

'Rich!' She gasped as she came face to face with her husband. Was she imagining things? What was he doing here?

Rich held up his hands. 'Look, I don't want to upset you. I'll go if you want me to, but I had to see you.'

Beth's heart ached. Every bit of her longed to throw herself into his embrace, but would he want that, after she'd left him so brutally? 'How did you know I was here?' she managed to get out.

'Georgie called,' he said in a soft voice. 'She told me what happened; said the police had brought you to hospital. She wasn't sure if you still had your phone on you or not.' He stepped forward cautiously. 'She said... she said you're pregnant. Is it true?' He met her eyes, as if he was afraid to believe it.

She nodded, and he sank down beside her. 'Beth, why didn't you tell me about the baby? Is that... is that why you left? Did it scare you?'

Beth bit her lip. He was so caring, and he deserved so much more than what she'd done to him. Not just leaving him, but hiding who she'd been. How could he ever forgive her?

'I wanted to tell you,' she said in that strange raspy voice that didn't feel as if it belonged to her. 'I really wanted to. But I didn't want to jinx it. I didn't want you to get your hopes up, and for me to let you down again.' Tears pushed at her eyes as she thought that she might have just let down her baby.

'Oh, hon.' Rich went to fold her in his arms, but he stopped at the last minute, and her heart broke into a million pieces. There was a distance between them that had never been there before – a distance she had created. But even if she could never erase the pain she'd caused by leaving, she could be open and honest about why she'd acted like that. Maybe he'd never see her the same way again, but at least there'd be no more lies separating them. At least he'd know the truth.

'But that wasn't why I left. Rich, there's something I need to tell you. Something about who I was before we met.' She paused, trying to gather up the story she'd buried for so long. 'When I was younger, I got caught up with some very bad people... people who were stealing, dealing drugs, and doing, well... other things.' She winced, thinking of the baby on the pavement. 'One drug delivery went wrong. I was the lookout, and the police busted us.'

Rich's jaw had dropped in disbelief, but she had to get this out. She didn't want to carry the burden of her past any longer.

'They gave me a chance,' she continued. 'Turn the leader in – my boyfriend – and they would let me go. So, I took it. He went to prison, and I moved on, tried to make something of myself. I met you, we got married, and we built this wonderful life.' She waited for him to say something, but he was still staring at her.

'But the man I'd sent to prison always said that he'd find me again, and that he'd make me pay. He called by the Nest, and I knew it was only a matter of time until he found out where I lived. If he came when you were all there...' She shook her head, trying desperately to keep the tears at bay. She couldn't lose it. She had to keep going. 'I couldn't put you and the kids in danger. That's why I told you I was leaving.'

'But...' Rich finally broke free from his stupor. 'You were going to leave, pregnant with our baby?' He stared. 'Why didn't you tell me any of this? I could have helped you. We could have gone to the police and told them you were in danger. You didn't think you could tell me?' Hurt was breaking through his disbelief, and her gut squeezed.

'I didn't want to think about what happened before I met you,' she said. 'I didn't want to remember what I'd done. I loved who I was with you – I loved our life. I couldn't bear to change how you thought of me.'

'Beth? Would you like to come through?'

Beth slowly got to her feet, her heart pounding. This was the moment. This was when she would find out if her baby was still with her, or if Curtis had destroyed everything.

'Should I come with you?' Rich's voice was tentative, and it broke her heart that he was asking. She knew how much he would want to. She could see it in his eyes. Pain gripped her that the easy, relaxed love they'd always trusted in had disappeared. Could they ever have it back again, now that he knew what she'd done?

'Yes.' It was his baby too. And no matter what happened after this – no matter what he thought of her – that was a connection that could never be severed.

She went into the examination room, climbed up on the table, and lifted her shirt under the midwife's instructions. Her mind flipped back to the last scan she'd had done, and how happy she had been when she'd clutched the ultrasound closer. She wished Rich had been there for that moment. She'd taken that away from him, just as she had taken away his future too – and maybe his child. Tears came to her eyes as she pictured that ultrasound photo she'd held so dear flapping in the wind outside Lenore's house, torn and tattered. That moment had been tainted too.

She squeezed her eyes shut as the midwife moved the probe over her belly, her pulse pounding in her ears as she waited. The room was small and stuffy, but the silence felt like a dark cavern waiting to swallow up any bit of sound. And finally... finally she heard a noise. A whooshing noise, fast and strong. The pulse of her child.

'Your baby is fine,' the midwife said, and Beth let herself give way to the sobs, the fear, the panic that had been inside of her. *Her baby was fine.* Oh, thank God. Thank God.

'The heartbeat is strong, and I don't see any signs of distress.' The midwife glanced from Beth to Rich and back again. 'I'll give you some time,' she said, and went out of the room.

'I'm so sorry,' Beth said, finally daring to look over at her husband.

Rich met her eyes. 'I wish you had told me about everything,' he said, a sad expression clouding his face, and pain racked her again. 'I wish you hadn't felt like you needed to keep it from me.' He dropped his head. 'I wouldn't have cared, you know. It wouldn't have changed how I see you. I know you, Beth. I know the woman you are: kind, caring, courageous. Strong.' He drew in a breath, and she could see how much emotion was inside of him, and how much he meant these words.

'I've seen what a great mother you are to the kids, and what an incredible wife to me. And what you were willing to do...' He glanced up at her. 'Leaving everything behind to protect us, well...'

He shifted in his chair. 'But you didn't need to go through this alone. We should have worked together, Beth. You should have let me in.'

A tear dripped down her cheek. He was right. She should have – should have trusted in him and their love.

'We had an amazing life,' Rich was saying. 'Nothing could have torn us apart if we'd stood together.'

Had an amazing life? His words echoed around the room. Did he mean it was over? That it was too late for them? Her eyes drifted to the screen beside them, and she blinked to clear them. This was their child, comfortably nesting inside of her, safe and protected. Despite everything that had happened, their baby was alive. The past had reared up, trying everything in its power to snatch that away, but it hadn't succeeded. Their child was still there.

And Beth was too. She was here, stronger than any secrets. She wasn't going to let the past take away another person so dear to her. She would fight for her marriage, the same way she'd fought for her baby.

'I want to come home,' she said, reaching out to grip Rich's hand. She blinked away a tear as she realised just how much he had become home to her. She'd always held herself so tightly, afraid the secrets might eke out. She could finally let go and allow the emotions to swarm over her; feel the depth of her love. 'I want us to be a family. To raise our baby... together.' She touched his arm. 'No more secrets. I promise.'

She held her breath as she stared at him, praying that it wasn't too late. But no matter what he said, she knew her life would be different. She wouldn't live in fear. The place where she'd shoved the darkest secrets and shame had been opened up. It was light now; it threatened no longer. She was free.

It felt like forever as she waited for Rich to answer, but it was probably only a few seconds. Finally, he smiled and squeezed her hand.

'I want to do this together too. I always will. You don't have to keep things to yourself any longer, Beth. You're not alone. Right?'

Beth nodded. 'Right.' And for the first time, she actually believed it.

THIRTY-SEVEN
GEORGIE

Georgie hurried down the hospital corridor, still trying to take in what had happened. She'd rescued Beth. She'd stood up to Alice. She'd heard the truth about the accident: it hadn't been her. She'd been so relieved, but though she may not have caused Florence to almost die, her actions had contributed to their daughter's overdose. Would Molly be okay? Georgie would never forgive herself if not. She never should have had those pills anywhere near the house.

She never should have been near those pills in the first place. She'd thought she couldn't do it without them, but she now knew that she was strong. She could do it, and although she knew it wouldn't be easy, she wasn't going to take them any more.

At last, she came to Molly's room and rushed inside. Kasper's familiar battered army jacket was slung over a chair in the corner, but he wasn't there.

'Moll.' Her voice was soft as she went to her daughter's bed, and Molly's eyes opened.

'Mum.' In an instant, Georgie was wrapping her arms around her daughter, tears streaming down her face.

'I'm so sorry.' Georgie pulled back and wiped her tears. God, Molly looked awful, her skin so pale against her black hair; dark rings circling her brown eyes. 'I should have talked to you more; got you some help. And those pills... They were mine, and I shouldn't have had them. You never should have found them.'

Molly squeezed her hand, and Georgie thought that as ill as she'd been – as she was – there was still power in that grip. 'Mum, it's not your fault,' Molly said. 'I could have talked to you, too, you know. I could have told you how I was feeling. I wanted to, but...' Her eyes filled with tears. 'I didn't want to make you and Dad upset.'

'So you thought this would be easier?' Georgie made her tone deliberately light, even as her gut twisted. Molly hadn't wanted to make her or Kasper upset, the same way she hadn't wanted to make Kasper upset. *Like mother, like daughter*, she thought. But that had to change. They couldn't get through this without being honest about how they were really feeling.

Georgie let out a breath. 'Nothing ahead will be easy,' she said, and at that acknowledgement, she felt a pretence drop between her and her daughter, as if by simply saying the truth, Molly could relax too. 'We can talk about all of that later. Right now, I want you to know that nothing you say or do could be anywhere near as bad as you not being here, okay?'

Molly nodded. 'Okay.' She squeezed Georgie's hand again. 'I love you, Mum.'

'I love you too.'

Her daughter's eyes slowly closed, her chest rising and falling as she drifted into sleep. Georgie sat for a minute, watching her, when a rustle at the door drew her attention. Her heart leaped when she saw it was Kasper.

She got to her feet and went over towards him. 'What did the doctor say?'

'She'll be okay. They pumped her stomach and gave her

some other meds to counteract the OxyContin. Luckily, she hadn't absorbed too much of it yet. If she had, it could have been a very different story.' His face twisted, and she felt the guilt grip her again so strongly, it almost took her breath away.

'I'm sorry.' That would never be enough, but she needed to say something. She met her husband's eyes, this man she'd known so long, and prayed he could see how much she meant it. 'It's just...' She paused, hoping she'd be able to explain. It wasn't an excuse, but she needed him to at least understand. 'I've been having such a hard time since Molly was diagnosed. Things have always rolled along like clockwork for us, you know? School, marriage, babies, a wonderful house in the village... We never had to face any difficulty. I didn't think I was strong enough to cope. One pill became another, and then another, and then I couldn't stop.'

A nurse bustled by with a stretcher, then silence fell as Kasper continued to stare at her. 'You could have talked to me,' he said finally. 'You should have talked to me. You should have told me how you were feeling.'

Georgie blinked, a tear falling from her eye. 'I would have, but you seemed so strong. I didn't want to be the one to bring you down. It made me feel... weak.' Her voice cracked. 'But I've realised that I don't need help,' she said, thinking of the past events. 'I'm stronger than I thought I could be.'

Kasper was silent for a minute, then he sighed. 'You're wrong, you know. I'm not doing well. I haven't been since we heard about Molly.'

Georgie jerked in surprise. 'What?'

He dropped his head. 'I've been seeing a counsellor to talk about it.'

'*What?*' Kasper had been seeing a counsellor? She'd been so certain that he was doing okay.

'I should have told you that,' he said. 'I didn't want to be the one to let you down either. But the real person we've let down through all of this is our daughter in there.' He jerked his head towards the bed. 'All this time we've been worrying about being strong, but in the meantime, our daughter has been struggling too.' Tears came to his eyes, and he swiped them away. 'Christ, Georgie, she could be dead.'

Georgie reached out to touch his arm, hoping he wouldn't move away. Instead, he drew her close, and the two of them stood like that as the people in the corridor bustled around them.

She gripped him tightly, realising that he needed her as much as she needed him. They should have come together, but instead they'd let their own fears and insecurities drive them in separate directions. But now, with everything revealed, they could do what they needed to care for themselves while being there for their daughter. There was no shame in vulnerability. To admit that, you needed the most bravery of all.

Georgie didn't know what the future held for her and their family. She didn't know what further consequences she'd face from admitting her drug use at the Nest. Whatever happened, it was going to be hard; it was going to be heartbreaking. But if they stayed open and vulnerable – being strong enough to be weak – she knew they could get through it.

THIRTY-EIGHT
LENORE

'Hello? Hello! Are you all right? An ambulance is on the way.'

Lenore opened her eyes. Where was she? Then it all came flooding back: Florence was in danger. James had been driving to the hospital, and then... then he'd floored the pedal and shot straight past it. And— she struggled to sit up, her heart pounding. He'd told her what he'd done. That he'd got Florence that day. That it was him who'd let her run into the road. Not her.

Not *her*.

That was the last thing she remembered before the car had sped off the road and everything went black. She winced as she turned her head to look at the driver's seat, almost afraid of what she'd see, but it was empty, and the door was wide open.

Had he just left her here? Where had he gone?

'I need to get to my daughter.' Panic surged through her. Was Florence still alive?

'Was she with you in the car?' The man looked surprised. 'I thought it was only you and the driver. He's not here, so I guess he went to find help.'

'No, she's in hospital already,' Lenore said. 'I need to go there. I—'

The man put a hand on her shoulder. 'You need to wait for the ambulance. You look okay except for that bump on your head, but the paramedics need to check you over.' He shook his head. 'You're very lucky the car went off the road where it did. The bushes slowed it down before it crashed into something that really could have harmed you. I saw your headlights and stopped to see if you were all right.'

The piercing sound of sirens filled the air, and within minutes Lenore was being gently lifted from the car and onto a stretcher. Before she could thank the man who'd found her, she was bundled into an ambulance and checked over for concussion and any internal injuries. Luckily, all was fine, and they agreed to get her to hospital as quickly as possible. She asked if a man had been picked up around the area, but they'd said no. She didn't have time to worry about James, though. If he'd been able to get out of the car, then he couldn't have been hurt too badly. She couldn't believe he'd just left her there.

Inside the hospital, she rushed as quickly as her aching body would allow to Florence's ward. She dashed into the room, heart beating fast, unsure what she would find. Her daughter was on the bed, the machinery taken away. Lenore looked wildly up at the nurse. Was she alive? What had happened?

'Florence.' She gripped the nurse's arm. 'Is she okay?' *Please let her be okay. Please.*

The nurse nodded, and Lenore felt the tension instantly leave her body. 'She is okay, yes. Better than okay, actually. We're reducing her medications. She should start being more alert, although she may experience more pain.'

Lenore furrowed her brow. What? 'But didn't she crash? Wasn't she...' She swallowed. 'At risk of dying?'

The nurse drew back. 'No, not at all. Who told you that?'

Lenore let out a breath. James had lied. He'd lied about his daughter, again. But why? She bit her lip, thinking how she'd told him she'd learned the truth about the accident. He must have thought she'd realised his role – she remembered his words that he wouldn't let her see Florence again. So he'd told her Florence was in danger to get her in the car, and then... She shook her head. Had he *meant* to crash the car? He hadn't wanted to hurt her – hurt himself – had he? She shuddered, recalling the shadows on his face and all he'd said to make her doubt herself. She still couldn't believe he'd done that, but it was too much to think about at the moment. She only wanted to be with Florence.

The nurse gestured to a chair by the bed, and Lenore sank into it. 'I can assure you that your daughter will be fine. It might take some time, but she *will* make a full recovery.'

Lenore nodded. *Thank God.*

Florence looked so small in the huge hospital bed, and Lenore knelt down beside her and kissed her gently. She was alive. They both were. They'd been through trauma and pain, but they were together. Love rushed over her, so strongly that she could feel it vibrating within her. This was the one thing that had remained constant, despite doubting her own abilities as a mother; despite drowning in confusion. She might have questioned her capability, but she'd never once questioned her love. Even at her lowest, she'd never wanted to let Florence go.

She wouldn't always know the right thing to do, she realised. Things might not always be clear; there might be panic and fear, just like when Florence was born... just like what had happened at the Nest. She might still doubt herself, like all parents did, she imagined. But she *was* well now, and she was strong enough to withstand a few cracks. If she just held tight to this love, if she believed in this love, then she would be the mother she'd always wanted.

Florence's eyes slowly opened, and she focused in on Lenore. She lifted up her arms, and Lenore leaned down and hugged her, breathing in the warmth of her child. This was all she needed. This was all she wanted.

Together, they would find their way.

THIRTY-NINE
ALICE

Alice awakened slowly, the harsh lights stinging her eyes. Where was she? She remembered standing in the heat of the flames at the Nest, watching the flickering dancing light, and then... then she must have passed out. She raised her head, taking in the white walls and machines. How had she got out of there? Who had brought her to the hospital?

She screwed her eyes closed as more memories flooded in. Simon saying he wanted to leave. The truth about the gate coming out. The cigarette in her hand and how it had caught the papers on the desk... and how she hadn't wanted to move. She'd wanted the flames to obliterate everything. And maybe, just maybe, to obliterate *her*.

And yet here she was. She moved her arms and legs gingerly, trying to assess what hurt, but she seemed okay. Her head was throbbing, and her throat felt like someone had scraped it with a razor blade, and she could smell the smoke clinging to her like a blanket. But somehow, she'd come through the fire. She'd survived.

'How are you feeling?' Malena stood up, and Alice blinked. She hadn't noticed her sitting on a chair in the corner. Her heart twisted that Simon wasn't here, but maybe he'd been by when she was sleeping. Anyway, she didn't need him, she told herself.

But what was Malena doing here? Had she come to question her already? Oh, God. She willed her brain to work. *Think. Think!*

'I'm not here to talk to you about the accident,' Malena said, and Alice sat up in surprise. 'It didn't happen because of the gate anyway.'

'What?' Her voice emerged raspy and hoarse.

'I know the gate was broken,' Malena continued, 'and it could very well have led to tragedy. But it didn't. Not this time.' She paused, and Alice could barely breathe. If it hadn't been the gate or Georgie, then what? Could it have been Beth? Was that why she'd been so invested in telling 'the truth'?

Did it really matter, though? It hadn't been her fault. That was all that was important. It hadn't been her fault! Alice shifted in bed, a tiny bit of hope stirring inside. Maybe she could get past this. Maybe she hadn't lost everything.

'It was James, Lenore's husband,' Malena continued, and Alice's eyes bulged. Lenore's husband. He hadn't been there... had he? How could he have caused all of this?

'He took Florence from the garden,' Malena explained. 'He was about to put her in the car when she got away and started running across the road.'

Alice was silent, her mind whirring as she processed Malena's words. She might have made a small error, yes. But it hadn't caused the accident. Lenore couldn't hold her responsible, and Malena couldn't charge her with negligence. And the nursery was gone, the tainted building burned to a crisp. She had nothing to worry about, and no more secrets to hide. This was perfect! The community would need another Nest, and she was ready to deliver. Maybe she could even start that chain.

She could rise from the ashes. She did have a future after all. She could barely contain her excitement.

'So that's it, then,' she said, holding Malena's gaze, trying to conjure up the power she'd always had. 'Now that we know what really happened, we can all move on.'

Malena tilted her head. 'Well, not quite.'

Oh, God. 'What do you mean?'

'You lied to me,' Malena said calmly, walking over to the bed. 'You lied to a police officer investigating an accident. I could charge you with perverting the course of justice. As a lawyer, you know that. You knew the risks, and you did it anyway.'

Alice tried to think of something to say. Malena was right, of course. She could do that. But would she? 'Malena, I—'

Malena held up a hand. 'I'm not going to bother. My team has more important things to focus on, and my commander agrees. I think you'll have enough on your plate anyway.'

Alice furrowed her brow. What did she mean? The new nursery the town needed?

'Because it wasn't just me you lied to,' Malena continued. 'It was everyone, and that will be enough. That will ruin you.' Malena paused, and Alice desperately wondered what she was talking about. She couldn't still be on about the gate, could she? Alice hadn't actually lied about it – no one had ever asked. And nothing had happened because of it. People would forget about it, if they cared in the first place. That wouldn't ruin her.

'The fire.' Malena stared hard at her, and Alice lifted her eyebrows. What did she mean? How it started? Her cigarette? 'The fire brigade managed to put it out in a few hours, and they noticed some fragments of material in the roof.'

Alice's heart started beating fast. Oh, God. Material in the roof. She couldn't mean they'd identified...

'They're fairly certain, given its appearance, that it's asbestos. They told me it should have all been detailed in the structural survey when the building was bought.' Malena leaned closer. 'And yet I don't remember hearing anything about it. I don't remember ever seeing the structural survey, actually. None of the co-op members does.'

Alice swallowed. She tried to speak, but nothing emerged.

'You told me that building was perfect. You said it was just what we were looking for,' Malena continued. 'We trusted you, time and again. Our mistake.' Malena looked like she was enjoying this, and Alice felt rage burn in her stomach. Just who did Malena think she was? 'To say we're all angry is an understatement. The Nest isn't yours. You don't get to make decisions about whether we potentially expose our children to hazardous material or not. It belongs to the community, remember? It's a co-op. That means we all own a part of it. We all have a say.' She towered over Alice. 'And after what happened with Lenore and this fire, you can be certain we'll never listen to you again. No one will.' She stalked from the room, anger in her every step.

Alice watched her go, then let out a strangled cry of frustration. How could this be happening, just when she'd been about to start over? She thought back to last night, when the cigarette had sparked onto the papers and she'd watched them burn, mesmerised as the flames devoured everything around her.

But they hadn't devoured her secrets. They'd only revealed them. Ashes remained, but nothing would come from them. Nothing would rise again. In a way, it felt like the ultimate betrayal: that the place she'd tried so hard to build and protect had reared up even after its destruction, extinguishing any hope that remained inside.

And though she had survived, she wished the flames had extinguished her too.

'Faster, Mummy!'

Lenore grinned as she glanced back at her daughter in the rear-view mirror. Florence loved when she zoomed around curves on the road. Although Lenore wanted to be more careful than ever with her precious cargo in the back, she couldn't help speeding up to see the smile grow on her little girl's face.

It was wonderful to see her so happy and healthy. The last couple of weeks in hospital had been tough. Florence had wanted to run around, but her injuries hadn't healed enough. Keeping her daughter entertained while staying in bed had been a full-time job, and Lenore had watched way more Peppa Pig than she'd ever thought possible. She would never complain, though. Not after what her daughter had been through.

Staff had told her that James sometimes crept in to see Florence early in the morning, before Lenore managed to get there from the Airbnb she'd booked in Guildford. They hadn't spoken since the night of the crash. He'd sent her a message saying he hoped she was okay, that he hadn't meant to go off the road and that he'd only left to get help. She hadn't responded. How could she trust anything he told her? Knowing the lengths he'd gone to to get her back was more than enough to open her eyes: about him, their marriage and their future.

She realised now that what she'd welcomed as help and support hadn't really been that. It had been control – James's need to control her, Florence, and their family. He'd drawn her into his vision of the perfect family life, and she'd complied because she'd wanted that too. He might have been able to mould her into the woman he wanted after the loss of her parents had unmoored her, but once they'd had Florence, everything had changed. God knows he'd tried to grasp the reins again, but her drive to be the mother she wanted and her love for her daughter had been too strong. And when she'd finally broken away, he'd almost broken her.

He'd almost broken their daughter, too, and after Florence's accident, Lenore wasn't taking any chances. She didn't want James to see Florence until she was out of the hospital, when Lenore could be with her at all times. She'd spoken to Malena, who'd updated the hospital staff not to let James in. Lenore had held her breath, waiting for an angry text when he was refused entry. He hadn't disappointed, bombarding her with messages until she'd blocked him. They'd need to talk at some point about the future – the divorce and how to move forward with Florence – but at the moment, Lenore wanted to focus solely on her daughter. To build their life together once more, starting from the inside out. Starting with trusting herself.

Trusting her love.

She'd rented a small flat back in London, close to the school she used to teach at before having Florence. They'd promised her some supply teaching work, if and when she wanted it. She didn't know yet if or when she would, but it was good to have options. She couldn't wait to see what was in store for the two of them.

The Nest came into view as she rounded a bend, and Lenore sucked in her breath. When she'd contacted Malena to tell her the truth about the accident, Malena had said the building burned down. Glancing at it, Lenore could barely believe her eyes. Black smoke climbed up the bricks. The roof was gone, leaving only a shell, exposing everything inside to the gentle rain falling from the sky.

Lenore shuddered as she thought of Alice inside the office, watching the flames consume her pride and joy. Had she been willing to die there? Malena had told her that Alice believed a faulty gate had been to blame – a gate she should have fixed. Would she rather burn in a fire than admit she'd been negligent?

Lenore bit her lip, wondering what Alice's reaction had been when she'd found out James was at fault, not her. Malena had reported that Alice had been dismissed from the board of the co-op, but that no one had seen her. Rumour had it that she'd moved out of the village. Only two weeks had passed, and it was still early days, but the co-op was thinking about starting a new nursery whenever a building became available. Malena had hinted with a smile that she might put herself in the running to spearhead the project.

And as for Georgie and Beth, well... Malena had said that neither of them could believe the real cause of the accident, but they were glad Alice had been kicked off the board anyway. In her quest to hide what she'd thought was the truth, she'd threatened them and lied, almost destroying their lives as well as her own.

But Georgie and Beth had lied, too, whether they'd meant to or not. Just like James, their stories were designed to tear Lenore down and protect themselves. Beth had apologised back at the Nest and tried to do right, but Georgie had yet to get in touch. Malena had said she was in therapy, doing her best to overcome her addiction and be there for her poorly daughter too. Given the circumstances, the co-op had decided not to pursue any further punitive measures for her drug use at work.

And while Lenore still felt upset and betrayed by Georgie's lies, it sounded like Georgie was going through hell already.

Lenore didn't want to hang on to the past; to any of the emotions this had stirred up. She didn't need to be haunted by it any longer. She'd been through hell, too, and she'd emerged stronger than she ever thought possible.

She watched as the Nest receded in the rear-view mirror, the building slowly replaced by her daughter's shining face. Then she pressed down on the accelerator, eager for the life that lay ahead.

A LETTER FROM LEAH MERCER

Dear reader,

I want to say a huge thank you for choosing to read *The Playgroup*. If you enjoyed it, and you want to keep up to date with all my latest releases, just sign up at the following link. Your email address will never be shared and you can unsubscribe at any time.

www.bookouture.com/leah-mercer

I hope you loved *The Playgroup*. If you did, I would be very grateful if you could write a review. I'd love to hear what you think. It makes such a difference helping new readers to discover one of my books for the first time.

I really enjoy hearing from my readers – you can get in touch through social media or my website.

Thanks,

Leah

www.leahmercer.com

facebook.com/AuthorLeahMercer

x.com/leahmercerbooks

ACKNOWLEDGEMENTS

First of all, a huge thanks to my readers, reviewers and everyone who has supported me since my publishing journey began. A big thank you to Hannah Todd for her continuing guidance and professionalism. Thanks, too, to Laura Deacon, Billi-Dee Jones and the formidable Bookouture team for their enthusiasm and hard work to get my book out to readers. Lastly, thank you to my husband and my son for supporting me in my dream career.

PUBLISHING TEAM

Turning a manuscript into a book requires the efforts of many people. The publishing team at Bookouture would like to acknowledge everyone who contributed to this publication.

Audio
Alba Proko
Sinead O'Connor
Melissa Tran

Commercial
Lauren Morrissette
Jil Thielen
Imogen Allport

Data and analysis
Mark Alder
Mohamed Bussuri

Cover design
Jo Thomson

Editorial
Billi-Dee Jones
Nadia Michael

Printed in Great Britain
by Amazon